BOY, GIRL, BOY, GIRL

BANTAM NEW FICTION

BOY, GIRL,
BOY, GIRL

DAVID MICHAELIS

BANTAM BOOKS

NEW YORK · TORONTO · LONDON · SYDNEY · AUCKLAND

I am grateful to Deborah Futter
and Joy Harris for their generous
contributions to this book.

BOY, GIRL, BOY, GIRL

A Bantam Book / November 1989

*Grateful acknowledgment is made for permission to reprint lyrics
from: "By the Beautiful Sea" copyright 1914 Shapiro, Bernstein & Co.,
Inc. New York. Copyright renewed. Used by permission. "Na Na Hey–
Kiss Him Goodbye," copyright © 1969 Unichappell Music, Inc. &
Little Heather Music. All rights administered by Unichappell Music,
Inc. All rights reserved. Used by permission.*

Library of Congress Cataloging-in-Publication Data
Michaelis, David.
    Boy, girl, boy, girl / David Michaelis.
        p.   cm. — (Bantam new fiction)
    ISBN 0-553-34761-6
    I. Title.
PS3563.I265B6   1989
813'.54—dc20   89-7007
                                                                CIP

Published simultaneously in the United States and Canada

*Bantam Books are published by Bantam Books, a division of Ban-
tam Doubleday Dell Publishing Group, Inc. Its trademark, consist-
ing of the words "Bantam Books" and the portrayal of a rooster, is
Registered in U.S. Patent and Trademark Office and in other countries. Marca Registrada. Bantam Books, 666 Fifth Avenue, New
York, New York 10103.*

PRINTED IN THE UNITED STATES OF AMERICA

FG   0   9   8   7   6   5   4   3   2   1

To
JULIE AGOOS
and
ALEXANDRA STYRON

CONTENTS

PART THREE
THE LAST LITTLE GIRLS

PROLOGUE

In September, to raise cash for the estate, my brother and I sold off the last of our mother's houses. We had grown up in Massachusetts, wintering in Cambridge, summering on Cape Cod, and the Cape house had already been stripped and surrendered when Murray and I shuttled up to Cambridge at the start of Labor Day weekend. It was a muggy evening, and our old street lay hushed and pungent under its August-swelled canopy of ailanthus. The house, a plump Victorian with a peaked slate roof, rose high above the privet hedge and oakembowered yard. Green acorns pebbled the path to the front porch. The sharp smell of our tree of heaven hung in the air.

At the door, my brother snapped open his briefcase and withdrew the shiny set of latchkeys the lawyer had given us. The traffic over on Concord Avenue sounded louder than I'd remembered, but the normal outbound din of Friday evening may only have been amplified by the vast, unnatural stillness of the uninhabited house. Across the street, the Bigelows' upstairs

1

landing light was on, cheerful as a candle. Next door, cloaked in hemlock, the Lessenhoffs' windows were dark, but theirs was the orderly darkness of weekends away—the hopeful, welcoming darkness of continuing life. Only our blackened house seemed to have lost its senses, to have quit life, betrayed its friends and neighbors.

The copied latchkey fit. The old tumbler gave the familiar, balky reply. The heavy Chinese-red door swished open, then stopped short, bumping up against a heap of mail. My heart lifted a little, and with a rush of homecoming, my brother and I barged into the front hall. We jostled each other as we fell to the mail, each of us seizing fistfuls of letters like clods of earth. Home-starved, we tore at the creamy envelopes until we saw that their glassine windows bore not the names of the quick, but of the dead, not the residents current, but long-ago and long-gone. Glumly, we stood. From the carpeted hush of the living room came the cool, minty breath of the hearth.

We spent the long weekend sorting through thirty years of possession. We had both been born to this house, conceived here, brought here from the hospital. Our mother, passionate, disorderly, tolerant—blissfully unmarried to the end of her life—had never thrown anything, or anyone, out. Yet Mom's stuff was the least of it. Some ten years back, the house had also absorbed her parents' things: yellowing heirlooms, sculpture by the crate, books by the ton; to say nothing of Dad's rejects: transatlantic steamer trunks and abandoned portmanteaux; as well as the unclaimed Sargasso Sea formed by family friends, guests, governesses, lodgers, leeches, housesitters, graduate students, lunatics, and full-fledged tenants whose flotsam had long ago floated freely into Mom's large, liberal domain.

The "tangibles," as the State Street lawyer had optimistically described this astonishing debris, had over the years settled into dense, Etruscan-like burial mounds. Fourteen rooms, eleven closets, two pantries, two attics, two cellars, one base-ment, and a garage. Everything had to be gone by Tuesday.

Murray and I have always been close, in an unreserved, argumentative way. Though we didn't become friends until Miss Little's School put us on equal footing, our fraternal rap-port, tested earlier by our parents' divorce and later by our moth-er's cancer, has always depended more on our differences than our sameness. We happen to have identical voices, which we like to raise in each other's company, but on that first night together, back in the house where we'd done so much of our finest shouting, there wasn't much to fight about.

For one thing, neither of us could take back to his one-bedroom apartment more than the tiniest of tangibles. For another, we almost never agree on matters of personal taste, and though Murray has long argued that I, the younger, received the greater share of Mom's love (and therefore that *he* deserves the larger wedge of posthumous pie), neither the functional items—rugs, furniture, household gadgets—nor appraisable as-sets, such as silver and antiques, gave much ground for argu-ment. Not even the rivalrous toys and bitterly contested games of our childhood prolonged or renewed the anguish.

Yet, early Saturday morning, when a frilly ostrich fan emerged from a trunk in the overstairs attic, we fell on it like vultures. The parentless halls of the house rang once more with our childish treble. By noon, we had had two more harsh exchanges—over a padded bedjacket and some elbow-length white kid gloves and the buttonhook that went with them. Then we quarreled over a suitcase full of perfumed silk scarves and garter belts. Then the foolish feathered fan reappeared. Throw it out? Store it? Give it to the Goodwill? Take it?

We stood at right angles to each other, sweat beading the ends of our noses.

"Chuck it," Murray declared, pulling his arm across his sooty, heat-reddened face.

"Better store it," I counseled.

"You would, faggot."

There was a certain guilty pleasure at going through the private things of women we would never see again. And there was so much of it: Dazed by the sheer smothering volume of female legacy, ambushed by a Labor Day weekend heat wave, we picked fights over handbags and hatboxes and hatpins. In babyish voices, we squabbled like lovers about an empty leather diaphragm case, each accusing the other of having already hidden the missing article in his personal luggage:

"Why would I want Mom's diaphragm?"

"Why would *I*?"

"Because you always did."

"No way, Myrrh Man."

"Yes way, Pieman."

"You're high."

"Face it, Pieman."

Even after we'd bickered over chamois nail buffers and eyelash curlers, even after we'd taunted each other with atomizers and applicators, pumice stones and hair removers—to the point of semihysterical tears—even then we kept unearthing distaff articles that had belonged neither to Mom nor to Grandma nor to Great-grandmother Murray.

"Smell this," I said.

"Smell what?"

"This," I offered, neutrally, and swept a long flannel nightgown with lace-cuffed sleeves out of the attic closet.

"Smell a nightshirt?" said Murray.

"Oh, man, it's a Lanz *nightgown*," I whined, extending the limp flannel arms to demonstrate its gowny voluptuousness.

Grudgingly, Murray leaned over and nosed into the generous folds at the bosom. He inhaled, then drew back, holding his breath. "Woo—*Pieman*," he leered, smirking at the phantom sleeping beauty.

It was his facetious leer, the one Murray reserves for people and things that remind us of our Little days. "Woo—*Myrrh Man*," I leered back.

All afternoon, we traded that sly, joyous leer, as we lifted from our attic tumuli the relics of a vanished people. Dripping sweat, I unearthed a Mason Pearson hairbrush still entangled with long, coiling strands of honey-gold hair, as well as several beribboned clove-studded oranges, some Rapidograph pens, and a tarnished silver christening cup, engraved *Mary Beryl Mansfield* in Belgrave script. Murray dug up a plastic Dial-a-Pack prescribed for "A. Johnston" by "Dr. L. Cox" and dispensed by the "Little School Infirmary."

"Face it, Pieman," he jeered, thrusting the drab, scallop-shaped dispenser under my nose.

Slack-jawed as a teenager, I peered into the busy wheel of discharged chambers and ran the tip of my finger around the empty slots, twenty-one in all, each marked by a day of the week. "Good God," I murmured. It was hard to believe that anyone had had that many chances—at age fifteen. My head reeled at the perpetual calendar of orgiastic days.

"Annie Johnston," Murray told himself in a warm, consoling voice. "Annie Johnston," he repeated, the way a still-hungry breakfaster, thinking aloud, might happily conclude, "English Muffin."

In the back of the master bedroom closet, I put my hands on a canvas duffel bag, and even before dragging it out into the light, I knew what it was and what it contained. At first, I put it aside. As the afternoon wore on, I found myself drawn to it. But not *directly* to it—beside it, around it, over it; but never *to* it.

It was nearly evening when I finally opened the bag. The

air was cooler, with just a suggestion of summer's end in the twilight haze. The brown canvas was faded, piped with leather. The big, plump zipper ran smoothly across its belly. I unzipped slowly, testing my susceptibility to the contents of the bag.

I happened to know, for instance, that every important item inside the duffel was blue—a summery shade of blue most anyone would associate with mussel shells and cornflowers and wild berries. For me, it was an almost pornographic blue, the color of my deepest adolescent foolishness and yearnings. I had once believed so devoutly in the everlasting sacred fact of that blue, that even now I expected the duffel to whisper to me like the chambers of a seashell. I plunged a hand in and tugged at the first thing I could seize.

A familiar aroma embraced me—clean, sweet, like moist September mornings after rain. I took a testing sniff. Miracle of miracles: I felt the breath but not the teeth of longing. I let out a long sigh. I had persisted long in my foolishness. *But when did it end?* When did the foolishness stop? Was it simply discontinued, or—?

Turning away, I filled my chest. Fresh air gave me confidence. Feeling sure-handed and cured, I reached back into the duffel. I dug around in the soft blue things, and then my hand brought forth, from among the rope-soled espadrilles and cutoffs and cotton tees, a certain blue bikini, and for the briefest of instants, I knew once more that I would die if I could not love the mermaid who swam the sea in those blue pieces.

There are still boys—grown men now—who talk about that creature from our past. Usually they claim to have seen her in midtown, or in someone's wedding, or at a dinner party where she had a fight with her date when the guy turned up from the office three hours late—or never showed at all. But how could they have seen her: Berry Mansfield, working in corporate midtown? Berry Mansfield, a bridesmaid? Berry Mansfield, stood up by a date?

Not *my* Berry Mansfield. Not the girl against whom I measured all the girls who came after. Not the most desirable girl in the school. Nowadays, when I hear news of Berry—in midtown, in a wedding, in a quarrel—I still tend to picture her as a senior. I don't even realize I am doing this, until, as the grown-up conversation continues, I look up and realize that I have been thinking about a big scary senior, fair of face, with long, lush hair the color of wild honey, huge blue eyes, a knowing smile, immense, splendid breasts. I am five feet six and ogling her at the water fountain. I am a freshman, watching her file into assembly between Lisa Mackay and Jane Melniker. I've just glimpsed her take her seat, with 249 other girls—and me—on the first day of school.

PART ONE

THE FIRST LITTLE BOYS

Having landed, they saw trees very green,
and much water, and fruits of diverse kind.

—Journal of Christopher Columbus
October 11–12, 1492

1. Lessons in the Mother Tongue

The day I entered Miss Little's School for Girls, I woke at dawn. Until that morning I had been a Ruxton boy—obedient, courteous, disciplined. Dressed in coat and tie, I had slaved for God and grades at the Ruxton School for Boys in Boston. I had spent more than half my life under the despotic rule of dew-lapped Dr. Crouch, the denture-breath of Mr. DePinna, the pitiless Roman laws of boys. I longed to escape. Mostly, I longed for girls—to know them, to be near them—and now, in just a few hours, I was going to get my wish. Miss Little's, one of the oldest and most distinguished girls' boarding schools in the country, had voted to open its gates to twenty-four freshman and sophomore boys. By 8:00 A.M., I would be fully enrolled in a school where girls outnumbered boys by a ratio of nine to one.

It was a Monday, I remember, because Monday was our housekeeper's day, and my mother had decided that before I left for school I should vacuum wherever Ozella, with her bad knees, could not reach.

"Sam!" Muz called in her low, chesty voice.

My brother had left the night before, and I was still sulking. He would enter the school as a sophomore boarder, having successfully argued in family conference that as the older, the "more mature," he deserved to spend his nights on a campus with nineteen-dozen women. Dad, who paid the bills and lived in Washington with his second wife, had said he saw "no practical reason why both boys have to be boarding students at Miss Little's Finishing School for Indecently Wealthy Girls." So I would live at home, a freshman day student, but I drew the line at vacuuming just the same.

"*Sam,*" Muz warned, standing in my doorway.

When she saw that I was still in bed—mouth ajar and drooling slightly—she straightened her back, as though guiding a tour past the Boyhood Bedroom at Hyde Park. She cleared her throat to announce: "The historically *fetid* odor of the growing boy."

I took this as a compliment. On the verge of entering a school for girls, I was glad at least I smelled the right way.

"But 'fetid' isn't quite it," she told herself. "It's more . . . Oh, what's the word I'm after, Sam? It has to do with 'lubricity,' with the unashamedly *lubricious* odor of every adolescent boy."

She was trying to make me feel better. Lately, I'd been worried about my height. Over the summer, my brother had shot up to six feet. Every time he came out of his room he'd grown another three inches. I was still five feet six, every morning, and that didn't feel tall enough for a school that was altering its name, for the sake of coeducation, to "The Little School."

Also, I didn't look much like a boy. I was skinny, with

mantis-thin arms. I had no muscle, no need to shave. I had pretty hands and long, curly eyelashes. My mother claimed that I had "a lovely masculine mien—if only you'd let us see your face." But this was 1971, when hair was grown on women by the yard and on men by the foot, and I wore mine to my shoulders. Hidden under fronds of sun-bleached hair, I appeared as a boy in outline only, like one of the monkeys concealed in the vegetation of the *Highlights* magazine puzzle at the orthodontist's office.

Muz strode over to my window and raised the shade. The morning was cool, charged with clean, pure light. Out along the tops of trees leaves stirred. A breeze puffed into the room, faintly metallic, scented by the rusting mesh of the window screen. From down the street came the laborious clanging of the neighborhood knife-sharpener's hand-rung brass bell.

" 'Lubricious,' Sam—?" Muz proposed in her best brisk voice, the one she used whenever she vowed to "lose ten pounds and write a memoir of the Kennedy years from a feminist point of view." A public-television producer, Muz usually succeeded in dropping many more names than calories.

She crossed back to my bed, tapped my shoulder. "Pardon me," she said sharply, "I was looking for my son."

"Fag word," I replied at last.

"Oh, 'lubricious' is not faggy at all. I'm surprised at you. That is exactly the sort of thing that *American* men would say."

"Well, what do you want?"

"I'd expect you to be a little more subtle, Sam. *European* men—the intellectuals, at any rate—aren't all hung up, all hung up about the size of their penises."

"Because they haven't got any."

"Oh, but they do," said Muz, straightening up and touching her hair. "They most certainly do. *No,* the one thing they *haven't* got is a lot of hang-ups about their bodies, which is why Europeans, for the most part, are so much better in bed." Muz lowered her voice, unnecessarily, and, with historical emphasis, added: "It's why your father was a far better lover than all the ghastly American men I was seeing in those days."

A silence opened up, and the knife-sharpener's bell filled it, ringing out as if in homage to Dad's continental competence in the kip. I tried to pretend I was looking at a water stain on the ceiling, but only got red in the face, and when Muz leaned over to kiss me, apparently to favor the ghastly Americans after all, I burst out laughing.

She giggled, too, bending toward me, her clean, sunny hair falling girlishly across her cheek. I raised a hand, obliged by custom to hold off the weight of her affection. She had a voluptuous, fleshy figure, my mother, and it was years before I no longer shied from her. Later on I was able to hold her, even to get into bed—a hospital bed—and hold her, but at thirteen I was too embarrassed by the desire her body caused me, and too befuddled by the pleasure she took in mine, to be truthful about how badly I wanted to love her back.

In a flash I rolled toward the wall. Muz pursued, planting kisses on my cheek—loud, joyful, smelly kisses. Despite the masking Elizabethan bouquet of tea-rose perfume and Dr. Thompson's toothpowder, I could freely inhale a full portion of breakfast kippers off her queenly breath.

"P-yew," I complained.

She kissed me on the temple, the chin, the throat, and as I yelped and wriggled and pretended to be very cross, she worked her way around behind my ear and laid her cheek on my neck.

"Forget you," I yelped.

"It's marvelous back here," she said. "I wish you'd be reasonable and just let me have a segment, Sam—this terribly smooth piece back here, at the nape."

"No way, José."

"Oh, it's all the same flesh. You'd just be saving your mother from going around looking wrinkled and prunish."

"No chance, Romance."

"You wouldn't want a prune for a mother, would you?" She nuzzled in behind my ear to renew an old offer: "We could so *easily* have a transplant done by that really good surgeon in London."

"How about getting him to fix your breath first?"

"Oh, *Sam,*" she gasped out. She had just parted the unwashed mop at the back of my head. "That hair . . . Your scalp!"

I plunged under cover. It had been more than ninety days since my last shampoo; I'd been trying, for no special reason, to set a personal record in unwholesomeness.

"You're caked! You're all caked with dandruff. . . . Please, just let me have a look. I won't *touch* it."

But a tour guide spoke from under my covers: "Ladies and gentlemen, we now direct your attention to that portion of the Simon household which dates from before the Civil War. . . . Note, especially, the fishy odor of the wrinkled old prune in the foreground."

"You're impossible," Muz said, assuming a businesslike, first-day-of-school posture. "What's more, you're all jazzed. That school and the idea of all those big buxom girls has got you all jazzed up."

Muz, the daughter of a women's college president, had had mixed feelings about the Miss Little's "experiment" from the start. I had spent half the summer trying to reassure her, and now, in my real voice, I told her for the hundredth time that I could handle it. "I can *handle* girls," I said, without much conviction. I wasn't about to admit to anyone, at this stage in the game, that I could hardly breathe whenever I thought about girls, let alone being on the business end of a nine-to-one ratio.

15

"They're terribly bright, terribly sophisticated," Muz warned. "Louisa Little's girls were always terribly, terribly—" She had turned to the window as if to a crackling, brass-skirted fireplace. "They always had a certain—and I don't say I had much appreciation for it when I was at boarding school—but a certain very particular high polish on their cordovan moccasins."

This seemed to put both of us at a disadvantage. "Well, I'm wearing sneakers," I decreed.

"You wouldn't if Miss Little were still in charge, I can tell you that. It was *her* school—I'll never forget Mother saying it—and they were *her* girls, and they were the best dressed, the best behaved, and they all went on to Radcliffe or Bryn Mawr or abroad. They were women of achievement, Sam—successful in their own right. You'll have to be very grown-up."

Grown-up I wasn't worried about. In our house, being grown-up meant having the sense not to ask the real grown-ups why they were all of a sudden speaking French.

"You've *already* grown up so fast," she lamented. "Murray with his gadgets, you with your blazer and your football— Oh, Sam, you were such a golden boy!"

"Oh, wazoo, Mom."

"Well, I'm concerned. I'm concerned for *you*. All those *girls* . . ."

"I can handle *the girls*! Enough with the girls!"

"Are you sure?" she insisted, seriously.

Downstairs, the dog was barking. T. K. Sethna, the Indian man who cooked for us and lived on the third floor, had let someone in at the front door.

"Ozella," Muz called down, "is that you?"

Puddleby's mean, convulsive barking rang up the stairwell.

"Oh, thank God," Muz said to herself in the same throaty voice she used after the first sip of a vodka martini.

The commotion got louder, Sethna reasoning with the dog

in sagely pacifistic tones, Muz joining in at the top of her lungs, Ozella calling back, "I don't pay him no mind," coathangers clattering to the floor, Muz calling down, "Please don't stoop to get those, dear! I'll get them when I come down—or Sam will get them!"

Turning back, Muz warned, *This minute, Sam, Ozella is here.* She dropped her voice: "Please do something with your dog."

Puddleby, once the family dog—a sweet-tempered, piebald mutt—had become my dog or Murray's dog ever since we'd discovered that he barked exclusively when black visitors came to the door.

"I mean it, Sam! I'm going to have her start in here. And for goodness sake take your own sheets down to the laundry, and put them *in* the machine. Ozella must not have to stoop—do you hear me?"

"Yas'm, Marse Muz."

"A little more action, a little less *Uncle Remus,* please."

"Mom."

"Oh, I'm not *looking*. No one is the least bit interested in looking at your penis."

I turned back the covers and slipped out of bed. Muz gave the room a last, reproachful look. Her gaze coasted along without a halt—the desk, the chair, the rug, the lamp—until finally it jounced over a small bump on the floor under my bed.

"Sam, what is that? What hideous thing have you got under there?"

In behalf of Ozella, we both stooped over to peer at my favorite whack-off rag—a hand towel, glazed, dried, structurally as sound as a sand castle—standing up by itself under the bed.

"Really, Sam," said Muz. "Can't you at least use Kleenex?"

2. The Great Elm

I never once made the trip to school without wanting to stop the car, get out, and, from sheer nervous excitement, puke. The Little School stood only eighteen miles from my house—eighteen miles out Route Two, a drab, workaday highway—but they were the eighteen most tantalizing, stomach-wrenching miles of my life.

That first morning, driving out with Muz, I sat very still as we skipped past the familiar highway eyesores, skirting motley Waltham and Armenian Watertown, steeply breasting Belmont Hill. By Lexington, when all traces of the known world had vanished, and with historical sites coming fast and furious, it was diverting to watch my mother turn from a blue-eyed beauty into a coarse old tourist, so pushy and shrill and embarrassing to be with I nearly asked to hitchhike the rest of the way.

"Oh, *Sam*," she rejoiced as we turned onto the Cambridge Turnpike, a bouncy country road leading into the town of Concord, "smell the *grapes*."

Not one particle of the pungent September scene escaped Muz's paeans of thanksgiving. Her eyes watered at the sight of loaded orchards, at unseen rills gurgling through the rain-rinsed meadows, at the madly waving arms of wild apple trees. Roadside stands bulged with bright squash and pumpkins; radiant white picket fences mustered in the sunshine. Muz reviewed and saluted them all.

"Hoo-hoo!" she yodeled to a white-clapboard manse standing in a pine grove. "It's Emerson's house—oh, and there's

Orchard House: The Alcotts! *Little Women*, Sam! And Wayside, Hawthorne's house, *right next door*."

The Lexington Road took us past the stern, colonnaded First Parish Meeting House and the somber Wright Tavern, directly into Monument Square, an oblong town green centered upon a white flagpole. I looked for movie theaters and pizzerias. Concord was a village of rustling trees and cool, dry cellars. The overburdened slope of the Old Hill Burying Ground rose up at one end of Main Street, which was lined on both sides with two-story clapboard storefronts. Farther along, opposite Sally Ann's Food Shop, the stores and curbstones gave way to a gritty, packed-dirt sidewalk that followed Main Street out past Nashawtuc Road to the fork where Elm Street veered right and Miss Little's augured her campus.

When we reached the school, Muz slowed way down. She cruised Elm Street, braking before each of the green-shuttered, white-clapboard dormitories, rubbernecking like a wedding guest bent on seeing all the bridesmaids.

"But they're charming, Sam!" she cried as we halted before starchy, peristyled Buttrick, then stout Oldham, next pretty Ordway with its morning glory creepers and window boxes, and finally slim, wisteria-clad Walton. "I think," said Muz, pointing at Brewster's hemlock-shaded portico, "Murray is in that one. . . ."

Between the adjacent Greek-revival facades I stole glimpses of a lush, river-girt campus. I spied golden-hued dogs and towheaded children racing in delirious circles on broad, unfenced lawns. I saw a knob-shouldered man riding high aboard a red tractor, mowing the grass. No sign yet of the friendly peoples who inhabited this uncorrupted green place, no lambs or maidens gamboling in the milky morning mist down along the willow-curtained banks of the Sudbury River.

19

Miss Little's School stood silent, keeping its secrets. So far, no girls.

But as we poked along Elm Street, my heart accelerated. Up ahead, above the roofs of Hoare and Hooker houses, a gigantic tree towered into view. I had never seen anything like it. To my boy's eyes, it seemed to be all things at once—animal, vegetable, mineral—not so much a single tree as a whole forest unto itself, a vast overspreading of wonder, childlike and primeval, a whispering of something half remembered from deep dreams.

In fact, there had long been question about whether the Great Elm was a single tree or two trees growing from the same root system. It certainly *looked* like two trees: Set inside the school's main gate, the base heaved upward, its deeply creviced trunk so solid and marmoreal that the bark appeared hewn from rock rather than from two or three centuries of ringed wood growth. At seven feet, the tree divided into Siamese parts, one tremendous lichen-bristled leg thrusting right, subdividing into three huge boughs that branched again and again and again, writhing upward, until a hundred thousand twigs and leaves had exploded under the sun. On the left, the matching limb stood defoliated, its blighted boughs sticking up like the sad, bare poles of a shipwreck. Sheltered from storms by the gabled rooftops of Hoare and Hooker, the diseased limb remained *in situ*, but with the ominous look of something sea-sunk and stripped.

When my mother and I pulled up and parked, the healthy branches cast a full complement of shade onto a fresh white sign whose green letters welcomed us to "The Little School."

"Well," said Muz, "you're really going to have to buckle down and work."

A summons of bells sounded across the treetops.

"Well, I'm late," I announced importantly, "I'm late for my first assembly."

"Nonsense," Muz rejoined.

Ahead of us, other latecomers were jumping out of station wagons and darting through Main Gate; I breathed easy. But when I noticed that among all latecomers I alone was male, the air suddenly seemed oxygenless. My throat constricted. I began yawning like mad, strangling on my own neck muscles.

Muz leaned calmly out the window. She smiled at the touch of sun on her face. She threw back her head. She issued a full-throated sigh. "Smell the tansy," she urged. "Can you smell it?"

I smelled nothing.

"Oh, Sam!" she burst out. "All those classes! All those *books*! I'm so jealous." She turned to face me with overbrimming eyes. "My beamish boy!" she whispered.

I noticed, critically, that she was wearing too much eye makeup.

"You'll need some pocket money—" she began, groping for her purse, while I, slyly disengaging the catch, worried the door handle.

"O.K., Muz, O.K.," I mumbled, accepting a crumpled, purse-fragrant five-dollar bill.

"O.K., Sam, O.K.," she mimicked, as I dismissed her with a fast kiss, then slid out the door.

She reached suddenly for her purse. "A comb—your hair—a comb."

I stood firm and shut the door. With body English I sped the car on its way. When the car gave no sign of leaving—when the driver began waving a long pink comb through her open window—I turned quickly and walked away. I remember that I kept a sharp lookout for girls with a certain high polish on their cordovan moccasins. I planned to tell any well-behaved girl who stopped me that I had no information concerning the identity of the woman parked in the jalopy at Main Gate. If pressed, I might venture that in all probability the old hag had just pulled over to comb her hair. But I could not have guessed why she was still sitting there, parked on school property, sobbing to herself in that shabby, ill-kempt heap.

3. Love's Lemon

No one had said anything about perfume. New students had simply been asked to report to assembly, neat and well groomed, and I found my way there by following the other foot-draggers down Old School Drive and into the bright, skylighted lobby of the ultramodern Lively Arts Center. Assembly had just started. A side door admitted latecomers to the cavernous amphitheater, but, once inside, none of us dared intrude farther than the first aisle. It was dark in there—the slightly scary duskiness of a sideshow tent. Up inside the concave ceiling, a tinted skylight dropped a strange blue glow over the rising rows of seats. I peered into the vast volume of warm, scented air. My eyes were slow to adjust, but when they did, I saw a remarkable thing. I was in a room with over two hundred women and every single one of them was staring at me.

There they were—the girls. In the misty blue light they appeared to me as a multitude: Freshman perched front and center, sophomores behind, juniors to the right, seniors to the left, row upon boyless row, shoulder to soft shoulder, wall to glorious wall—*girls*, dozens of girls, hundreds of girls, all arrayed in graduated tiers like hosts of angels and archangels. I would still swear that I glimpsed Berry in that first impression, yet how could I have singled her out? Every girl in the school seemed to have long, thick, lustrous hair, parted in the center, and every time the side door opened to admit a newcomer, all the girls faced right. Every time they turned, their hair jiggled a little, and every time that long, thick, lustrous hair jiggled, the intoxicating scent of herbal shampoo rose into the auditorium, unfurling like a welcome banner. Apparently, every student at the Little School had lately emerged, perfumed and pink, from a long, lingering bath.

The American boy, finding himself like that—inside the green gates of paradise—is supposed to react something like this: First his Adam's apple should bob up and down. Then his eyeballs should spin in their sockets like the wheels of a slot machine, displaying a blur of bars, bells, and fruit, finally settling—bong! bong! bong!—on a quivering line of cherries. Then, just as he shouts, "Hot dawg!"—falling away into a dead faint—his eyeballs should shoot out of his head, goggling like a lobster's.

I felt only a decisive tremor in my legs. To me, at thirteen, shampoo was an aphrodisiac. And *herbal* shampoo—well, let me just say that herbal shampoo had more or less lubricated my entire fantasy life since puberty. The moist, gingery fragrance of my mother's Clairol Herbal Essence had stoked every erotic whim I'd ever tried out in the shower at home. To find it here, *at school,* and on my classmates, was terrifying. The day had scarcely begun—it wasn't even recess—and already my most private cravings had been aired in assembly.

With a thrashing heart and slick palms, I groped for the door, desperate to find a water fountain. Just then, to my enormous relief, a formidable, short-haired woman stepped forward, all trim and trig in a dark green cardigan, white silk blouse, and tailored skirt. She was Edna Brickley, dean of

23

students, and, so far as I could tell, Edna Brickley wore no fragrance of any kind.

Unscented, the dean had been calling the roll and issuing seat assignments, and now, though she consulted no clipboard, she summoned each of the latecomers by name. I had the distinct impression that a clipboard would have been beneath Edna Brickley, and superfluous besides. The point was, she already knew us. She knew our faces, our names, our family backgrounds; she knew things about us and about our parents that many of us didn't yet know about ourselves. When the dean called out my name in her crisp, collected voice, she gave it in full: "Simon, Edward Sampson!"

My middle name drew a laugh—to me it sounded like a shriek. I was named after my mother's grandfather, a Congregational minister in Somerville, Mass., but I would bet that the Reverend Edward S. Murray never once faced a congregation as rowdy as the one I stood facing at the Little School. Shrieks of laughter broke out everywhere, including squeals from the sophomores and screeches from the juniors—louder than any hubbub I'd ever heard in boys' school—and I stood rigid in the aisle, paralyzed with shock and embarrassment.

Dean Brickley sprang to my side and took me by the elbow. Looking me square in the eye, she said, "Food for thought," adding firmly: "I'm sure that tomorrow morning you'll join us promptly, and with a more appropriate hairstyle."

I raised my hand to my head, but the dean, with her lidless eye, had already drawn a bead on my unclean scalp.

"A word to the wise," she warned. "Long hair is a privilege for men or women. Long hair requires constant care. Even the crowned heads of Europe, who were not always as clean and well groomed as this school will require you to be, finally decided it was a nuisance."

Here she shot me a look that told me I was too smart and

she was too smart for either of us to exchange another word about grooming.

"I suggest," confided Dean Brickley, dropping into a lower octave, so that I had to strain to hear her: "I suggest that you pull yourself together at once." Then she stepped back, lifted her voice, and dismissed me warmly: "Off you go, spit-spot, spandy clean—Frosh S's, Samperton-Stott."

"Pardon?" I replied.

"Sam Simon; clean slate; Freshman S's; second row, between Sara Samperton and Jenny Stott."

She smiled, her eyes twinkling, as she pointed the way.

Happily, Dean Brickley's mnemonics landed me in an aisle seat. To my left sat Sara Samperton, a pale, expensively dressed girl whose gleaming mane of yellow hair was hitched up with an ice-blue Hermès silk scarf. To my right lay the aisle—an open path to the door, the lobby, a bathroom.

No sooner had I sat down beside Sara Samperton and her clean yellow hair than I started to gag. For a moment I thought I might actually vomit, right there in front of all those hundreds of potential girlfriends, which number had just been reduced by one. There is no way to say this nicely: Sara Samperton reeked.

Still, I should say, by way of explanation for my problems with Sara, that at Ruxton I had always been afraid of choking to death—on the bottom of a football pileup, at the end of a forkful of refectory stew. All through boyhood, I had been so terrified of something blocking my windpipe that I had never once allowed myself to puke; I'd always managed, at moments of peak nausea, to resist the menacing urge by sitting perfectly still, shutting my eyes, and gagging. So I was sort of a virgin of vomit, all spandy clean, when I took my place beside Sara Samperton in Frosh S's.

Sara reeked of lemons. And not fresh lemons, either—not the brisk lemon of a tart iced tea. Hers were thick, inguinal, syrupy lemons, manifest neither as fruit nor fluid, but as a gas whose fumes emanated from the entire body, the hair, the clothing, and probably the soul of Sara Samperton. She seemed, frankly, to have been born of lemons, though I later learned that her parents were New Yorkers. Of course I had no idea that she was also carrying around more or less the entire consumer products line (including shampoo, conditioner, rinse, hand soap, bath beads, hair gel, body powder, nail polish, lip slicker, blush-on, and travel spray) of a popular fragrance called Love's Lemon.

That first morning, I knew only that Sara Samperton stank, and stank so badly that it was physically impossible to sit beside her and claim my share of the neighborhood's oxygen. Within seconds, I was gagging—the long, greedy fingers reaching into my gullet—and as assembly continued, Sara's teasing citrus scent and my ceaseless gagging so wholly occupied my mind, I hardly heard or saw the rest of the program. I dimly remember the two peppy captains of "Yeas" and "Nays," the school's intramural athletic teams, jumping to lead simultaneous cheers—screeches, really. I remember Topsy Johnson, a biology teacher, objecting, in a loud, pseudo-male voice, to "the counting of the quorum," and calling for "a show of hands." I remember Coach Sanfred Worrell displaying the first official boys' varsity soccer uniform, and the giggle-storm that swept the auditorium when everyone suddenly saw that we would have to face the enemy ranks of Groton and Middlesex wearing shorts and shirts emblazoned with one word: "LITTLE."

And of course I remember Dr. Cox, the school's first resident physician, who stood before us exhibiting the infirmary's new "specialized services," including the Condom ("Slips on just like a nylon stocking"), the Diaphragm, the Pill, the

IUD—and the somber mood of the senior section, where Dr. Cox's services had been received, I noted, with a uniform look of bulletproof indifference. For my part, I sat gagging, my confidence badly shaken. I had never before seen the copper-sheathed, .22 caliber sized IUD, which was going to be implanted in the soft, pink parts of girls my own age. It looked mean and sharp, and its miniature size was disconcerting. It didn't seem to correspond to any private part I knew anything about. It looked like it belonged to the phone company.

Mainly I remember Frederick Harr, the new headmaster. Lean, shrewd, nervous—bald as a condor at thirty-eight—Fred Harr seemed an unlikely successor to a saint. He sported a "mod" necktie and "flared" slacks, and as he addressed Miss Little's School on its historic first day of coeducation, the headmaster did not speak so much as he quipped. He also jested, joked, chortled, and leered.

"Hello! Hello!" he called, jackknifing out of his seat to welcome us all to the new Little School. "Greetings! Greetings! Ha! Ha! Old and New! This morning, you old girls are going to see a lot of funny things happen on the way to the quorum! One of them is me—your first male head! Eight of them are the first six-foot mattresses in the history of the boarding department! Twenty-four of them are the very first Little boys. . . ."

Wild applause took over, and lemur-eyed Fred Harr goggled at the school from behind thick-lensed glasses. "Well," he deadpanned, his lips spreading into a lordly leer, "we certainly hope they're not *too* little!"

From that moment on, Fred Harr leered indefatigably—leered the way a more traditional headmaster might shake hands. And though later his leer came to stand for a kind of jocose mutual understanding, at the beginning it seemed only to endorse the male cause, to ratify my hopes, to certify that every Little boy was hereby enrolled in an orgy of untold enravishments.

4. Milk and Honey

My first morning at the Little School still rings in my ear. Across the soft green lawn of Senior Garden, the chapel bell tolled the end of each period, and at the first lick of the clapper, the quiet, cozy classrooms erupted. Then, for the next ten minutes, the creaky corridors of Louisa Little's Old School Building—a converted barn and stables—would shake to the rafters with the thrilling tumult of girls changing classes.

At recess, at the bake sale outside Senior Cloakroom, I found myself surrounded by frank, gabby seniors each of whom had a nickname: Sarah Knight introduced herself as "Starry" Knight; Janet Daley, known as "Planet" Daley, was also "Daley Planet." Andrea Waples and her younger sisters preferred to be called "Waffles." But trickiest of all—for boys, at any rate—were the open wooden cubbyholes that honeycombed the upstairs hallways of Old School Building. Each of us had been assigned one of these small, snug spaces for our books and supplies, but how were we supposed to say this word—*cubby*—and still sound like boys?

In third-period art class, Ms. Wilkie, fresh from her first maternity sabbatical, announced that she had made, from scratch, some natural ice cream, and that when we finished molding our clay into significant forms, we would use the remainder of the period as "some get-to-know-each-other time." What happened next seems, now, pretty farfetched, yet I distinctly remember my eager credulity when, as we freshmen artisans were laughing and talking and noisily lapping up the natural ice cream, I heard one of my classmates approvingly tell Ms. Wilkie: "Wow. Your own breast milk. Cool."

At lunchtime, the buzz of voices and the clatter of dishes and silverware came to a standstill. Each time a boy entered the dining hall, chewing mouths closed and closed mouths opened. Nimble eyeballs followed us as we sped our trays along the buffeteria. No one knew exactly what to make of us. We resembled none of the familiar New England schoolboys. We had none of the Groton boy's capacity for clannishness, nor the all-around team spirit of postgraduates at Andover and Exeter. We weren't clubbable, like Hotchkiss boys, nor muscular and Christian, like the choristers of St. Paul's. Whatever we were, we were popular—Miss Little's girls begged us to sit down *here,* and, after we'd taken seats, also *here* and *here* and *here.* Fed on honeydew melon and milky tea, we basked in the kind of attention usually reserved for firstborns.

Everyone automatically knew our names. The whole school knew that Frank Purvis was a slack-jawed sophomore who wore a silver stud earring and came from St. Bernard's in New York. The entire junior class, plus Madame Jones, had a crush on Brad Wentworth, our sardonic State of Maine year-rounder, who had become, since first period, Madame Jones' *chéri,* the unrivaled, "tutoyed" favorite in the old French teacher's soufflé-soft heart. (Wentworth was like that: he didn't even take German and Mrs. Muenzinger called him *Liebchen.*) Brilliant Paul Winslow was so admired for the idealistic remarks he had just made in American Studies—third period, Mr. Laidlaw—that he personally could have founded and populated a vast utopian community made up of barefoot followers in black leotards and dungaree skirts. Charlie Crocker—Charles Bowditch Crocker— and his sidekick, Danny Armbrister, escapees of Groton School's third form, skipped lunch, but showed up for dessert; Charlie

Crocker had scarcely set foot in that sunny cafeteria when he became universally known as "Betty" Crocker.

I had not seen my brother since the bake sale at recess—when he'd introduced me to his new boarding department buddies, "Pinky" Thaarup, "Trinka" van Winkle, "Tipsy" Twistleton, as well as a very large girl in overalls, called "Roo," whose real name I still don't remember. I'd also swapped cupcakes with one "Bunny," two out of three of the "Waffles," and countless girls with skinned-back hair and wide-open eyes who urged me to have seconds on brownies before I'd had firsts.

In the dining hall, Murray, attended by all the Waffles, ignored the buffeteria and strode confidently to the organic foods table. He seemed all of a sudden to love brown rice and yogurt. The Waffles, who could hardly keep their hands off Murray, heaped his plate with large brown lumps, then ushered him to a table, smothering his body with hugs and his yogurt with granola. My shy, gawky brother, after twenty-four hours at the Little School, had reached heights of popularity known only to rock 'n' roll stars.

I barely touched my food. Outdoors, beside the dining hall, a patch of lawn had been set aside for smokers, and this glamorous spot held my eye. Girls were sunning and smoking out there, and from my table I kept catching glimpses of one: She was barefoot and wore cutoffs, and she lay flat on her stomach, resting her chin in the V of her palms, now and then rolling luxuriously onto her back, like some sky-gazing peasant girl at the top of a hayrick.

That was how I first saw Emma. Even now I tend to picture her not as the world sees her today, but as she was when I first saw her smoking. Safe in the dining hall, I watched how she ducked her chin to inhale, then hooked her hair behind her ears to exhale. She rubbed the ashes into her blue-jean cutoffs, and when she was done, she sat up, plucking grass from her hair, and a full yard and a half of thick, fawn-brown tresses tumbled over her shoulders and blue cotton tee.

Deftly, she tilted her head and tossed the hair. It swirled around her torso, twisting in the sunlight, the ends spreading like iridescent plumage. At the last second, she inclined her head forward, breaking the flight of the tresses, which fell in velvety clusters, curtaining the seat of her rump. Then she drew her suntanned legs to her chest and hugged them.

Watchful, absorbed, she peered over her kneecaps with large, pale, melancholy eyes. She frowned at her small, squarish feet. She wrinkled her nose, which was freckled and peeling slightly, and I could see, above her knitted, disdainful brow, little wisps of fleecy hair—tiny curls—high on her forehead.

5. Vague Fears

In the first sun-drenched afternoons, after sports, when I needed privacy to sneak cigarettes and say aloud her name, I would climb into the Great Elm. It was the spot I singled out to be of solemn and everlasting importance to me and Emma Mansfield. It was the place, I felt certain—this great cathedral of leaves—where we would one day marry, our love too big for ordinary churches.

Daily, I paused under the nave of ancient timber, all black and sinewy against the archivolts of golden leaf. Up in the cleft between the twin boughs, a clump of soil had long ago gathered, and in its mossy mound, beside some woody fungus, a currant bush had fructified. As an act of faith, I would always stop and eat a single red berry as I climbed up into the secondary branches. Then, following the widest, levelest branch to its outermost fork, I would dare myself to stand up to full height.

The best view lay to the east, between the chapel and the Lively Arts Center, down across the lower fields to the river. In the margins of the Sudbury, weeping willows draped golden yellow filigree into sedgy pools. Between the lacy branches, I could see the boathouse, with its small board-and-batten canoe shed and its rickety dock, listing slightly in the topaz-tinted waters. Beyond the dock's rail, a withered beech, gray and elephantine, knelt beside the river. Far beyond, across the sinuous Sudbury, the low, grassy meadows rolled away to the birch-haunted woodlots of Nashawtuc Hill.

As the afternoon melted into its highest pitch of blue and gold, Louisa Little's moccasined tribe would enter that view. Without any doing on my part, without a single act of imagination or fantasy or will, girls would simply *materialize*—whole teams of brown-limbed girls, gliding in formation across the burnished fields, swatting at one another's legs with their primitive sticks. There ran the varsity in green middy blouses, and there the J.V. in bloomers, and there miscellaneous rebels in hemmed blue-jean cutoffs held up with neckties: the zebra-bright, red-white-and-black Groton School tie—trophy of some springtime conquest.

My gaze returned most often to Emma Mansfield and her circle of friends, who, after practice, liked to lounge under the sycamores at field's edge. I would stare at those girls, my mouth dry, my chest aching, and in my heart would burst sweet pangs of unfulfillment. I had never in my life longed so much for something so within, yet so out of, reach—never in my life seen girls like these: girls who would lie around in the grass, rapturously entwined in each other's sunbrowned arms; girls who, seized by delight, would touch each other all over, heedless of what anyone might think; girls who already knew more of intimacy than maybe we would ever know; girls by themselves.

Sometimes I wondered if somewhere, deep in boyhood, deep in some boys' first book of history, I had seen or dreamed all these girls. It was months before I glimpsed a photograph of Louisa Little—in pigtails and tennis sneakers, building the chapel, circa 1949—and when I saw her sunbaked skin and examined her wistful, weathered eyes, I all at once found my way back to that first red race of men and women who fished for shad and herring in the swollen spring streams of Massachusetts.

From my lookout in the square-rigged Great Elm, I could see pigtailed Emma Mansfield and ponytailed Lili Hooper, their cheeks dimpled with pleasure, innocently flaunting themselves in front of Miss Peters, who stood by, a protective duenna, corked with a whistle. I could see Hannah Gustin and Hilary Fraser and Tizzy Tucker sitting all in a row, braiding each other's hair into ropy plaits. I could see Hattie Bancroft and Berry Mansfield, panting, leaning against each other, buttocks to buttocks, their deep, breath-catching gasps swelling their chests.

I could see Hattie and Berry conversing in single-word exchanges, understanding each other perfectly, their shimmering gold hair tied back with dark ribbons and bows, their cherry-cheeked faces flush with after-practice dew. Berry, the sachem, was right in the middle, with all the others around her, and all their heads rimmed with sunlight, and all their long shadows—big as Amazons—sliding along in the sun-gilt grass.

That was the view from the Great Elm. That, and my ever-increasing adoration and fear of it. For even when all the brown-limbed girls dashed, shrieking, back into the trees—even with no girls—that view stood for girls. It came to mean everything I did and did not know about girls, and everything I feared about the not knowing.

6. *Perfecto Bazoom*

Those first popeyed days puzzled everybody. After all, we were in the midst of plenty, surrounded by wonders and delights on every side. Bosoms here, behinds there. Everywhere we looked, boobs. In math: an asymptotic inch of cleavage. In chapel: nipples rising into the chilly morning like steeples in the countryside. In biology: a perfectly whole, rounded, active mammary, observed inside a lab partner's open shirt. The more we sighted, the greater the embarrassment of choice. Yet glimpses remained the limit of our daring.

Late in the afternoons, I would often miss my train and join Wentworth, Winslow, Armbrister, Crocker, and my brother on the widow's walk atop Brewster House. There, with field glasses pointed at varsity field hockey practice, we would gawp at the swelling shapes before us, turning to one another with a wild surmise, like Balboa and his men, stupefied upon an isthmus peak, realizing for the first time that no matter which way we turned, no matter which course we took, some greater, more beguiling sensation would always be discovered in the next hour.

Discouraged, wonder-stricken by the diversity of size, shape, and cup, we did the normal thing. We ranked them. We had gone to summer camp as papooses (first year), braves (second year), warriors (third year), sagamores (fourth year), and sachem (fifth year). We had swum New England ponds and bays as "tadpole" and as "dolphin." Children of status and privilege, we had grown up in an endlessly classifiable world.

Now, as freshmen and as sophomores, we drew up a taxonomy of busts:

The lowest division—*Null Set*—covered everything from the flat chest up through the training bra and the pushy little A-cup, of which my brother was the great champion. Murray favored flatness, inextension. He loved the Null Set's hoyden virtues. Snobs, the rest of us held out for the upper echelons, but I always admired my brother's democratic attitude toward breasts; it seemed to offer him unlimited freedom with girls.

The next bracket brought forth the *Booblet,* a B-cup group, last stop for Murray; still no interest from the other widow's-walkers. No one was hanging out bunting for Booblets.

At *Boobs,* however, Winslow started to sound acquisitive, and even Charlie Crocker, in whose big-boned life everything customarily came in Extra-Large or Family sizes, sounded all of a sudden proprietary about the C-cup class. For a very brief, almost insignificant period, which none of us but Wentworth could later remember, there even existed sub-phylla to classify oddball C-cup shapes, such as *Cone* and *Conelet, Bulb* and *Bulblet,* and the *Spheroids: Oblate, Prolate,* and *Pancake.* Nobody but Wentworth fussed much in the subkingdom of Boobs.

Up in the D-cup family—*Booswam*—certain of the boarders grew exacting as an admissions committee:

"Gustin is definitely Booswam," proposed Crocker.

"No way."

"Come on, wussy, look at her!"

"Way too big."

"Can you clarify your objection?"

"Pendulosity too great . . . excessive aureole radius . . . protrubo-mammiform excurvation . . . viscosity. . . ."

"Potential spontaneous lactic secretion?" Wentworth asked hopefully.

"You wish."

"Gross me out, man."

"Barfulation."

"O.K., douche bags," Wentworth submitted: "Lili Hooper?"

"Booswam."

"*Quasi*-Booswam."

"You're high."

"Look, man, she's nice and round."

"Can you clarify?"

"Um . . . dangleability; um . . . randomized cleaving action; um . . . visibility of erect rectractile bovine lactation units; um . . . negative iscosity."

"Yeah, but . . . *Booswam?*"

Armbrister broke in with the crucial question: "Does she touch? Does Hooper *touch?*"

We had observed that a true Booswam, ashamed at the perfection of her bosom, rarely, if ever, touched her own breasts, much less acknowledged in any way that they existed. Booswams, we'd discovered, were the trickiest of all breasts (one man's Booswam might be another man's Boob), and we'd developed the touch-test to separate forever the Booswam from the Boob. Paul Winslow, fond of plumbing these verities, often posed the koan: "If a Booswam falls out of its brassiere in the forest, does anyone see it?"

Higher up, above *Booswam,* in the next officially sanctioned bracket—*Mondo-Booswam*—only Armbrister, Crocker, and I cared to confer. Winslow argued that anything above a Booswam should be considered outright pornography—grounds for immediate and complete confession to Dr. Ditsky, the school's new psychiatrist. Wentworth protested that he was "more interested in pussy anyway." Murray objected to the very flab required for the Mondo: "What would you *do* with it all anyhow?"

Finally, up at the acme and pitch of the bosom world, high

above all known hemispheres, up where flesh and flab merged into great bovine globes and cherub-pink udders, up in the rarified, oxygenless air of the *Mondo-Mondo Bazoom,* I alone scanned the sky. I alone remained vigilant. Mind you, I had never in my life seen a Mondo-Mondo Bazoom, much less had anything to do with one. Dead-eyed as the Great White Shark, primordial as the Loch Ness Monster, atavistic as the Abominable Snowman, matriarchal as the Great Elm itself, the Mondo-Mondo Bazoom hovered in the heavy air of my earliest thoughts—a visitor from dark, Germanic dreams, swollen as a zeppelin, tinted pink, trailing the steamers of a fevered, festering sunset.

"Hattie Bancroft?" Winslow nervously proposed one afternoon.

"Boobs."

"Solid Boobs, no question."

"What are we talking?" I asked.

"We're talking Harriet Bancroft's boobs—where have you been, Pieman?"

"Lactating," predicted Wentworth.

"O.K., faggots," I countered, imitating Wentworth, whose rough, easygoing way with friends and girls I admired: "Emma Mansfield?"

"Booblet."

"No way."

"Possible Boobs?"

"*Likely* Boobs."

"Wentworth's moist for Mansfield. . . ."

"Listen, I'd drink her bathwater," vowed Wentworth.

"You guys are crazy," Winslow struck in angrily. "If Hattie Bancroft qualifies as Boobs, then Emma Mansfield cannot, objectively speaking, be put in the same class."

"Winslow's wet for Bancroft. . . ."

"Fuck you," Winslow flashed at my brother. "You clarify, then!"

"It's Pieman's fault," Murray complained. "He screwed us all up when he started drooling over Starry Knight." (Who had arguably the largest breasts in the school.)

"Total inflation!"

"Mondo!"

"Go, van Gogh!"

"Wait a minute," pursued Paul Winslow. *"Wait just a minute . . ."* Then, breathlessly, as if broaching the unbroachable: "Aren't we talking . . . 'Mondo-Mondo'?"

"Almost, man—not quite. But, good call."

Someone said: "Berry Mansfield."

Everyone shut up. The boarders all blinked, exchanged owlish looks. We had never tried to classify her. An involuntary sigh escaped someone's chest.

"Booswam?"

"Booswam."

"Booswam."

"Booswam."

It was unanimous: *Booswam.*

"Just Booswam," lamented Paul Winslow. *"Berry Mansfield?"*

Intense disappointment befogged the air, as if we'd squandered our entire allowance on one stupid game at a summer carnival.

"I got an idear," said Charlie Crocker in his pukka Boston voice. "Put her in a class by herself."

"Like *Première* Booswam."

"Booswam *Extraordinaire.*"

"How about *Globoidal Perfection?*" Wentworth suggested gleefully.

"What about just . . . *Perfect Tits?*"

"Hey!"

For a second we thought we had it.

"Negatori," said Danny, disgusted.

Another long pause swept the rooftop.

"Can anyone clarify?"

"Come on, you rectums, clarify, clarify!"

"Someone's got to spherify first."

"Paul?"

Winslow stared off into space with the goopy look he got whenever he was thinking about something that made him anxious. He took a deep breath, then flung it at us:

"*Perfecto Bazoom.*"

"Whoa . . ." we echoed.

We cocked our heads, as though listening for something in the sky. We heard the percussive sonic boom (Per*fect*—O Ba—*zoom!*) and smirked.

"Second."

"Vote on voting?"

"Affirmatori."

"Nays?"

No answer.

"Yeas?"

It was unanimous: Berry Mansfield was in a class by herself.

"*Perfecto Bazoom!*" we all whispered, hugely relieved, and strangely satisfied.

7. "Romping"

On the third afternoon of the first week, I had visitors beneath my lookout in the Great Elm.

"Are you spying on us?" Harriet Bancroft called up. "Because we're spying on you."

Hattie, dressed in field hockey cleats and middy blouse, was singing Gilbert and Sullivan as she dragged along Emma Mansfield and Lili Hooper, with Hannah Gustin, in mufti, bringing up the rear. Under the tree, the droll procession fell apart.

"Forget you guys!" cried Hattie, ditching her companions, and bounding up into the Great Elm.

I can still see her scrambling over the currant bush and the woody fungus, her small mouth wide open, teeth and gums gleaming, her hair the color of a gingersnap. In that first sunlight, the corolla encircling Hattie's frizzy head shone like gold. Tied back loosely, knotted at the nape, Hattie's hair formed a nun's wimple around her longish, irresistible face, her sticky, watermelon smile: all pink, all wet, featuring dark flecks of whatever food she had sampled most recently.

She was such an oddball beauty that boys like me were always missing a lot in our first impressions of Hattie: her terrific hourglass figure, of which she made nothing; her hidden, Carthusian ears, of which you never saw much (when I finally got a good look at Hattie's ears, one night in 1978, I was amazed at how small and dainty they were—like tiny pink bud roses pressed into a bible). And most of all, her fascinating face, of which you had to become a student before you could recognize, much less interpret, its two sides: on the right, the goofy, daffy, gleeful girl (and, invariably, the chocolate frosting from the bake sale cupcakes); on the left, in her narrowed eye, the ray of judgment.

When Hattie left off with Gilbert and Sullivan, no one seemed to know what to do, or say, next. Gussie, peppery as a hash-house cook, called up to me: "Did you know you're sitting in the largest surviving elm tree in all New England?"

"Elm is the traditional wood for coffins," Emma commented. "It rots sort of slowly."

"That's very bleak of you, deary," Gussie said in the finishing-school voice of the girls' favorite housemother, Ducky Wigglesworth.

"Mum says that elms wait to drop their branches," Emma persisted. "They wait through a whole winter storm, for the first peaceful summer's day, when a man's passing underneath, and then—"

"*Splat*," finished Hattie, shinnying up the bough, closer to my perch.

I couldn't take my eyes off Hattie's nose. It was my mother's nose—the same trim aquiline beak—and I wanted to make some gesture to indicate my familiarity with it.

"We have to ask you some questions?" Emma called up, apologetically.

"For the paper," explained Gussie, the only one of the four officially on the staff of the *Ulmus*.

"We're here," Hattie announced with aplomb, "to waylay you."

"We're sort of, um, 'roving' reporters?" said Emma.

"*Romping* reporters," corrected Hattie, "and 'Three little maids from school are we . . .' " And back she took us to

41

Gilbert and Sullivan, only this time in broad parody—bobbing her head as if it were a rock 'n' roll song.

"We put on *The Mikado* last spring?" began Emma.

"And the faculty were in it, too," Hattie broke in, "and Miss Grocock wore Band-Aids over her nipples because she wasn't supposed to wear a bra with her costume."

"Hattie!" Gussie said sharply.

"Ew," agreed Lili, opening her crowded, snaggletoothed mouth for the first time. Lili—a cutoffs rebel—was blond and broadshouldered, with a great, graspable behind.

"But we've got to ask you sixty million questions," pursued Hattie, "because we've been told that you are M–A–L–E."

"Such as, do you feel discriminated against?" Gussie asked seriously, and waited for my reply with the open microphone of a portable tape recorder.

"And are the faculty treating you differently?" appended Hattie. "And do you like it here even without football? And have you noticed our Lebanese faction, such as the prickly-legged Miss Peters and the peachy-cheeked Miss Pregnall?"

"Ew!" said Lili.

"Hat, this is *taping*," warned Gussie.

But Hattie was uncensorable: ". . . And we forgive you for living, and will you be our friend? And are you cuckoo for cocoa puffs? And do you think Barney Rubble prefers being a blonde . . . ?"

I never knew how to reply to Hattie's rhetorical flights, with their strange, satiric mixture of prudishness and sensuality. I was always afraid I wouldn't be witty enough or charming enough, or, in later years, moral enough. But, that day, I didn't have to say a word; she just soared on, inspired:

". . . Because we want to know you, Mas Nomis, and all the facts about you, such as, on account of your big brother and my big sister, you and I are both second eggs."

"Well, so's Emma," Gussie commented coolly.

"So am I," said Lili, "and Gus, you too."

"We're *all* second eggs," said Hattie, eyes widening, agog, bursting with the importance of it all. *"Les Oeufs Deuxièmes!"* she cried, as though she'd just discovered a cause to champion, and for a second, I really thought I might be more in love with passionate, hot-blooded Hattie than with beautiful, melancholy Emma. Hattie blazed in my eyes with all the ardor of a Joan of Arc, and when she raised her arms, cupping her hands around her mouth, she looked very nearly winged.

"We're all going skinny-dipping tonight," Hattie whispered. "At a secret pond. After lights-out."

"Great," I said, "great!" But I was only showing off. A day student, I had no place to sleep over.

"Not to worry," Hattie advised. "First we're going to do our garden chores; then we're going romping by the river; then we're going to meditate; then we're going to fast at supper; then we're going to behave ourselves in study hall; and then, Mas Nomis, you are going to get permission to spend the night so that you may illegally accompany us for a swim in the noodle."

"You can stay," suggested Emma, "in your brother's room in Brewster."

"And bring your brother," Lili added.

"And at midnight," continued Emma, "we'll throw pebbles at the window."

"And Bam-Bam, too," said Hattie.

Within minutes I was out of the tree and into the school's kitchen-greens garden, a large, zinnia-bordered patch cascading over a sunny stretch of soil on the south side of Hoare Barn. By the hand, Hattie led me through the ripened rows, "each one broken off in the middle, like a bar of music," I remember her remarking as she introduced me to the staked, sprawling tomatoes, the leeks and scallions, the unruly bouffants of lettuce.

I was supposed to harvest butterhead lettuce, but I found it impossible to concentrate on any one row of heads long enough to do the job. I kept following my eyes down hanging rows of corn.

Loitering along the marigold borders, I found Emma, a handbasket in the crook of her arm, crouched among some veiny, blue booswam cabbages and some mondo yellow zucchinis.

I came upon Lili and Gussie in a wildly overgrown patch where fantastic orbs lay underfoot, yellow, orange, mysterious, linked umbilically to one another by twisted, ropy stems. Every time I turned around, tall sunflowers were peering over my shoulder.

Hattie looked up from the shade of a furrow and smiled at me. She was pulling onions, potatoes, and carrots out of the swollen brown earth, and I remember feeling, as I watched her, that I had finally arrived. My bare toes, wriggling with pleasure in the soft soil, seemed on the verge of splitting open like heavy seeds, sending forth empurpled green shoots deep into Louisa Little's earth.

"Here," said Emma, holding up to my mouth a fat, succulent tomato. "Bite," she commanded, and I bit, and the musky flesh made my lips tingle, and gobs of seedy juice spurted from the wet opening, running down over my chin and into Emma's cupped, unflinching hand.

In the final unfolding of afternoon, we all joined hands and "romped" by the river. Then we sat down cross-legged in a quiet, needle-carpeted spot under some pitch pines. It was like rest period at camp, with the soft chittering of the birds, and the muddy breath of the river stirring the warm, sweet air, and the shallow respiration of the meditators. The girls all had their own private Transcendental Meditation mantras, and they sat there under the evergreen boughs with closed eyes and decreased metabolic rates, drifting off into six or seven stages of calm and restful contemplation before becoming one with the universe.

Emma shared her mantra with me.

"You *can't*," Hattie hissed, annoyed. "Maharishi said sharing was against the rules."

All the same, Emma leaned over and whispered hers into my ear. But when I closed my eyes and concentrated, my breathing immediately quickened and my metabolic rate increased sharply. I could feel my pulse drumming through my neck. Behind closed eyelids, I couldn't seem to picture anything but the bodies of the other meditators. No sooner had I pictured Emma than my thoughts drifted restlessly to Hattie, and from Hattie to Gussie, and from Gussie to Lili and to Lili's wonderful wide stable seat. . . .

"Sam?" whispered Emma, and it was a shock to find, when I opened my eyes, that she still had her clothes on.

"Was it O.K. for you?" Emma said in a husky voice, apparently very much gratified herself by the meditation.

"I don't know," I whispered. "I think I was just getting started, actually."

"It's hard," she agreed, stretching out in the sticky needles and landing her head in my lap. "It's hard your first time."

"You're all jazzed up," said Muz, when I called to get her permission to spend the night.

"I've been meditating," was the reply.

"I can hear that," said Muz.

In study hall, I sat sightless, sleepwalking through the same paragraph again and again, repeating to myself, as if it were my own authorized mantra: *"Four girls and one boy . . . four girls and one boy . . ."*

I had always hoped that my destiny would include a ménage à trois, but I had neither counted on one so soon nor suspected that, thanks to the school infirmary, everybody in my ménage would come equipped with her own prepaid contraceptives.

"Romping?" said Murray, looking up and rolling his eyes back into his head. "You went *romping?"*

My brother was sitting on his bed in the room he shared with Paul Winslow in Brewster. In his lap lay one of his roommate's KLH stereo speakers. There were tools scattered around on Murray's quilt.

"Exactly how do you 'romp'? Just tell me that, will you, Pieman?"

"Actually, I thought it was fun."

"You would, faggot." Murray drilled me with an eyeball, shook his head, and fell back into mesmerized study of Paul Winslow's malfunctioning woofer.

"Are you coming?" I pressed. "They're going to be here at midnight, you know."

Murray pointed with his chin to a pair of pliers on his comforter.

"Are you coming or not?"

"Just hand me the tool, tool."

"Lili Hooper wants you to come."

"I hope you know, you're going to get kicked out."

"Think about it?"

"The tool, Pieman."

"Just think about it?"

"We'll see," he granted, and I handed him his pliers.

After a statesmanlike interval, I volunteered the subject of black sweatshirts. I had decided that for my getaway to the secret pond, I would need a black sweatshirt and black corduroy pants. Black, I told myself, would demonstrate experience in matters nocturnal. Unfortunately, my brother in those days enjoyed a mania for locks and keys and secret combinations. Murray had the soul of a janitor. He kept all his possessions, including his toiletries, under lock and key, and when he could not find a secure closet, he resorted to the more artful, yet somehow still seedy, world of strongboxes, safes, and footlockers.

"What's happening these days to *which* black sweatshirt?" said Murray.

"You know: the one Mom got at Expo '67."

"Oh, no, Pieman. Not *the* black sweatshirt—"

"O.K., *your* black sweatshirt. Wazoo."

"I wouldn't advise you to wazoo me, Pieman. In fact, I would not advise you—" Murray was suddenly unable to suppress his glee. "Duh, I get it!" he gloated, his voice dumb and cartoony. "You think it would be, like, espionage and camouflage and everything to wear a black sweatshirt out to this pond!"

I told him he was out of his mind.

"Pieman!" he exulted. "Oh, yes! I bet you want my black corduroys, too! Oh, oh, *yes,*" he trumpeted. "Pieman wants my sweatshirt and my corduroys so he can sneak around in the dark all dressed in black!"

The clothing I needed lay cached inside an old portmanteau of Dad's—origin: Berlin, 1932—which now resided at the foot of Murray's bed and which had, built into its dark, fussy, Teutonic lid, a triple-digit lock whose combination Goebbels himself could not have tortured out of my brother. It seemed to steady Murray, that footlocker, with its old-world smell of paraffin and iodine, and he guarded it methodically.

I circled nearby, attempting to appear as if I were merely

zeroing in, however gradually, on a place to sit down for a minute.

Murray manned his bed—steady, opaque, unreadable as a spider.

"I see what you're near," he said, without looking up.

"I'm not near anything," I protested. "What am I near?"

Murray reached out and flipped a toggle switch on a boxlike contraption positioned beside his bed. A powerful floodlight suddenly sent a blazing high beam onto the perimeter of Dad's portmanteau.

"The Controller," said Murray in a deep voice. "Stops 'em dead. Every time."

I rolled my eyes. "Would you just let me have the combo, please?"

"I don't know if I know that combo, Pieman."

"You know it, Murray."

"You may have to say the words," he said dispassionately.

I told him I would never say the words. He replied that he had ways to make me talk.

After a while, I said: "Then will you let me have the combo?"

"Say the words."

"Murray!"

"No one's listening, Pieman. Just say what you want to do."

"You're such a tool."

"Say it: *I want to be cool. . . .*"

Swallowing as much of the sound as I could, I parroted the words. Murray singsonged my next response:

". . . *And sneak around in Murray's black sweatshirt.*"

After I'd submitted, saying every word out loud, Murray took a deep, satisfied breath.

"Just because they went 'romping' with you," he resumed, "doesn't mean they'll let you do anything else, you know."

I told him he was a chicken-shit asshole. "Anyway," I hedged back, just in case nothing did happen at the pond, "it's only swimming. It's just skinny-dipping. It's just *natural.*"

"Natural! 'Natural,' my foot, Pieman. Emma Mansfield and Lili Hooper may be sneaking out for a little nature walk, but we all know what part of nature you're going for."

"You better tell me that combo, Murray."

But now he wouldn't look me in the eye. All of a sudden, my brother had lost interest. Bent over the back of his roommate's speaker, bristling with screwdrivers, Murray had pried open a panel of solid Masonite. Never mind that the manufacturer, the KLH Company of Cambridge, Mass., stated explicitly, right there in a printed warning stapled to the Masonite, that under no circumstances should anyone open the panel. Never mind that Paul Winslow had not authorized the procedure.

"Just come," I said. "Why don't you come?"

Murray's eyes were glaucous, unseeing, glazed with the forbidden pleasures of woofers and tweeters.

"You're my brother," I said, seriously.

Without comment, Murray made an O with his lips and pretended to have learned some vital piece of information from a tiny copper coil.

"Just let me have the combo," I begged, but Murray would not reply—would grant me nothing. I could see in his darting eyes all the sounds of the dormitory: the hissing of the shower and the flushing of the toilet and the howling of the shower-taker; and the unidentifiable whomping above us on the third floor.

"No one's listening, Murray."

Just then, a cloud of radio static burst from the speaker in Murray's lap. Unsurprised, expectant, he coolly adjusted a switch on his private control panel. The static increased in volume. Then—thorough to the end—Murray lowered his voice and said:

"Muz's birthday."

I had somehow forgotten our old code—childhood cipher for tricking grown-ups and outwitting passersby—and I had a moment of panic before I realized that the numerals 3-15 would open Dad's portmanteau.

8. In the Noodle

On the stroke of how many summer midnights had Murray and I, with Sandy Bullman and Bobby Bradford—our Cape Cod gang of four—tossed pebbles at a girl's window, then waited, moonstruck in a rose-hip bush, as the girl descended a trellis? Here at Louisa Little's school, the four pebble-tossers huddled with their bikes in the night shadows under Brewster's hemlocks, and as I crept down the fire escape and stole into the bicycle shed behind the house, emerging stiffly with the first bike I could find—a girls' three-speed with wicker basket—I felt strongly the unsettling, persistent illusion that I was the girl and they were the boys.

We were away quickly. A Little girl, Emma told me, had been raped the previous spring, right on the campus, in one of the Elm Street houses (Emma would not say which); and since then, the school had hired its first security guard, whose name was Ray Roy and who packed an enormous flashlight. ("Beware Ray's ray," Hattie intoned.) But Ray Roy was not abroad and the streets of the village stood silent. Frock-coated Concord was all buttoned up to its chin.

In convoy, we flashed past darkened storefronts, rounded the luminous white flagpole at the end of town, escaped the clinging, sweet and spicy gift-shop smell around the Country Store, and pedaled away on Monument Street. A suppertime rain-shower had left wet leaves pasted to the roadway; I made loud, leisurely S-curves among the cuneate markers. As we glided past Hawthorne's melancholy Old Manse, a sleepy breeze blew in off the Concord River, and Emma, pedaling easily beside me, reached over and laid her long knuckly fingers on my sweatshirted arm.

"Smell the grapes," she whispered, lifting her nose to the wind.

I obeyed, taking in a big whiff. I filled my lungs, nearly blacking out from hyperventilation, but when Emma squeezed my arm, I smelled grapes, all right.

"And alderberry," she urged, squeezing again.

I think I even smelled some tansy. Pedal-happy, unable to stop, I kept taking in autumnal scents by the gulp, and Emma Mansfield, coasting beside me with the wind in her long flowing hair, kept squeezing her approval deeper and deeper into my forearm.

Punkatasset Pond lay a couple miles out of town. Emma and I were the first to arrive at the tire-rutted sandy lane that trailed into the woods and down to the pond. While we waited for the others to catch up (Lili had run over a toad and persuaded Hattie and Gussie to stop and help her bury it), Emma showed me where to ditch the bikes, where to hide from the high beams of passing cars, and where to look up and see Orion thrusting his spear into the flanks of Taurus.

Heads tilted back, lips parted, marveling at the starry, plum-colored sky, we crouched down in some thickets, our shoulders touching. Emma pointed out Jupiter, and Cygnus the Swan, and the pole star, and she described the difference between polar north and magnetic north, and I learned that a blue moon was a real thing—a moon that happened to be the second full moon to shine in a single calendar month. And I discovered that I liked it when Emma pretended to stammer:

"Orion? This handsome hunter? Who Diana loved?" Emma squeezed out in her tremulous, querying way. "She was on the verge? Of marrying him? But, accidentally? She killed him first? And now, forever, he stalks the sky," she concluded sadly, and I was all of a sudden so awed by the infinitude of tragedy in the heavens that when Emma took my hand, slipping it between her cool palms, I gasped, appreciatively.

"Yah," Emma agreed, her voice gentle with sympathy, "I know."

I could not have articulated what she knew or what I knew, but it made my head spin. It seemed uncanny, the knowing. It seemed as if the very laws of nature were changing —as if, with this cool-handed girl (so confident in celestial affairs!) I had entered another hemisphere. I suppose that in school or summer camp someone must have taught me the elementary, geographic difference between magnetic north and true north, yet on Emma's lips it all had a new and astonishing sound. I felt in my vitals a jolt of dismay, a primitive sense of alarm: I was conscious, all at once, of my limits.

Emma, meanwhile, had turned my trembling hand palm-up. She worried the flesh of the thumb-ball and, with almost maternal concern, peered into my palm as though studying the lie of a splinter.

"I'll do a reading down at Punk," Emma offered darkly, as much as to imply that these roadside manipulations were but preliminaries to the more serious fatidic business that lay ahead.

"Great," I said, "great!" And to let her know how profound was my regard for palmistry the world over, I added: "*Great.*"

It was perhaps the first and last night of my life during which absolutely nothing escaped the touch of greatness. I had never, for example, been cut in on before. But when Hattie and the others arrived, Hattie seized me by the arm and swept me into a sort of pondward Yellow Brick Road jig. Emma got left a couple steps behind, but when I looked back to protest—to show Emma my innocence, to prove I'd been hampered against my will (a fine coquette I would have made; my dance-card would have been in shreds)—Emma shrugged the shrug of a middle sister: "So you're going to dance off with Hattie?" the gesture seemed to say. "Well, then, fine. Just don't come crawling back from the floor when you've got splinters that need tweezing."

The shadowy, tire-rutted lane gave way to a trail of loose sand and loam, the pine needles studded with rocks. A thick tunnel of fir overarched the footpath, playing tricks on our eyes. Soon the darkness was mesmeric. As a cat uses its whiskers as an organ of touch, so Hattie used her vocal chords to lead us through the woods, starting off with a couple of verses of "Lions and tigers and bears—oh my!" and then veering off into a recitation of "The Lake Isle of Innisfree."

At the edge of the woods, a moon-bright pasture broke into the clear, sloping down to the copse that encircled the pond. Without a word, we joined hands and, five abreast, burst forward into the light. Underfoot, the squishy turf gurgled with meadow tea. Emma guided us to the sumac-shadowed path that led through the copse and into the clearing favored by Little girls.

It was exactly as I had always pictured the morning of creation. The pond brimmed with silvery light, its smooth, unruffled surface fringed with ringlets of mist. Behind us, a host of bright-white birches shimmered in moonglow. Birds now and then fluttered in the branches. Mice rustled under ferns and fallen leaves, and from deeper in the woods came the emphatic notes of a whippoorwill. The clearing was lush and grassy, resonant with (said Hattie) the "belches of horny frogs" and the "*Sedg-wick* chirp of Massachusetts crickets" (said Emma). The air felt as clear and new as if we'd been the first creatures on earth.

On the bank, a stout tree dipped its roots into the black, moon-spangled water. A rope swing, knotted at its lower end, dangled gamely above the shallows. I was glad to see it. No matter what happened—say I'd lost my nerve on the ride out—I still knew how to show off on a swing, and I ran over to get the feel of the rope, to see for myself what kind of arc it would offer. No sooner did I have it in my grasp than Lili advised:

"That's for Estabrook boys."

"Yah," Emma seconded.

"Not you, Nomis," said Hattie, sighing, disappointed, as though she had expected me to have outgrown or abandoned all boyish urges after only three days at the Little School. But it wasn't just Hattie. They were all looking at me in a pitying sort of way.

"They kind of *hang* from the bottom," reported Gussie, as if, in ways that twentieth-century scientists could only guess at, the knotting of the rope had carried some deep meaning for the Estabrook Boy.

"Oh, yah," reproved Emma, shaking her head at the swing, as though at some primitive appendage that had passed into disuse in the unfolding of evolution.

Feeling somehow lewd and scolded, I let go of the rope and watched it swing limply away. So much for being a boy.

The girls had begun to strip. Surprisingly, I found myself unable to watch. I turned the other way, my whole body stiffening with a sudden, unexpected pang of modesty. My palms had moistened, and now my flesh began to tremble, to quiver all over at the very idea of nudity. But my companions never gave it a second thought. Emma shucked her jeans, stripped off her panties.

"Little girls are terribly sophisticated," I heard my mother say.

Braless, Emma pulled off her shirt, neatly folding the cotton tee, then laying it, just so, on her rope-soled canvas shoes. Slowly, luxuriously, she stretched in the moonlight.

"You'll have to be very grown-up."

Lili kicked off her paddock boots, then peeled off her putty-colored painter's pants and clean white drawers. Hattie stepped out of her flip-flops, dropped her skirt.

"You'll really have to buckle down and work, Sam."

Off came Gussie's corduroys, Hattie's boxy silk panties, Gussie's shirt. Hattie's blouse.

"All those classes! All those books!"

Lili's shirt. Gussie's panties.

"My beamish boy!"

Gussie's bra!

My head swam. I searched my memory for what to do next. I had skinny-dipped with girls only once before, at eleven, in Provincetown, and only with Hilary Moseley and Alix Wiegelmesser. In the knee-deep water by the bulkhead, we had all peered at each other like smart little scientists, and I, prepubescent, my privates utterly hairless, had pasted to my glowing, wormlike baldness the nearest available toupee: a handful of dark, matted seaweed.

At thirteen, at Punkatasset, even with hair of my own, I was staggered by my fellow nudists. With four fully developed sets of bare parts to examine, I was cross-eyed with frustration: Was I supposed to just *look*, openly and naturally? Or pretend (while stealing glimpses of the big stuff) to observe some lesser body part—the clavicle, the ribs, the navel, or (schoolboy's last

55

resort) the epidermis? Would I be expected to keep up my end of a conversation? And what about the dreaded and unpredictable, the importunate boner? Would the pond be cold enough to suppress it? Or would the water be *too* cold? Just when I most needed a show of competence and general humongousness, would my dick retract like the mandibular head of a shrewd old tortoise?

I was the last one in. For the entrances of the girls, the pond lapped gently, encircling each bather's head in rippling rings of radiance. For me, it rocked and rocked, as if my masterful dive were a hilarious joke. Still, I was in, and the pond was warm with silt and summer, and the moon was making luminous, cosmetic improvements in my skin.

"You guys—the pole?" I heard Hattie suggest in a secretive sophomore's voice.

"Yah," agreed Emma. "Let's."

Ahead of me, the girls swam a strong crawl. They were bold, graceful swimmers, and when I caught up, they were already at the pond's equator, circling something on the surface. An obsolete telephone pole, drifting along like an old crocodile, had drawn them out there. The girls slid aboard, one behind the other, and I straddled the rear. The pole, saturated and smooth, made skin-soft by the water, sank under our weight, then corked back up, resilient and ready.

The object was to stand up, all at once, like five log-rollers. But the point of the game, I giddily discovered, was the aftermath of each attempt: the giggling free-for-all, the happy frolicking and splashing, and also, after a while, the happy accidental tickling and touching and feeling. Curiously, though, the more I tickled and touched and felt—the more I experienced every natural, accidental delight of pole-play—the more foolish and chaste and *un*natural I began to feel. Treading water in the middle of Punkatasset Pond, I began to wonder: Was something happening to me—some terrible, irreversible change?

The girls, breathing easy, swam their strong crawl back to shore. I followed, paddling softly so that I could watch them emerge, glistening, from the water. But my heart sank when I saw them jump straight from the pond and run for their clothes, their lustral rites completed. I drifted in, pretending never to have given a moment's thought to moonlight orgies or mossy-banked ménages. I pulled myself onto the bank and remembered that we hadn't brought towels.

"You're shivering, hon'," said Emma, coming over to me at once and laying her cool hand on my forehead. Instinctively, I pulled back, and I remember how grateful I felt when I looked down and saw that Emma was still nude. Her warm, naked body gleamed at arm's length. Her solicitous hand wavered at my forehead, moved to my cheek, stroked the edge of my jaw, came to rest on my shoulder. I scanned her face for some sign of what was happening—a signal of encouragement to return her caress?—but all I found was a troubled look.

It was years before I finally acknowledged that Emma's endearments and caresses, innocent, unbidden, were no greater than, or equal to, the same "hon's," "dearys," and "dear hearts" she reserved, along with a tender stroke, for her three younger brothers, the family pets, her closest friends, and her paternal grandfather. I never got used to it, any of it, and though in later years I trained myself to resist the simultaneously arousing and belittling force of Emma's touch, I look back on my thirteen-year-old self a little helplessly.

"Are you feverish, dear heart?" she asked, and when her fingers fluttered back up to my forehead, I half expected her to shake down a thermometer and pop it under my tongue.

9. A Show of Hands

Warm as flesh, the rocks at the edge of the clearing had conserved some of the day's sun. Emma and I, naked, drip-drying, straddled the largest rock so that Emma could read my palm. Gussie, twisting the water out of Emma's hair, smoked a cigarette, now and then allowing us drags. Lili, twisting the water from Gussie's hair, peeked over all our shoulders.

"You have beautiful hands," Lili told me in her hunt-country drawl.

"Yah," Emma agreed, and held up my moonlit fingers for all to see.

"They're like Em's," said Gussie. "Piano hands."

Across the clearing, Hattie pretended to sun herself. Brooding, moody, she had clasped her hands behind her head and now reclined like a poolside movie star, face cocked toward the moon, tapering toes pointed skyward. Eyes closed, she sang the entire theme song of *The Beverly Hillbillies*.

"You guys?" she called, unaware perhaps that Emma, tracing my lifeline, had just fingered my first big romance (not until college!); and when none of us answered, Hattie sat up and stared at us, unsmiling.

"You *guys*?"

We all looked up.

"Is Christopher Robin really a boy?"

"A girl, I thought," said Lili.

"She *is* a girl," declared Gussie. "She wears dresses."

"—And smocks," continued Lili, "and she has those queer little lips."

"No," said Emma, "she's a boy. They're all boys, except Kanga."

"What about Piglet?" said Lili. "Piglet's a girl."

"Piglet's a neuter," said Gussie. "Piglet got spayed."

"But, you guys?" Hattie insisted, as if her next question actually followed. "Don't you hate the word mature when it's pronounced 'ma-*toor*'? It's so prissy, like saying you want to blow your nose with a '*tiss*you.' "

It almost didn't matter how we replied. "But, you guys?" she called again, moments later: "Didn't you always think Tampax was something that would help you swim and sail and play sports?" And then, only seconds later:

"But, you guys? Does anyone really *like* the Existentialists? They are so mopey, that crowd."

Emma, meanwhile, served as parliamentary chairman. When Hattie asked, "You guys, during a make-out, should you keep your eyes open, or closed?" Emma fielded the question, saying, "So. What do we think?" Then, with oscillating eyebrows, she stated the question and opened the floor to discussion.

When Lili volunteered, "Closed. . . ." Emma shot back: "Closed? Why *closed*?" And when Gussie followed up with, "Open, what the hell?" Emma demanded, in an equally critical tone: "Open? Why *open*?"—as though discussion had now reached a philosophic-artistic plane on which opinions alone would no longer suffice.

Eventually, she turned to me, placing her fingertips on any handy part of my body. With great solicitude she encouraged my reply, caressively asking, "Hon?" as though predisposed to understand me, to favor my judgment. But when I faltered, then spoke too glibly, and then too sentimentally, Emma smiled sweetly (so sweetly I never knew I was being gibbeted) and hoisted up my jejune opinions for all to scorn:

"Um, I'm not sure," I began.

" 'Not sure'?" she summarized, eyebrows ascending.

"Well, I guess open. Yeah, open—open all the way."

" 'All the way,' hon'?"

"Well, I'd want to see everything, wouldn't you?"

"I don't think so, deary."

"But, you guys?" Hattie resumed from her side of the clearing. "What about French kissing—how long is long?"

"So," stated Emma. "Duration of a French kiss: what do we think?"

"Ew," said Lili.

"Yah, but what do we think? A minute or two?"

"About two-and-one-half *seconds*," Lili countered nervously.

"But why, Li?" said Emma.

"Who wants some boy's tongue rammed down your throat for half an hour? If a boy kisses me on the lips, I'm like: 'Yeah?' But French kissing, I'm like: *'Gross.'* So it's weird, I don't know; God!"

"O.K., Li, O.K.," Emma soothed. "Gus?"

"I don't mind it," said Gussie. "It's a little gross, I guess, but if the guy brushed his teeth, it's all right."

"Hat?"

"Even if a boy flossed, first base wouldn't make me go borneo, but then neither would second, third, or fourth base. I like baseball, though. Compared to football or hockey, the players are so polite to each other."

"Hon'?"

"It's—you mean Frenching?—it's great," I proposed.

Emma looked doubtful, but she smiled and cocked her head at various judicious angles, as if to see the question from my point of view. " 'Great,' hon'?" she said. "Great—the same way Monet is great?"

"Monet?" I said.

"What about butterfly kisses?" said Hattie.

"What about blow-jobs?" said Emma.

I nearly fell off the rock.

At first, it was impossible to tell whether Emma was just being offhand, and no one but me seemed to want to break down into small study groups to clarify the situation.

"So. Blow-jobs," persisted Emma. "What do we think?"

Mute, grinning a little, I just sat there, all asprawl, dumbstruck (and flattered) that I was present (and naked) among silky-haired women at a parliamentarian debate about blow-jobs. Of course, it would be difficult to explain later. There was no base in the sexual infield to mark blow-jobs, far less the act of debating them. But at least I would have something tangible to report to Murray.

"I don't like the swallowing part," moved Gussie.

"Same," Lili seconded.

"Oh, Li," Emma broke in, objecting sweetly, "you've never given one."

"Have so—had to."

"Oh, *Li*."

"Have not," agreed Hattie.

"Have so."

"Come on, you guys," inserted Gussie, which shut everyone up. "I mean, once you've gotten over the basic idea, what's the big deal? So it's a little throbby, who cares?"

"So, what else . . . ?" pressed Emma, unwilling to limit debate. "Hon'?"

A dozen fresh points of view seemed to rise in my gorge. The tongue's view of the depressor. The swallower's view of the sword. The tunnel's view of the train. The sharpener's view of the pencil. And so on, through the orificial world. Gussie's authority in things throbby seemed so unimpeachable that I had no amendments to add except a brief sudden attack of gagging. Maybe it was sympathetic response, I'm not sure. In my entire life I have never felt less excited about blow-jobs.

"I'll tell you what *I* think of blowfish," Hattie offered.

"O.K., Hat," said Emma.

Poised, Hattie dipped her feet into the pond and soaked them while we waited. Then she removed them to dry land and sang: "Fake out! I don't know anything about blowfish. I have," she announced, "no adequate information on the subject. Anyhow, it's boring. Doesn't it bore everyone to tears to always be talking about S–E–X and I–U–D and pieces of A–S–S? I get bored just thinking about it. I certainly don't care to *talk* about it."

"Then what do you want to talk about, Hat?" Emma said in a not unfriendly voice.

"Anything important," she replied.

"Like what?" said Gussie.

"Like the formality of the curtain call at the ballet," declared Hattie. "Like how the dancers try to have these extremely modest expressions during an ovation:

" 'No, no, no,' " Hattie stage-whispered in the Slavic voice of a ballerina: " 'Really, Nishkabish, you were the best!'

" 'Oh, no, no, no, I *insist,* Flatulatov,' " she took up on the other side of her mouth, tensing her neck muscles, flaring her nostrils: " '*You* were the more exquisite, the more formidable, and I insist that you receive the much louder applause!' "

Hattie broke off, spread her toes, and plunged them into the pond. "Of course," she said, "there's also the expression on the boy's face when he's *getting* the blowfish."

"Yah," said Emma, warming to the question. "What do we think?"

10. Beware Berry

A rack of ragged yellowish clouds had gathered over the pond, darkening discussion. We ignored the threat. Consideration of time and weather had been temporarily suspended. We had just deferred action—on throbby blow-jobs and boys' facial expressions therefrom—to debate the question of pubic hair and boys' anxieties therein, when across the pond, in the rising wind, the feathery tops of trees signaled distress.

"It's about to rain," Emma decided. And that was that. No debate, no vote, no voting on voting. Emma had predicted rain.

On the way back up to the road, I fell behind the others. Hattie and Emma were trading what sounded like secrets in some droll strain of pig-latin. Hattie was perfectly fluent:

". . . *Beebeewabare Beberrebee* [Beware Berry]," she told Emma. "*Beberrebee ibis goboibibing toboo gobo cubuckoo fobor cobocoboa pubuffs obovober Nobomibis* [Berry is going to go cuckoo for cocoa puffs over Nomis]. *Hebee's veberibee cubute* [He's very cute]."

Later, I was able to pick Berry's name from the chatter in a noisy room—just the sound of it would pinch my heart. But there, on that hushed, muted trail, it had no impact. In the first place, I did not then speak or understand Ubbidubbi, native language of the Little girl. Moreover it was not Berry but Berry's younger sister who paused on that hushed trail and waited for me with lowered eyes.

Hattie went on ahead, and when I came abreast of Emma,

63

she neatly slid her arm around my waist. I was not sure what Emma Mansfield meant by that arm, but I certainly was not going to stop and ask. I shot back a skinny answering arm and waited to see if the spell that had brought me there in the first place would now wear off, turning me back into a frog.

But my form remained, and Emma's curvy right hip and my bony left hip adhered, charm-bound, and I let out a whoop of pleasure that echoed through the woods. It seemed to me that the universe might have a purpose and I a place in it after all. Joined at the hip, Emma and I were able to roll along without a single faltering step, as though gliding to victory in a three-legged race. Every synchronized step suddenly seemed a step in the right direction. It felt fantastic. And when I squeezed Emma's waist—soft and warm as custard—she replied with a squeeze of her own.

"So," I almost said, "what do we think?"

But Emma spoke first: "Bizarre," she said in a low, awed register.

All around us, life had come to a standstill. A terrible, deep-down absence of sound and speech had claimed the heart of the woods. Even voluble, giddy Hattie now held her tongue. Everything stood suspended in dead silence. Then, with a rushing sigh, the rain hissed through the leaves. The springy loam beneath our feet rapidly blackened, and all at once, before I knew what was happening, Emma drew away.

Ham-handed, I followed, trying to turn the last membranes of our Siamese gait into an embrace. But Emma skipped ahead to the bikes, and when I drew up alongside her at the roadway and attempted, however foolishly, to refasten myself to her waist, she shied away, releasing herself into the dark soothing freedom of the cloudburst. "It's so beautiful," whispered Emma. "Let's just feel the rain. It's all so beautiful."

*She said to him, "How can you
say you love me when you do
not confide in me?"*

—Judges 16:15

1. "Hugging"

I didn't know what to do about Emma. She liked to share cigarettes with me at recess and to mete out caresses on the way to lunch. To all my bungling attempts at getting her alone in the afternoon (always on the pretext of going down by the river—"to have a cigarette") she was considerate enough to take me seriously. And one evening, when I stayed on campus, we shared an armchair in study hall. Emma held hands all the way through the last seven chapters of *The Scarlet Letter*. But we never kissed.

Whenever we went down by the river, Emma would crimp her brow at the first touch of my shoulder. We would position ourselves on the dock behind the canoe shed—notorious trysting spot for Groton boys and Little girls—and if I put my arm around her, she would reply by looking into my eyes in her pinched way. If I brought my face closer to hers she would search me with a wounded, troubled gaze, as though somewhere in the past I had caused her untold agony. The closer I crept toward a kiss, the deeper Emma's mood sank, like the claws of a cat being carried toward water.

I could never figure out what she wanted me to do. Every afternoon I failed and every afternoon we ended up talking about art: Emma murmuring deep-felt remarks about the Impressionists, while I, feeling clownish and ineffective, stood with my arm around her, posed in an embrace no more carnal than the standard Christmas-card format for displays of filial affection.

One afternoon, to vary our routine, I steered Emma away from the canoe shed and led her up into a beech whose broad, barkless bough overhung the river. The sun had plunged into its most lurid, fiery phase, burnishing the birches on Nashawtuc Hill, making copper of the river. Emma's hair, especially the little curls at the peak of her forehead, burned with the color of flame. At my elbow, her long locks fell loosely, covering our arms, and when I reached over to touch the reddened stuff, I felt suddenly bashful—the beauty of her hair, the obviousness of my gesture—and I found myself reaching forward, instead, for the safety of her hand.

Emma started to give it to me. She turned her wrist and placed her palm gently in mine, but I had reached too quickly (*lunged,* was more like it), and in my haste and gracelessness I overshot her offered hand; and, overreacting, pulling back, I ended up with her wrist in my grip.

Now what to do? I was holding Emma Mansfield's wrist. But, fool that I was, instead of covering with a joke and taking her hand properly in mine, I did the stupidest thing possible: Solemnly, I squeezed the wrist. And then again, with feeling.

Now it looked as though I *liked* to squeeze girls' wrists. Too proud to play the fool, I had turned a bungled move into an erotic act, and for a second, in my panic, I had a flash of hope: Maybe this was brilliant. Maybe in the outdoors I had stumbled onto a truer, more artistic technique to arouse Emma Mansfield's passion. Maybe—?

But, no. *No,* I told myself. It just looked wimpy and perverted—to be holding a girl's wrist and squeezing the daylights out of it. So what should I do now? Drop the wrist? Try to get a better purchase on the hand? Slowly slide my fingers down onto the back of her knuckles without breaking contact? Apparently, I did not have the guts for any of these maneuvers, for I did something much more daring—the sort of thing at which I can still look back from the vantage point of decades and blush.

The savage glow of sunset had faded. Evening was coming on. Soon the dinner bell would toll across the cooling fields. Emma, plainly less than overjoyed to find me wringing her limbs like an octopus, had turned her attention to the calm blue eastern sky. The first stars twinkled over the horizon. "Look," Emma urged. "Make a wish." But I did not look. I did not make a wish. I did not lessen by one pound per square inch my death grip on Emma Mansfield's slender wrist.

Gallant, full of grace, I bowed my head. Puckering slightly, I kissed the back of her hand. Emma pulled back sharply, and for a wild moment I thought the better part of my kiss was going to land on her fingernails. But I held on and dropped my lips safely behind her whitened knuckles (there was very little blood left in that hand).

Emma stirred uneasily.

"What's the matter?" I said, popping up to find her eyeballs searching my face like klieg lights.

She sighed deeply. "Nothing—that was—" She attempted a smile, then frowned. "It's—nothing?" she faltered, turning her corrugated brow to the indigo sky. "Just—*nothing,*" she insisted, flinging me a sad, sorry look. And then she broke away to face the river with such finality that I was now too timid to try and kiss her anywhere.

So we sat there for a while. We lighted cigarettes and talked about art, and when the bell rang, we climbed out of the tree and went to supper and sat apart at a big table—Emma flanked by Armbrister and Crocker, and I, by Lili and Gussie and Wentworth and Winslow. Usually it was free seating in the cafeteria, but at dinner boarders were encouraged to sit boy, girl, boy, girl whenever they could.

I longed to be a boarder. Those were palmy days for the boys of Brewster. They lived the lives of gods. All that fall, they were fussed over, sought after, celebrated—merely for being male. Overnight, their names had changed. On the way to dinner every evening the leafy campus pathways resounded with some new pet name:

"Poopsy!"

"Wenty Bird!"

"Myrrh!"

"Betty!"

"Wait up, you guys!"

Occasionally, Wentworth would grumble to himself, almost wistfully, "What's wrong with 'Whipper,' or 'Whopper,' or 'Hooter'?"

"Or 'Sluggo'?" Poopsy Winslow would put in.

But, just then, some seniors, gamboling along the path, would cry out, "*Poops*y! Hiya, *Poops*! Howza li'l poopsy tooth?"

And Poopsy Winslow would have to stop and open his mouth and show the tiny little baby tooth that he still retained between two full-sized adult molars. "It just never fell out," Poopsy would explain to any girl who hadn't yet seen the freak molar. Then, later that night, Winslow would find under his pillow in Brewster some little coin or treat or favor, wrapped in tinfoil or tissue or ribbon, left there by some "Tooth Fairy" who'd taken pity on Poopsy for never having collected on the itsy-bitsy poopsy tooth in childhood.

I now begin to see why my mother started every schoolward journey of that semester with,

"You're being spoiled rotten."

"Not exactly."

"But exactly, Sam: Girls calling on the telephone at night. Girls flocking to you first thing in the morning. Girls watching your every move in class and on the field. Girls feeding you at lunch—"

"They do not. We fast at lunch."

"They feed you every chance they get, Sam! You have absolutely no appetite of any kind!"

This, in fact, was true. Between bake sales at recess and fasting at lunch (to say nothing of between-period cubby cupcakes), I was living on a diet almost entirely composed of sugar. There continued to be ice-cream parties in art studio, and once, when Ms. Wilkie brought her infant son to class in a Greenlandic papoose, it occurred to me that, technically, that kid and I were both subsisting, albeit at separate feeding times, on the same breast milk.

"When do you *study*, Sam?"

"I study at home."

"You do nothing of the kind. All you do at home is *sleep*."

True, I had lately been wiped out. But how to tell about "romping"? How to describe the backrub sessions given by "the Hookers," the sure-handed girls of Hooker House? How to explain "Big Sisters"? I had not dared tell Muz that each of us had been assigned a "Big Sister" to welcome us to the Little community. Nor had I revealed that *my* Big Sister was a shy, golden-hearted junior, who, three weeks into the school year, was still delivering to my cubby a weekly plate of warm sugar doughnuts and a glass of grape Kool-Aid. There was simply no way to wear out my welcome with Kathy Cardew; she even waited until I'd gone home for the day before busing the empty plate and sticky, grape-stained glass.

"You stay at school till all hours, Sam, yet your grades don't improve. What are you doing with your time?"

In fact, as a day boy, I lived in dread that every evening, when I tore myself away from campus to catch a train, I was missing out on some fantastic new development in study hall. In the morning, I would hear daily bulletins: *Poopsy Winslow* . . . wedged into a study carrel with *Hattie Bancroft* . . . had *spoken his first words in Ubbidubbi.* . . . *Myrrh Simon* . . . spent study hall *locked into a listening room* with . . . his Big Sister, *Diana McFeeley.* . . . *Betty Crocker* and *Danny Armbrister* . . . elected to the staff of the *Ulmus* . . . *were promoted* to the position of *Ecology Editors,* which entitled them to spend legal late-nights at the printers, getting *hugged by Starry Knight.* . . .

I wasn't entirely left out of the hugging. Each morning, when Muz and I pulled up to Main Gate, there, in the clamorous moments before chapel, a delegation would be waiting to hug me. At many boarding schools, students acted as official guides and greeters. Open-armed, barrel-chested, moon-faced Starry Knight was the Little School's unofficial hugger. A senior from San Francisco (doctrinal birthplace of hugging), Starry was the most knowledgeable hugger in the school.

The theory, of course, was that you and I and the earth could be "friends." All people on earth, regardless of race, age, gender, or religion, were now supposed to be great, great friends; and we, the students of this enlightened era, were supposed to be especially free to express our friendly feelings. All of which meant that in the name of global love we got to feel each other up like mad.

"This sort of toozling is *allowed*—?" Muz would say,

incredulous, as every morning, before we came to a full stop, Starry Knight and several other seniors would spring to the passenger door.

"Mom, would you keep your voice down?"

"—Condoned? During *school hours*? In full view of the headmaster?"

"It's not *toozling*."

"Sam, I understand your sincere, if somewhat misapplied desire to accommodate the *zeitgeist,* but does this kind of thing really have to start first thing in the morning?"

"We're just hugging."

"Before you've even been to class?"

"It's no big deal, Muz. We're just friends."

"Why can't you hug your friends a little later—*after* you've been to class?"

"We hug whenever we feel like hugging. It's a free will situation."

Muz lifted her hands off the wheel and brought them down with such force the horn sounded. "You're being *pampered,*" she shouted. "I want you on a schedule, Sam! I want you on a rigorous study schedule at once! You have simply got to stop this toozling, or I promise you, young man, I will pull you right out of this school!"

2. A Word With Berry

To be exact, it happened at five minutes past eleven o'clock on the morning of October 3, 1971—the morning of my fourteenth birthday. The mail had just been sorted and delivered to the boarders' mailboxes in the Hoare House mailroom. The air was dry and crisp. Above the Great Elm's sunbright canopy, the sky was so blue it hurt. Louisa Little's chapel looked white as cuttlebone. We might have all been walking on clouds—and probably were.

Berry emerged from the mailroom with a handful of letters, and chose the uneven flagstone path between Hoare House and Old School Building. I happened to be using the same path, inching toward the headmaster's office in Hooker. Ray Roy, the night watchman, had nabbed Emma, Hattie, and me after a recent excursion to Punkatasset, and our punishment was to make up our own punishment and report back to the headmaster. I had been elected by the girls to advise Fred Harr that for one week, every afternoon, we would pick up litter around Walden Pond. Which sounded great to me: anything to stay in Concord and spend every afternoon with Emma Mansfield.

When Berry and I caught sight of each other, some thirty feet of flagstones separated us. She was wearing narrow cordovan loafers, a thigh-length mini-skirt of gray suede, and a crimson turtleneck sweater that was not exactly angora and not exactly cashmere; I still don't know what kind of wool it was (alpaca? llama? vicuña?), but it had the softness and pungency of a rose petal, and if today you opened the door to Berry Mansfield's closet and led me blindfolded to the pillowy, sandbagged shelf of sweaters, I would be able to sniff out the very one.

In passing, Berry and I exchanged a total of twenty-five words (Berry: 24; Sam: 1). We spent exactly six seconds in sight of each other before proceeding to our scheduled destinations. After passing, Berry did not look back; I did. I saw the thick, sun-spangled hair, color of wild honey, cascading over the cadet shoulders. I noticed the strong back and slim waist, the fearless upright carriage, such as you would see on a no-hands bike rider. I knew the rest without looking: knew that the buttocks in their taut suede skin would tattoo my heart; knew that the legs would be smooth and suntanned, the color of toffee; knew that the ankles would be bony and slender.

But I did not know then as I know now that the emotions she trafficked in would be as potent as poppies. By the time I wobbled into the headmaster's office, my bloodstream may have shown no traces—or a virtually inadmissible quantity—of a legal substance called Emma Mansfield. A new narcotic, twice as overpowering, had entered my veins.

Take away everything else, and what would still have introduced Berry to my system was the way she carried herself. In those days I almost never noticed a girl's walk. I was too single-minded. A girl's walk, like the invisible pulse of a wave, seemed inessential compared to matters like breast size and shape. But Berry's stride—smooth, unbroken, systolic—had somehow brought inland to Concord a vibration from the ventricular chambers of the sea.

Thirty feet up the flagstone path, it showed itself in rolling suede hips. At that distance, I could feel the first intimations of trouble, of mortality, the complete knowledge and acceptance of the approaching, inevitable scene of drowning.

At twenty-five feet, the sun suffused her skin with caramel colors and rosy tints. In 1971, Berry's flesh was the flesh of a brand-new egg-filled woman: vibrant, fecund, aglow with the hourly release of vital essences and fluids. Obviously the drowning would be rather cozy, amniotic—a farewell and hello to Mom.

At twenty feet, a flash of teeth. Berry's smile shone in that sunny autumn as a singular, steady outpouring of brilliance— certainly the most direct source of light I had yet encountered outside my mother's bedroom.

At fifteen feet, the corners of her downward-turning, long-lashed eyelids crinkled, and the aquamarine eyes fixed their crafty, comprehending look upon me. If, with Emma, the knowing had seemed uncanny, with Berry it was mathematical. No hocus-pocus involved. Pure math: Berry's shrewd gaze let me know instantaneously that she knew that I knew that she knew that I was already enslaved to her.

At ten feet, she called out, in the first of her voices, "Skinny-dipping at Punk with my little sister—naughty, naughty!" And so began my long-standing acquaintance with Berry's toilet-training voice, which was, I am sorry to report, her most tantalizing: There was always the suggestion that in the next moment she would command you to take down your pants.

All of Berry's voices were forceful, effective, sometimes bossy, but she was neither a covert scold, as Emma was, nor a declaimer of selfhood, as Hattie was. Berry Mansfield was a careerist, a woman of affairs, a banker's daughter who straight away invested a voice in you and watched the interest grow. She always kept you guessing. For speaking to boys, the Mansfield sisters had as many tongues as there are generations in the Bible. Emma's tended to be Old Testament: unpredictable and full of doom; Berry's were New Testament: full of the good news. Both had a lashing Mother Superior tongue and a flat, grocery-charging, diaper-changing timbre—the logical phonetic mix for the two oldest of seven offspring from the marriage of lace-curtain Irish (Mrs. Mansfield, née Mary Shanahan) to North Shore Yankees and North Shore money (Henry Lee "Harry" Mansfield, Groton '44, Harvard '48; Lee, Higginson Trust Co.; Myopia, Somerset, St. Botolph).

At five feet, the wavy hips and the voluptuous bosom, rising and falling with the eyes and the smile, surged forward from swells into breakers, giving me about two more seconds to escape, to duck, to swim for shore, or simply to pretend I hadn't seen what I had seen—to get away, far, far away, on dry land, with a nice normal girl.

At four feet came the smell of her hair, a lush, entangling aroma, moist, faintly intercrural, but clean and sweet.

At three feet, she appeared to have facts on me that even Dean Brickley might not have.

At two feet, give or take a few inches, she owned me: "Yup," she said, laughing lightly, relishing the stupefaction on my face, "I know who you are, dummy! *Happy birthday*," she sang, a twinkle in her eye.

"Me?" I croaked.

But of course *me*. The truth was, I had long suspected that something like Berry Mansfield would happen to me, and her flirting, sibylline smile, now just a foot away, seemed only to confirm our appointment.

Methodically, she replied, "Edward Sampson Simon, October Third," as though flicking into motion, like the plate-and-stick man on Ed Sullivan, one more plate in a series of smoothly spinning plates.

And finally, here she was, right beside me.

For the whole of the last six seconds, I had been standing my ground, straightening my spine, squaring my shoulders, lifting my chin—getting taller. And now, all at once, in the great rip and boil of Berry's passing, I felt a queasy sense of diminution. I was sinking. My lungs popped in panic, my heart sprang into my throat, and I went up on tiptoe.

But even buoyed up to maximum height—and bobbing up and down—even then Berry Mansfield topped me by four inches.

3. Friendly Customs

When leaving school grounds, every Little student had to sign his or her name and destination in the Old School sign-out book. During free periods, Berry and I began to sign out to Friendly's, one of two local ice cream parlors. Brigham's, downtown on Main Street, was the more established; cliques convened in Brigham's booths. Friendly's, uptown on Thoreau Street, faced the railroad depot. Racy, adventurous, Friendly's was for couples—hand-holding couples who might need to hop a train at a moment's notice.

Berry and I, meeting at Main Gate, would link fingers and run to Friendly's through the fallen yellow leaves. Before sitting down, I would stake out the lavatories.

"You dummy," Berry would say, "she isn't here." Then, sharply: "She likes you, you know. Emma really likes you."

"I like Emma."

"Then why don't you do something?" Berry would arch her eyebrows, make it look as simple as ordering soup.

"I did do something. Emma won't do anything with me."

"She's shy; she likes you."

"I like her."

"And? So—?"

"So—what about this?"

I would gesture hopefully toward our booth, our cutlery, our plump sugar shaker with its silvery mons veneris. At Friendly's, Berry and I had a booth. We had a flavor. We were known. And Berry knew the waitresses: Here was Geneva and here was Hazel, beaming under pewter helmets of hair, and the minute we reclaimed our booth, those large smiling women with their large swollen hands would present us the laminated menu as if they were issuing a marriage license.

"Butter Crunch, please," Berry would start. "Oh, and tea?"

"Young man?"

"Same."

Geneva would then ask Berry, "Will that be all, dear?"

"Ask the growing boy," Berry would answer, smiling back at the waitress, while looking pointedly into my eyes. Mock-serious, she would explain our project: "We're trying to fatten him up, Geneva. We're hoping he'll grow."

"Won't be long now," Geneva would say, casting a friendly eye over my skinny limbs.

Smarting, I'd duck behind the menu and order for bulk: "Um, some fries, with gravy. Big Beef Cheese, lightly toasted, heavily buttered. Some onion rings, very crisp. Some extra mayonnaise. Large Chocolate Fribble. And a side order of scrambled eggs with toasted bran muffin—"

"No eggs, young man."

"Bummer," Berry would say, without irony.

"But it's only five after," I would argue.

"No breakfast after eleven," was the answer.

"Is there ketchup?"

"On the table, young man."

When Geneva had left, Berry would nail me with a sly look and order: "Butts."

We had a brand. We smoked filtered Old Golds. I had never had a brand with a girl before, and every time I slipped the white king-size pack with the blue-red-and-gold insignia into my breast pocket, I felt as if I'd been decorated by a royal order. Berry, an old hand at outwitting guilt, had designated me Keeper of the Pack.

"I'm quitting tomorrow," she would regularly announce as I stripped off the cellophane and tossed away the coupon.

"Forget it, you can't."

"Yah," she'd insist; "I only smoke for fun."

Reverently we'd reenact our ceremony: Berry would give the word, I would doff the pack. She would wield the butts, I would strike the match. She would light two, hand over one. We'd puff.

Squinting, Berry would watch the first plumes of blue smoke uncoil from the tips of our cigarettes. Then I, exhaling a plume of gray smoke, would watch her watching the blue plumes. Then she would exhale a gray plume through which she would watch me watching her watch the blue plumes, and all the while I would be thinking: *She wants me to think she knows what I'm thinking.*

"I know what you're thinking," she'd say.

"Do not."

"Do so; I know you better than your wife will ever know you."

"O.K.—what?"

"You think I want you to think I know what you're thinking."

"Do not."

"Do so. You also think I think you're too short."

"Well, you do," I'd protest. "Don't you?"

"Do not."

"Do so."

I had to be watchful. With Berry, the wind was always shifting into a new quarter:

"So what am *I* thinking?"

"I wish I knew," I'd reply humorlessly.

"I love your hair," she'd mention, offhand.

"You do not."

"Do so!" she'd protest, and then reach across the table to tousle my hair.

After the first couple of cigarettes, I would reach for Berry's hand, which she would let me hold across the tabletop. Then, with unconcerned, forgetful fingers she would shake loose, saying, "But wait: So why don't you like Emma anymore?"

"I do like Emma."

"But you like me better."

"I like you better."

"You're not telling me something," she'd challenge, fastening her eyes on mine.

"I *am* telling you something."

"You'd better be!"

"I am! I like you much better!"

"That's better. But wait: So what else?"

In Friendly's, impounded in our booth, I felt for the first time the irresistible suction of Berry's demand for all the news:

"Come on," she'd coax, inclining her head forward. "What'd you do?"

"What'd I do when?"

"When you thought Emma didn't want to do anything."

"I'm not really sure."

"Come on, Sambo: *Entre nous.*"

The more I didn't tell her, the more I held on, the lower she'd incline her head and the more her breasts would push forward.

"Come *on*," she'd whisper hoarsely, peeking out from under her brow.

Never had I before, and never have I since, felt so strongly the urge to tell someone everything I knew. But to make the tautness between us last, I would pay out my information as slowly as I dared:

"I didn't do anything, really."

"Then what'd *she* do? Did she say anything?"

81

I'd let Berry wait. Five seconds. Ten seconds. I'd fondle the sugar shaker. Finally, I'd lose control, giggling a little—"She told me to make a wish!"—and at the first sound of a genuine fact, Berry's head would rise, her larynx would relax, and some of the first exquisite tension would be gone.

"So this was down by the river," she'd summarize briskly, as though she'd been briefed long ago and needed merely to compare accounts. I have a hunch Berry knew she could always depend on a factualist like me to correct the guesses that she disguised as statements:

"So this was behind the boathouse."

"We actually sat in that tree."

"So this was the time you were doing stuff."

"Well, there was only one time."

"When you were arm-in-arm."

"Well, we were always arm-in-arm. This time we—"

The more Berry knew about anything, the more she seemed to have the right to know everything:

"This time," she'd continue, threading the needle for me, "you guys were getting very lovey-dovey, and then you did that thing."

"What thing?"

"You were bad."

"I was not."

"Were so. You guys were getting all lovey-dovey and then you reached over and groped Emma."

"Groped? How do you *grope*? Who told you that?"

"I just know."

"You do not."

"Do so! You were very naughty."

"Did Emma tell you I—God, I've never heard anyone but my mother say that—*naughty*? How was I *naughty*?"

"I'll tell you what Emma told me you *didn't do* when you tell me what Emma told *you* right after what you did do."

"What'd I do?"

"What'd she say?"

"You mean when I was holding her hand?"

"She didn't say it was her hand, buster."

"What'd she tell you?"

"We're sisters; we tell each other everything."

"So what'd she tell you?"

"What part of her hand?—You're so cute when you get nervous."

It was always a little like a bad dream when the last of it came out, as if, under local anesthesia, I were being allowed to observe the surgical removal of my own large intestine. In those days, even when I made an absolute pact with myself not to tell Berry that one last thing, I would always find myself moments later telling her every last thing:

"I held her wrist."

"Wrist? Her *wrist?*"

"Yeah." (There would always be the slightly sickened feeling after it had all come out.)

"You dummy! You were putting the moves on Emma, and you just sat there, holding her wrist! What'd she say?"

"About what?"

"About you holding her wrist!"

"What's the difference? I don't know. Nothing happened. We talked about art—God, I wish I could barf."

"Oh, yah, you have that thing—that gagging thing."

I did not often fall for Berry's next maneuver: To rope me back in, she would begin to sound vaguely bored with me and my problems. She would tilt her head to one side, root under her hair, weed an earring, and, in an incurious, dull voice say, "Yah, I know," to whatever particular I mentioned. Meantime, she would drift back to worry some earlier bead of information, and, though preoccupied, she would continue to ask routine questions, barely acknowledging the replies, monitoring the flow of incoming news with a radar-like blip: "Yup . . . yup . . . yup . . . yup . . . yup . . ."

One afternoon in our booth, while Berry was weeding earrings and generally pretending to be bored with me, I counterattacked with a long, seemingly irrelevant story about that morning's chapel, which Berry had missed, but which she also claimed to have heard about:

". . . So Mr. Harr was getting up to make announcements . . ."

"Yup . . ."

"And he was joking around with Dean Brickley . . ."

"Yup . . ."

"But he tripped in the aisle . . ."

"Yup . . ."

"And his dick fell off into the pulpit . . ."

"Yup . . ."

"And then, in front of the whole school, he announced that I love you . . ."

"Yup . . . wait: What?"

For one full, triumphant second I had her—completely. Outside, across Thoreau Street, a boxy Boston & Maine locomotive rattled into the depot, bound for Fitchburg. The sun streamed through fake colonial windows. Our tea smelled of tar. The world had just shrunk by one size and it was going to fit me. Berry Mansfield was mine.

"What?" she shrieked, eyes asparkle.

I shook my head: No, I was not going to tell her again. And with that, her pleasure and curiosity grew so gargantuan there didn't seem room for both in the booth.

"But, wait!" she cried, leaning forward across the tabletop

and rocking with excitement. *"Come on,"* she coaxed, and again I shook my head.

Now we locked eyes, and Berry gave me her special crafty look. She spaced out her words evenly, firmly: "What did you say."

A command, not a question. If I did not tell her, I was going to get the spanking of my life.

Holding her look, I said: "I love you."

"That's not what you said. Come on, Sam."

"That's exactly what I said!"

"Come *on*," she begged, her voice cracking, her eyes overbusy with the effort of trying to appear cunning and careless at the same time.

"I love you," I repeated stubbornly.

"You do not."

"But I do," I protested, flailing around to find a voice equal to my adoration and pitching headfirst into a hoarse, choirboy's contralto: "I do!"

Berry gave me a serious, questioning look—halfway to sympathy. Then, abruptly, she leaned to her left.

Hanging over the linoleum floor, she shook out her long honey-gold hair until a yard or more of it flowed free of her scalp. For an instant, she seemed perfectly suspended, as if a magician had levitated her out of the booth.

"Why can't you be four inches taller?" she asked, sideways, adding airily: "Can't you grow any faster?"

I sat motionless, rigid with humiliation.

"Only *kidding*," said Berry, resuming vertical position. "You're not mad, are you?"

Without waiting for the answer, she signaled for our check.

4. Danny in the Void

The first cool, apple weather lapsed into Indian summer, and for days it was puzzling just to get dressed for school, for fall, for Berry. I needed someone to talk to about her. My brother was out of the question. Murray prided himself on being as practical about girls as he was about money. He thought I was a fool to spend even one penny eating ice cream with a girl whose heart I could never hope to win. ("Anyway, you just want her for her tits" was the standard fraternal rejoinder.) In Murray's book, the fool who persisted in his folly became not wiser, but broke.

"Why don't you go after *Emma* Mansfield?" complained my brother. "At least she's your size."

Poopsy Winslow was too full of his own anxiety to help sort out mine. Afraid that he wasn't being taken seriously—anxious about becoming a mascot for seniors, an easy target for Tooth Fairies—Winslow launched a program of self-improvement. While the rest of us were thumbing through *The Joy of Sex* on the cheesy sofa in the Brewster common room, Poopsy was upstairs in his room, wrestling with Beckett and Sartre, pinning down Genet, Pinter, and Stoppard. His mind expanded so fast, grew so bulky with doubt and dread, you could see the stretch marks.

"What *is* reality?" Poopsy would bellow after a light work-out with *Being and Nothingness*. "How can we know? Am I real? Are you real? Is this book real? Is that book real? Is Hattie Bancroft real, and if she is—if she's not just my 'illusion'—then why won't she do anything with me besides meditation?"

"Shut up and come down here, Poops. This book is real. Take a look: The pictures are unbelievably real."

"How can they be? They're an illusion."

"They're making us horny, for one thing."

"So you're horny? Ergo what?"

"Ergo, reality. Look at the Pieman: He's fourteen; he's horny. How much more real can you get?"

"But how do we even know 'fourteen' is real? And if it is—if it's not just some illusory speck in the void—then what? 'Fifteen'? What if 'fifteen' doesn't *exist*?"

"But, Poops, look at us—look at Betty Crocker, look at the Bird. . . ."

"What if we're all just *waiting*?" Poopsy would stammer, haunted. "What if sixteen *is* real? What if it *does* come? Then what? *Seventeen*? And then, at seventeen, we start waiting all over again—but for what? *Eighteen*? Eighteen! How do we even know *reality* is real, let alone *eighteen*. Oh, it's all so . . . *bizarre*. . . ."

At this point, Poopsy's pink-rimmed eyes would bug out. "Existence is so *undecided*!" he would wail, and then he would step up to some nearby object, such as the door to the Worrells' apartment, and kick it with his blunt-toed Frye boots.

Betty Crocker, on the other hand, had the easy, cheerful warmth of a country feed merchant. Unfortunately, Crocker knew more about Berry Mansfield than I was ready to buy. He had gone to North Shore Country Day School with three of the Mansfield sisters, and his sunny face and deep browridge would darken whenever Berry entered our conversations:

"Mansfields are bad news," he'd warn, softening the laconic voice of Yankee caution only slightly: "Do what you have to do, but don't forget, Berry Mansfield is queen of the hive. She'll never do anything with you except bite off your head. She eats drones like you for breakfast."

Wentworth, meantime, was too clownish for close friendship, too relentlessly the common room cutup. And Purvis was too cool, too unhappily sophisticated, in that quarrelsome, slack-jawed way in which New York City kids were always too sophisticated—always, for instance, insinuating that you didn't know anything about anything just because you had never spent the night eating peyote buttons with a bisexual junkie at the Chelsea Hotel. Sophisticated stuff like that just *happened* to guys like Purvis. Something sophisticated was always happening to kids who lived in New York.

Beyond Purvis, prospects thinned out. I had made no real friends among the forlorn band of Brewster boarders whom Wentworth and Armbrister called "the Dinks." For if the rest of us were bedeviled by the paradox of our new Eden—the gnawing of continuous want amidst unending exposure to plenty—our condition was all but unknown to loony Tad Gillespie, who talked to his sandwiches at lunch; eager Peter Hemmerdinger, who blew frothy bubbles with his own saliva (Hemmerdinger lasted only till second semester, when he became an Alice Cooper clone and dropped out); brainy Albert Ackerman, who had rubber animals for erasers and pet names for the animals; Euro-faggy Sergei LaFarge, who wore a high-collared black opera cape, addressed his father as "Pa-*pah*," and never (as far as we knew) varied his weird toilet habits, among them: standing up to wipe himself.

All of which left Danny. He was the first friend I'd had who'd lost his virginity—on an oil-drilling rig in Prudhoe Bay—and who had also read more than me. ("That's all there is to do on a rig, man—read and ball.") We had both read all the obvious stuff—modish writers like Camus and Vonnegut and Brautigan and Hesse. But Danny had read Joyce, and not just *Dubliners;* he was intimate with *Ulysses.* He had "done" *Portrait of the Artist,* gone all the way with *Finnegans Wake.* Danny had also read Freud, Kafka, Marx, and Malraux. His room was a world in paperback, and he would sit me down and make me read slim Grove Press volumes and cool, slightly scary-sounding authors—Borges, Bowles, Handke, Hamsun, Pynchon—on the grounds that I was worthless and these guys were art.

But more than Danny's tales, Berry Mansfield's breasts provided the idiom in which our friendship began. After sports, in fog, in frost, on bright days and in dark, Danny and I would huddle on the dock of the boathouse, smoking Balkan Sobranies, staring into the sluggish river, hypnotized.

"God," one of us would start.

"Oh, *God*," the other would agree.

"Unbelievable," argued the first.

"Fucking unbelievable," amended the second.

"God, she's amazing," declared the first.

"*She's* amazing?" countered the second. "*They're* amazing."

"They're amazingly un-fucking-believable," we joyously told the river together.

Danny admired Berry's bust almost as much as I did. He alone was unafraid to confess the full extent of his adoration. Danny had realized, quite sensibly, that there was no reason to be private or possessive about Berry Mansfield's breasts. Untouched, wild, immeasurable, they were beyond our control and therefore functioned as a kind of public enterprise—a precious natural resource to be set aside as permanent wilderness, enjoyed and respected by all, like the National Parks.

Apropos of nothing except the trust we had begun to place in one another, Danny might murmur,

"Berry Mansfield's breasts."

And I, returning the shibboleth, would solemnly reply,

"Berry Mansfield's breasts."

They seemed palpable.

"God, I want to suck *Berry Mansfield's breasts*—just *one* of them," Danny would generously offer, "I don't need both!"

And my admiration for anyone who would say something like that—out loud—was almost as great as my desire to fasten my mouth to the other of Berry Mansfield's breasts, the one Danny hadn't laid claim to. But all I could bring myself to say was,

"Perfecto Bazoom."

"Yeah, 'Perfecto Bazoom,' my ass. You want to suck them as badly as I do, man."

"Yeah," I'd agree, jittery, ashamed, "no kidding."

"Did you beat off last night?"

"Yeah."

"You are such a dink, man. You've got to save yourself."

A great advocate of Fred Harr's new humanities course, "Myth, Dream, and Symbol," Danny had developed a theory that when one abstained from masturbation before sleep, one would dream more deeply carnal dreams, producing sexier, more revealing images of one's true unconscious desires.

"You've got to save yourself for your id," Danny would remind me when I left campus in the evening. It became our parting cry: "Save yourself for your id, man!"

I almost never managed to save anything for my id, but occasionally some fragment of a dream would emerge into my waking thoughts at school, and I would find Danny at recess:

"Had this weird dream last night," I'd begin, and the instant I mentioned Berry's appearance in the dream, Danny would break in peremptorily:

"They're just your mother's breasts, you know. That's what we're all wishing for: We just want to go back and suck a breast as big as our head."

"My mother's breasts aren't as big as my head."

"They were when you first started sucking them, man."

After Danny had listened to the whole dream, he would frown and interpret:

"Obviously you're wish-fulfilling about Berry Mansfield. She's your devouring, castrating, voluptuous mother-figure, your *anima*. I'm not sure what the blunt object is—probably a phallus. The swimming pool is your unconscious, and Henry Kissinger is obvious: You were dispatched to murder him because he's your father-figure, but you didn't succeed because you couldn't decide between the castrating mother, for whom you have conflicting feelings of rage and lust, and the power phallus, which scares you because it means killing your father and balling your mother."

Danny would invariably get bored with the whole "Wet Dream and Symbol" business long before I would. Disgusted, he would say: "Forget this *vagina dentata* shit, man. We've got to get *pussy*—pussy that wants to ball."

"Like who?"

"Like any chick who wants to ball."

"Like *who*?"

"Get 'em wasted," Danny would muse. "Wasted on Boone's Farm. Then ball like crazy."

5. Hattie in the Barn

Louisa Little believed that an educated woman should know how to change a tire and plant a tree. Not for the Little girl the etiquette lessons and maid service of the classic girls' finishing school. Up with the rising bell, the resourceful young woman chopped wood, tended the garden, fed the animals, mucked the stalls. Miss Little's girls had stopped just short of milking cows and making butter, and though boarding students were no longer required to take turns on the tractor, they were still asked to perform light chores around the houses, barns, and garden.

In the clear, dewy chill of those first October mornings, I would often take an early train to school just to watch Hattie doing her chores in the barn behind Hoare House. Huddling in a square red wheelbarrow, and wallowing in warm composty smells, I would ask Hattie a million questions while she fed the houseparents' geese, tended her pet turtles, Abélard and Héloïse ("The only doomed lovers in the amphibian world"), and greeted the day. In Ducky Wigglesworth's tall green rubber boots, with the ruddy glow of morning overspreading her fair skin, Hattie wore high on her cheeks the round red badges of a seasoned greeter of the day.

"I don't know what to tell you, Mas Nomis," Hattie replied one morning after I'd asked for advice about Berry. "I think she likes you very much and thinks that you are *veberibee cubute*, but I don't know if her heart is going borneo. Dig me, pygmy?"

"You mean I'm too short."

"Nooo," said Hattie, scrinching up her face. Hattie, on the verge of telling you something, would pucker her lips, slit her eyes, harden her chin, drawing her lips downward. When she continued, she looked like a mandarin of old Cathay:

"No, Nomis, it's the way you think of her. The one thing Berry hates more than anything in the world is being thought of as perfect. She told me about your vow."

"It was a pact, not a 'vow.' "

"She said a vow."

"She did?"

I was stunned. In Friendly's the previous afternoon, Berry

and I had agreed that no matter what ever happened between us, we would meet at the top of Mount Katahdin on the last day of the last year in the century—December 31, 1999—so that when we awakened next morning we could be the first couple in the entire continental United States to see dawn break over the new year, the new century, the new millennium. We had also sealed the agreement, though not, as I had hoped, with a kiss. Chastely protected from me by the obstruction of our booth's tabletop, Berry had leaned forward and mouthed the smacking sound of a kiss—"Mwaah!"—and then instantly resumed normal conversation.

The anticlimax in Friendly's had pained me deeply, but now, here in the barn, I was floored. I couldn't believe that Berry, for all her grace, beauty, and sound, tasteful judgment, had cheapened our solemn pact by retailing the secret to someone else—*anyone* else, even Hattie, her best friend.

"Did she tell you what I said?" I had told Berry that she was "perfect."

Hattie nodded curtly, and I felt an itchy crimson balaclava roll down over my face from the top of my head, leaving exposed only the eyes and nostrils.

"She told you what I said about her?"

Again, Hattie nodded, this time squinting with her stern left eye.

"She couldn't have," I decreed. "She *wouldn't* have." I was now more angry than dismayed. It seemed unjust that my ideal woman could also be a blabbermouth.

Hattie's face, the left side especially, had turned stony, and she replied once more with a harsh eye.

"But why?" I begged, blinking. *"Why?"*

"Maybe," Hattie ventured, "to make you think she's *not* so perfect."

"I didn't *say* she was 'perfect.'"

"Yes, you did, Nomis."

My eyes smarted—watered with the truth. I thought I was going to cry. "Well, I don't think so now," I stammered

"Yes, you do, Nomis. And you will. And I know you will, because I believe in perfection, too—and sentiment—and we are alike that way, Mas Nomis. We are the same genus, same species, same soul, just different genders. Come—" She took my hand and pulled me out of the wheelbarrow. "—I'll show you perfection."

Hattie led me across the main floor, past the goat tie-ups and the dusty feed passages and the low-beamed gallery of mangers, into a sheepfold where a gray goose hissed a greeting. The goose belonged to Ducky Wigglesworth. Her name was Honoria.

"She made her first egg yesterday and two more this morning," Hattie whispered. "Look," she urged, and her eyes cried at the sight of two perfectly formed, whitish eggs huddled in the straw.

"How long," I said clumsily, "before they hatch?"

"She's not sitting, silly."

"What do you mean? Where's her mate?"

"She doesn't need one. You've got it all mixed up, deary. You are one of the millions who carry with them the misconception that girl geese make eggs only with the assistance of boy geese. Girl geese, like girls of my species, make eggs anyway. To make a gosling, she has to have a boy goose, a mating pond, some flapping, some angry-sounding gabbling, and then it's over and the egg is fertilized."

"Oh," I replied.

"The trouble is, whenever anything gets L–A–I–D, boys like to think they know what's going on. Such as the other great misconception, which is that the Immaculate Conception refers to Jesus' conception when in fact it refers to Mary's. Her mum's womb was pure, too."

"Oh."

"I don't blame boys, though; when you think that they make two million ravenous sperm a day, and we roll out only one defenseless egg a month—no wonder something's out of whack between us."

"You can say that again."

The chapel bell was clanging across Senior Garden, and for a moment we listened to school come to life beyond the barn.

"Just don't think too well of her," said Hattie. "And don't be sentimental. Berry has a horror of puppy dogs swarming around her, licking her hand, lapping her face."

"But I don't!"

"But you do, and you will, and she'll hate you for it." Hattie slit her eyes, puckered her mouth, hardened her chin: "I don't think she minds wolves," counseled Hattie, "but Berry hates puppy dogs who think she's perfect."

6. Berry in the Common Room

How I worshiped her! Every day at recess I made the first of three daily pilgrimages to the common room in Hoare. It was legal to smoke there, and that was one good reason to go. But the real enticement, the whole point of my faithful attendance, was the tingle I would feel upon being received in the room where Berry Mansfield sat enthroned. Overheated, bristling with loaded ashtrays, reeky as a hamster cage, the common room was a squalid, turbulent place, all nerves and excitation, and whenever I poked my head in there, I always held my breath. I knew I had arrived in no ordinary, no common room.

Berry conducted her affairs from the important, shawled sofa beside the hallway door. With her retinue ranged around her, she sat by the hour, deep in the purple, waiting for informants to bring her the news. It came in many media: From leather Levi's labels Berry apprehended significant facts such as waist and inseam sizes. From a brand-new magazine called *People* she would soon be reading as if to a mob. From primary documents—letters, diaries, dream-journals, address books, report cards, teachers' comments, student self-evaluations, notebook marginalia, and blue-jean graffiti—she fashioned her own history. You could always find Berry's fan mail (a mash note penned by some breathless, high-strung Groton sophomore) discarded beneath the sofa, inviting all readers. You had to be careful about what you let drop in the common room: Anything that came before a Mansfield's eyes and ears eventually found its way to her vocal cords—and then the floor.

As a rule, Emma sat on her older sister's right, with Hattie on Berry's left. Though each Mansfield deftly maintained her own sphere of influence, Emma always gave the signal to smoke:

"Come on, you guys," she'd say in her wise, tragic voice. "Let's have a cigarette."

And then everyone, except Hattie, who never smoked, would put down her homework, reach for packs of Old Gold, and light up. Gussie usually served as Mistress of the Match, with Lili as Cracker of the Window, and Tizzy Tucker and Hilary Fraser as Ladies of the Ashtray.

Berry, seated in laurel-headed, numismatic profile, her shoulders wreathed in robes of ermine smoke, would then turn to me as Keeper of the Pack. Accepting an Old Gold and a light, she would answer with her crafty look.

"I've got a TL for you," she'd announce coolly.

TL's, or "trade-lasts"—another name for exchanging

compliments—served the daily purpose of renewing Berry's authority, as well as offering a controlled system for flirting: Berry would reveal a compliment about me only if I first supplied a compliment made by a third party about *her,* for which she would "trade last."

Emma, who flouted TL's, would in her turn announce— mid-cigarette—that she was quitting smoking for a week. She would then spend the rest of the day languishing on the sofa, head pillowed in Gussie's lap, complaining of cramps and headaches and constipation. She always made it through the first day without a puff. But, as the hebdomadal ordeal went on, and as everyone grew gradually accustomed to Emma's abstention from the daily cigarette rituals, Emma would begin to belittle herself (as only Emma could belittle: in the voice of New England Conscience), announcing that she felt "pathetic," and "fallen," and "defeated by vice." A terrible cloud of Calvinist gloom now enshrouded her every word:

"It's . . . it's . . . it's . . . just—so *hard.*"

Berry, rolling her eyes, would blurt: "Little Miss Merry-thought is just trying to get attention," and Emma, swift and silent as a cat, would stalk out of the common room, straining everyone's loyalties.

Even then, long before all of New York became their common room, the Mansfields and their friends would discuss each other in one's absence from the circle. Even then, Berry and Emma knew the trick of gossiping and being gossiped about while appearing for all the world as if one were only passing the time of day.

"Emma's going to be the one to lose her virginity first," Berry foretold when Emma had slipped away for one of her sullen, solitary walks on the Squaw Sachem Trail.

"No way," chimed Gussie and Lili.

"I bet money," said Berry. "She said that in her dream last

night she did it with Brad Wentworth and that it was weird because he 'moistened' her nipples, like one of those towelettes you get in Maine after eating lobster."

Another day, when Hattie had gone off by herself to audit a "consciousness-raising workshop" in the media department, Emma decided, "Hat just needs a boyfriend."

"She likes Poopsy Winslow," said Gussie.

"Not anymore," Berry reported.

"Yah," said Emma, "she does."

"No," returned the older sister, "she doesn't. It's over."

"As of when?"

"*C'est fini*. She's not borneo."

"*Beberrebee* still has my best *ubunduberwebear*," Hattie thought to mention one evening when Berry had gone to borrow some laundry detergent from the Wigglesworths.

"She's had my grandmother's pearls since that alumnae singing thing in Boston," Hilary Fraser complained.

"I'd just like to know what the hell happened to my sheepskin gloves," put in Gussie.

"Or my cashmere turtleneck," added Lili.

"You can't leave your stuff around Berry," Emma said bluntly. "She's got sticky fingers."

To myself I always wondered: What do they say when *I* leave the room? If Emma Mansfield has no trouble calling her sister a klepto, then how hard could it be to pillory me?

But of course that was the compelling thing, wasn't it? That was the thing that always brought me back for more. It wasn't, let's face it, the Old Golds, or the trade-lasts, or the irresistible excitement of the Mansfield circle that drew me back to that smelly room three times a day. It was the fair expectation that I was going to be discussed. The minute I left the room, I knew I was going to be their next victim.

*   *   *

Late one afternoon, after wrenching myself away from the common room, I missed my train to Cambridge. All the way back to campus I debated whether to drop in again, or just to wait at the depot for the next train. I couldn't decide either way and ended up more or less in the middle: I walked back to Hoare, but entered neither through the front nor the back, but the *side* door, which led past the mailroom and into the rear hallway adjacent to the Wigglesworths' apartment.

As I passed through the cold, tranquil mailroom, loud, heated voices penetrated the wall. Berry's was hottest of all. She was fuming: "So get him home! Just get him to come home! It's no big deal!"

I stopped in my tracks, electrified. Blood pounded through my ears. My heart cannonballed when I heard Emma concede, apparently in her turn, that if she *had* to choose . . . if the Bomb *had* dropped . . . if every man in the world, including Robert Redford, *had* been killed or sterilized . . . if the entire contraceptive supply *had* been vaporized and Dean Brickley *had* been forced to issue weekend slips to every Little girl of childbearing age . . . in short, if Emma Mansfield were forced to take home one Little boy with whom to lose her virginity and repopulate the planet, then from among all twenty-four able-bodied specimens she would pick . . .

"Sam Simon . . . I guess. He's the cutest one."

"So do it," proposed Berry. "He likes you. He'll do it. Just put in a pink slip. Tell Brickley that Mum and Dad are home. Or just say Mum's not feeling well and Dad's away on beeswax."

"No, *you* say," Emma demurred, her voice shrinking.

"I can't," replied Berry. "Brickley can always tell with me. But it's cinchy: Just say that Mum's feeling fluey—*a touch of the flu,* say that. Whatever you do, Emma, don't mention you-know-what. Be *cazh* when you hand in the pink."

"No," Emma concluded. "Just—*no.*"

99

"Fraidy cat," said Berry.

"There's always Switch Night," I heard Gussie say.

"Yah," Berry took up excitedly. "Get him to ask you to Cambridge for Switch Night."

"What about the mother?" said someone.

"It's a big house," reported Berry, "and the mother is typical Brattle Street: liberal and cool, et cetera."

Skulking in the mailroom, I wondered how Berry knew anything about my house or my mother. Then I heard Emma comment:

"Sam's nervous, in a way."

"So make the first move!" exclaimed the older sister. "You're the one who's on the Pill!"

There was a long pause over this consideration. Emma broke the silence:

"So what do you do if the guy is horny?"

"Just pretend you're the girl," decreed Berry.

7. Switch Night

Louisa Little had always urged boarding students to put out the welcome mat for day girls, and day girls to invite boarders home for an overnight. In theory, each girl would profit from seeing how the other lived, and the boarder would get a nourishing home-cooked meal into the bargain. One night each semester—a school night—had always been set aside for the switch, and in the new era, a show of hands at all-school meeting had ensured the survival of the custom.

"It sounds like a lovely idea," my mother said when she got home from a Congressional fact-finding mission to Angkor

Wat. She was reading the mail. "How many," she asked vaguely, "shall we expect?"

"I'm not sure—maybe five? Maybe six?"

"Lovely," she murmured, scanning letters and invitations. On second thought, she looked up, taking me in with narrow eyes: "Sam. How many did you invite?"

I had very quietly invited Emma and (for obvious reasons) only Emma. Emma (for protection) had then suggested that it "might be good" if I asked Lili and Gussie, and (for politeness' sake) that I "just mention it to Hattie," who Emma assumed would beg off when Hattie learned that Berry hadn't been invited. But when I "mentioned it" to Hattie, Hattie went away feeling very invited; and, only minutes later, when Berry learned of all the invitations sponsored by Emma, Berry got mad, declared Emma a "fraidy cat," called off all bets, and invited herself to my house. Dumbfounded, I assented, and only minutes after that, Emma, with Lili and Gussie in tow, declined my original invitation and retreated for a sullen, stoic walk on the Squaw Sachem Trail.

I couldn't believe it. And neither could Muz: "Five girls?" she said. "It isn't very practical, is it?"

"Well, if there are five, they'll all have homework to do."

"Do you really think you need that many, Sam?"

"Probably, there'll just be two," I finally confessed.

"Sam, this doesn't sound very well planned. This sounds," said Muz, "all rather *ad hoc*."

I told her that my Switch Night happened to be extremely well planned. "It's no sweat," I insisted.

"What about dinner?" said Muz. "I'm concerned about dinner."

"*No problémo*, dinner."

"And the sleeping arrangements? Isn't it, for example, the same night as my African Museum fund-raiser—when we'll have Dan Schmermer up from Washington and the Rostislav-Ratsheskys from New York?"

Muz could hardly cavil with the thoroughness of my sleeping arrangements. With Emma as my guest, I might have tried a more relaxed approach, but when Dean Brickley posted the official Switch Night roster, announcing that Beryl Mansfield, along with Harriet Bancroft, would spend the night at my house, I didn't want to take any chances.

I drew up charts, planned refreshments, laid in supplies. From an orange-haired, mildewy hippie on Cambridge Common I bought an ounce of pot. From a kid at Palfrey Street School I got a couple grams of hash, and then settled on Duncan Hines' "Double Fudge" as the brownie mix of choice. With the help of another, older, mildewy guy—this one retching outside Sage's—I obtained a selection of fine wines. At Nini's Corner, I bought a carton of Old Golds. On my bedside table, for the decisive post-coital cigarettes, I positioned, just so, the yellow "Ricard" and the red-and-white "Martini" ashtrays my brother and I had snitched from cafés in Paris. I even changed my sheets.

I remember washing sheets almost endlessly the week before Switch Night. I had begun to look at my bed with new eyes (as the scene, for example, of a crime), and I'd decided that it would have been one thing if my sheets showed signs of manly discharge. But who wanted Berry Mansfield to see his drool stains? Who wanted to be thought of as a *drooler*? One drool could blow the whole night.

My plan broke down into five parts. Phase one, "the Dash," involved spiriting the girls back to my house as quickly as possible after sports. As I did not have a driver's license, this could only be accomplished by train. If we sprinted to the depot, we would depart Concord, 5:10, arriving Porter Square, Cambridge, 5:32. A ten-minute march—over Avon Hill, down past the Radcliffe campus, across Concord Avenue, and through the Lessenhoffs' hemlock hedge—would bring us to my back-yard at about a quarter to six. Once inside the house, the second phase would start immediately.

"The Duck" entailed philtering Berry with Strawberry Cold Duck, among other festive wines in my private stock. Hattie, I knew, would want to meditate in a quiet room as soon as we arrived; I planned to stash her in Murray's room—way down the upstairs hall. Then, with a certain amount of spontaneity, as though pleasantly surprised to find myself in the neighbor-hood of my own room, I would suggest to Berry, *"Maybe you and I ought to meditate in here,"* adding with a shrug: *"We can use the bed."* If for any reason Berry refused to join me, I figured I would pretend to have alarming but noncommunica-ble symptoms: dizziness, partial hearing loss, maybe even a bloody nose. But if all went well and Berry submitted—why then I would simply dole out the seduction supplies: the Cold Duck, the Mateus rosé, or, *pace* Boone's Farm, the raspberry Ripple. I must have set great store by these wines, because for the next two and one half hours no other diversions and cer-tainly nothing solid, far less "nourishing," had been planned.

At 8:30 we would move directly into phase three: "the Dead." The Grateful Dead concert at the Boston Garden, for which I had bought a trio of scalpers' tickets, would begin at nine. We would be home, I figured conservatively, by midnight.

Phase four, "the Dope"—back in my room after the concert—would see the rolling of joints and the decanting of many additional fine wines. For a nightcap, I had set aside a gallon of Almadèn (I guess we were still boycotting Gallo, even in my plans).

The fifth and final phase of the big night (evidently I assumed we would all still be ambulatory) required almost no preparation. I knew that for "the Double Fudge" I could count on Hattie to fade first, leaving Berry unprotected. As I saw it, I would now move in on my dream girl, putting my arm around her, while with my free hand I would casually reach down under my bed and produce the square cake tin containing the Duncan Hines "Double Fudge" hash brownies.

And how could she refuse? Positioned on my bed, besotted with wine and song, invested with any or all of Dr. Cox's contraceptives, Berry, by this point, would also be starved. She would be *ravenous*. She would gobble up the aphrodisiacal brownies, and once their effect had taken hold, there would be no limit to the sleeping arrangements. From there on out, at any rate, I planned to wing it.

The day proved to be gusty and crisp, full of reddening maples holding down their skirts. At five o'clock sharp, I picked up my guests at Hoare. Their hair was brushed and tied back, and it shone in the quick, apple-fragrant air. Berry wore a fleece-collared leather flyer's jacket, black turtleneck sweater, gray corduroy skirt, black tights, and pumps. Hattie was dressed in a quilted blue-jean jacket, scarlet muffler, blue-striped French sailor's shirt, homemade blue-jean skirt, argyle knee socks, and tennis sneakers whose rounded rubber toes had been marked with the reminders, "L" and "R."

My breath was clean (I had even brushed my tongue), and I was fortified with huge amounts of cash—something like seventy-five bucks, mostly in ones and fives, time-released over a period of ten days from my mother's purse. I remember feeling grateful, almost to the point of tears, that I had so much money and such a masterful plan of action to carry us through all the hours ahead. For though I had increasingly come to admire the ingenuity of my multi-phase strategy, I could already feel, as we set off for the depot, my heart punching against my ribs.

Each girl had packed her overnight things in a canvas sail bag with loop handles of royal purple. Neat and organized, each insisted on carrying her own bag—a sure sign, I decided, that dial-packs and diaphragm cases were meant to stay discreetly out of sight until the crucial moment. This steadied me, but it also took my breath away. To think that I alone had to get these girls from Elm Street, Concord, Mass., all the way to Cambridge, and then to Boston, and then into separate beds— who was I kidding? On the other hand, whenever I began to hyperventilate, I simply reminded myself, in a reasonable tone of voice, *Listen: they're the ones with the contraceptives.*

A two-minute walk separated the depot from school. I had us there in forty seconds flat. On the way, I kept checking to make sure I still had the seventy-five bucks. All but five of the dollars happened to be concealed in my left boot, rolled up in a tight wad—so tight that whenever I couldn't feel it moving around in there, I got nervous, broke stride, hitched at my pants, and shook out my leg until I could feel the money again. Naturally, I tried to make this look as though I were shimmying in the street for the sheer exuberant hell of it. By the time we reached Thoreau Street, I was plucking at my pants, wriggling my legs—more or less doing the hula-hula. Berry flung me an astute, sisterly glance. She said:

"Do you have to go to the bathroom, or something?"

The train was twenty minutes late out of Fitchburg. When it finally arrived, hissing, spluttering, weaving into the depot like the town drunk, I happened to be second in line at the Friendly's take-out window, to which I had been sent for Butter Crunch cones. I could see Hattie over on the platform signaling like mad; I could hear the train conductor bawling; nevertheless, I waited. Perversely, stubbornly, perhaps hoping that the girls would carry on the plan without me, I waited. The counterman said:

"You're going to miss your train."

When at last I had the cones and paid for them, I bolted across the street, dodged through the depot parking lot, and raced down the platform, noticing, with only yards to go, that the train stood motionless. The driver's head popped in and out of the engine cab, the puzzled faces of city-bound passengers appeared in the sooty windows. And there, at the steps to the silver coach, stood Berry, chatting up the conductor, a crane-necked, bandy-legged man with a shock of snow-white hair and a wonderful bright pink nose. Berry had the whole place tied up and waiting. She chanted:

"It's about time," and then added, "Bummer," when I pulled up short and one of the ice cream scoops sailed off its cone and into the steamy, enuretic world under the train.

"You could probably get another," offered Berry. "He has time, right, Dave?"

The conductor said, "Like to leave sometime today, darlin'," and shepherded us aboard.

"What are you, nuts?" I hissed at Berry, red-faced, abashed by her cool-headed control.

"Dad commutes," was the whispered explanation.

"What—?" I shot back, suddenly helpless before Berry's superior understanding of the ways of the world.

"My father is an old friend of Dave's," she said, spacing out the words neatly, as though for an unruly child.

And our conductor, it developed, was indeed a very old friend of Harry Mansfield's—and of a few other Mansfieldian things besides. As Dave O'Donnell stood by to let us pass into the gently rocking coach, I felt his eyeballs on us. I knew what he was staring at, and felt a pang of jealousy when I realized that under the guise of watchful duty, the conductor was allowed to keep his balance in the companionway by canting his eyeballs to the meridian line of Berry's boobs.

Hattie was holding our places. We had two pairs of seats facing each other, and Hattie and I sat on the country side, facing Berry and the distant, unseen city. The girls looked out the window and polished off the ice cream cones, and then each girl untied and re-brushed her hair, bending forward and worrying the darker nether tresses for at least but not more than twenty-five strokes.

Brushing, Hattie said, "You looked so gallant running into the station, Nomis. You looked like you were in *Doctor Zhivago*."

"You should never cut your hair," Berry told me.

Inside the car, the girls' voices sounded so persuasive, so pure and new, I felt as if I were hearing them, unobstructed, for the first time. Then their reflections appeared in the window, backed by rushing pastures, and I freely studied the astonishingly simple loveliness of their un-made-up faces.

Sunset blazed in the treetops behind; dusk stole up the trunks. Swallows, scared up by the train, swooped across the soot-scored window. Luck was in the air, surrounding us like music. Everything was working. Everything was working according to plan. I could have wept for joy: These goddesses were coming home with me.

Dave O'Donnell, canvassing the aisle like a ward heeler, stopped to collect our fares. He lingered, flirting with Berry in a courtly South Shore voice, and when he continued up the aisle, calling back over his shoulder, "You be good now, deah," everything fell into place. Life opened up to me in the gathering of evening. The world seemed to beckon, to invite me to penetrate its warp and weft, and I seemed to see inside the shady shapes of things, to glimpse as never before the hidden pattern in leaf and tree, conductor and train, tie and tracks, Berry and Boston, Boston and Maine, Maine and Mansfield—all seemed interlaced in some gentle, dreamy way.

And as the 5:10 from Fitchburg clattered toward the city, silver as a needle, I gave Berry long, deliberate looks. Hattie serenaded our reflections in the window, and Berry matched me, look for look, serene and steady. Somehow, I took courage from Berry's strangely impersonal gaze.

When Dave O'Donnell called out our stop, I reached over and grasped Berry's hand. Impatiently, she shook me off, and for a second I could measure, in inches and feet, the staggering length of the night ahead. But Berry only wanted to start over: She shook off my sweaty, ineffective clasp, re-weaving, right up to the knuckle, tight as twill, the dry fingers of her hand and the damp fingers of mine.

The sky over Porter Square was black when we got off the train. The walk to my house should have taken, as I've said, ten minutes—fifteen at the most—and with Hattie singing and Berry and I still holding hands, we managed to clear Avon Hill more or less on schedule. But as we flanked the landscaped Radcliffe campus, our progress slowed to a shuffle, then a crawl, and then, at the corner of Garden and Linnaean Streets, Berry dropped my hand.

Out of the shadowy Cambridge evening, on foot and on bicycle, came friends and relations, old Little girls, older sisters of North Shore neighbors, cousins of Dark Harbor friends, friends of Dark Harbor cousins—even the silver-haired daughter of Mr. Mansfield's Groton crew coach, whose name, I seem to remember, was Cogswelp.

Berry knew them all and they all knew Berry. It was uncanny. Literally every face that flashed under the amber glow of a streetlamp was familiar, or related. Naturally we were obliged to stop, chat, and catch up with every single one. It was like carrying a message from the front to the back of a parade. Berry had a word *about* everyone, *for* everyone, *from* everyone, and she broadcast her news to and about New England's sons and daughters with a grace that astonished me.

"Hi, you guys," she would call out, almost offhandedly, as she greeted a person she hadn't seen in months. Her lack of ceremony was part of the trick, for it implied the kind of familiarity that is immediate, continuous, forever unbroken. Within seconds, she knew how many karats figured into an engagement ring, how many months remained in a pregnancy (to say nothing of how many had elapsed since the wedding), how many dollars were at stake in a contested will, how many weeks or days or hours a dying patriarch was expected to last. The facts of life came magically to Berry's fingertips, yet I still couldn't understand how she moved into and out of all those intimacies so easily.

"O.K., you guys," she always concluded, with a smiling, valedictory toss of her head. And then, in the parting touch of a hand she would glean one last bit of information, such as why one Cogswelp granddaughter was now working in the curatorial department of the Fogg Museum while the other had taken a year off to mop floors at Zum-Zum. ("Expelled from Farmington— for drugs," she would whisper later.) Meantime, as Hattie and I inched away, Berry would call out, "Bye! . . . Bye! . . . Bye . . . ," sustaining the illusion of inseparableness all the way down the street. Every Mansfield leave-taking I ever witnessed was a matter of prolonging the good-byes until the next corner or the next hello, whichever came first.

The hour was nearly seven when we reached my house. A welcoming light blazed between the pillars of the front porch. The front door stood slightly ajar. Usually placid at this hour (or, at most, murmurous with the evening news), my house was tonight positively chatty. The windows were full of pep. Beckoning circus shadows—stilted Uncle Sams and elongated fat ladies—strutted across the ceiling in the front hall. Discarnate trapezists flew to the edge of the transom, then slid down the opaque panels of rice paper in the doorway sidelights.

Lifting the mail drop, I smelled instantly what was wrong. Instead of the usual living room scents that wafted out to greet me after school, there now emerged in warm puffs the smoky, lamplighted haze and cheddary perfume of grown-ups having cocktails at dusk on an autumn evening.

Before I could straighten up, the door swished open. T. K. Sethna sprang forward, all gussied up, smiling a sickeningly obsequious smile. "Our Indian man," as Muz invariably referred to Sethna when she entertained, instead of loitering around the kitchen—sipping pale teas, suspended in Shetland-sweater limbo—was tonight costumed in his state-dinner embassy whites—the coat with the tall stiff collar, the pants with the machete-edge crease. He bowed importantly from the waist and I found myself idiotically bowing back.

"Yes please, hello," said Sethna, inviting us in, and when no one moved, he lowered his eyes and offered the variation, "Hello, yes please."

Flustered, I piped out: "What are you doing here?"

"Yes please, hello," Sethna took up again, for I had failed to cue him for his usual speech about coats. But just then Hattie offered her warmest mystic greetings and stepped forward to surrender her jean jacket. Berry followed, drolly, while I alone remained on the threshold, ready to make a run for it.

Coatless, we were trapped, and to our left, in the thick of living-room action, several grown-ups were already making gestures to acknowledge our entrance—the ducking of chins, the shooting of the elbows, the weird little bows—all the motions of rising without actually rising at all.

"Oh, there's *Sam!*" came my mother's voice, just as if we were expected. "Sam, darling, bring your friends in to meet everyone!"

The babble of cocktail voices hushed as I slunk forward and peeped in. Stiffening, I glanced around the chamber of horrors, noting the more familiar tableaux:

Dominating the davenport: the dreaded Rostislav-Ratsheskys, Sasha and Alex, both Russian émigrés, both geniuses, both incessant smokers and talkers, both with black turtlenecks and incredibly bad breath. Sasha, the man, smiled an unvarying, self-satisfied smile: the Pulitzer smirk; Alex, the woman, never smiled, and though I had no idea what the Rostislav-Ratsheskys did, except win prizes and grants, at that moment they were curling the ears off lucky Howard Rosenbloom, a Nieman Fellow.

Pretending not to be impressed: the unfortunate Rostislav-Ratshesky children, Irina and Rudolph, with whom Murray and I had been flung together at grown-up cocktail parties since age three. One special feature of the Rostislav-Ratshesky children was that they always had educational pets, usually reptiles, always much beloved, and they named these pets, one right after another, "Ibid." The present Ibid, a four-foot-long milk snake, and the only voiceless creature in the room, was now coiling itself around Irina's wrist and arm.

Holding forth at the hearth: Daniel Schmermer, the China hand and foreign policy troubleshooter, up from the nation's capital this evening, wearing African beads with his faded blue Mao cap, and grinning every third or fourth sentence with his mouthful of stumpy yellow corncob teeth.

Ensnared by (but not listening to) Dan Schmermer: Karl Ozankan, neckless astrophysicist and Nobel Prize winner, with teal velour shirt buttoned to the chin and a nose like a raw sausage pinched free of a whole string of raw sausages; plus, the Klopstocks, Hans and Edie, Wellfleet friends known to Murray and me as the Chopsticks, he a painter, she a sculptor, both with B.O.; plus, a tall, tanned man in a very white shirt, whose name I don't remember, but who had had something important to do with foreign aid in the Kennedy administration. In those days there was always some guy in our living room who used to have something important to do, and he was always the one with the white shirt and the tan.

"So!" Daniel Schmermer boomed, interrupting himself at the hearth. "Your mother tells us you're a pioneer at Miss Little's School for Girls! You must tell us about it! How is life among the other half?"

An unyielding silence gripped the room, during which Berry remarked under her breath, "Boy, are you in trouble."

"I see you are doing quite well!" Schmermer persisted. "Something of a ladies' man, eh?"

Just then, beaming, Muz emerged from the heart of the cocktail haze, floating forward like some inscrutable Ethiopian empress. She wore a loud, bright, orange-vermilion African tribal tunic, and she was so pleased with herself she was on the verge of levitation.

"How do you like my dashiki, Sam?"

Everybody waited, then Hattie spoke up: "Cool," she said.

"Yah," Berry agreed, and stepped forward, rather field-hockey-captain formal, grasping Muz's hand, pumping it vigorously. "How do you do, Mrs. Simon, I'm Beryl Mansfield, and this is my roommate, Harriet Bancroft. We've heard a lot about you."

"I've heard a lot about *both of you*," Muz returned.

"It's really nice of you to have us for Switch Night," Berry said, while Hattie, glancing at the guests, added: "We hope it's no trouble."

"On the contrary," said Muz, introducing her paste-on smile to the conversation. "It's marvelous! Sam's been looking forward to having you for weeks. He's been terribly excited about everything, talking all about the Mansfield sisters, cleaning up, getting us all ready . . ."

These remarks, together with my mulish silence, threw everyone off balance, but Muz pressed gallantly on: "Sam, don't you want to introduce everyone to the smashing Mansfield sisters?"

I threw my mother a murderous look.

"What—can't I say that?"

"We'll come down later," I growled.

"Don't you want to give Sethna your drink orders?"

Twice, stealthily, I bounced my eyebrows at Muz.

"Wouldn't you like to try some 'soul food' for dinner?"

Sharply now, I bounced my signal, and Muz, as though listening to an interpreter who just barely spoke Eyebrow, followed along: "You want me to *what*? . . . *Now*? . . . Oh, *Sam* . . . Excuse me," she said to everyone within earshot, "my son seems to have an emergency."

"*Muz,*" I bleated, once I had her corralled into the study.

"Now don't you start 'Muzzing' me."

"But I told you! I told you Switch Night was Wednesday!"

"Thursday. You told me Thursday. I distinctly remember you telling me Thursday because I changed the date of the fund-raiser, not once, but twice—*twice*, Sam!—to accommodate your schedule."

"But I need the house!" I stammered, stalking wildly to an indefinite point on the rug and flinging my arms into the air like a Bolshevik.

"Well. I'm sorry, Sam. I really am. I know you're disappointed."

"Then do something!" I roared.

"Sam, you can't very well expect me to do anything now, clearly. . . ."

"It's perfectly clear!"

"Stop bullying, Sam."

"I'm not bullying, just get rid of them. Get them out of here!"

"You've got that tone."

I shouted that I had no tone.

"That irrational tone . . ."

I shrieked that *she* was irrational. The calmer my mother sounded, the tetchier I became, until, watching her flattened hand demonstrate in midair a descending octave of notes, I whispered: "O.K. . . . Please . . . just . . . get . . . them . . . out . . . of . . . here."

"Much better," said Muz, beginning again: "Now. You'll have a lovely evening; you can serve your guests a very chic buffet dinner, *with wine;* you can introduce them to Rudolph and Alice—"

"Her name's Irina, Muz."

"—And if you don't want to stay downstairs when all the guests are here, you can go up afterwards and . . ." Muz groped for the really attractive, the truly glamorous after-dinner activity. . . .

"Parcheesi," she proposed triumphantly. "You can all go up and play Parcheesi, and I'm sure your friends would love to chat with the Rostislav-Ratshesky children, who've gotten terribly sophisticated, you will see, after their new school in Switzerland."

One thing I knew my guests would not love to do was chat with Rudolph and Irina. Rudolph, fat and pathetic, with wrinkly little iguana eyes and a long, vigilant tongue, hated his strict parents and made a practice of overeating just to get back at them. ("Rudolph eats to punish Sasha," Muz always said with an air of pride.) Irina, on the other hand, a glassy-eyed zombie, attired always in something black and shroudlike, had found an even more systematic way to square

114

accounts with prize-winning grown-ups: Irina had not spoken a word to anyone—no one human, that is, except her psychiatrist—since age eleven. I suspected that her three years of Absolute Silence had probably made her a rather imposing Parcheesi player.

"But the Rostislav-Ratfaces aren't staying here, are they?"

"Sam, I told you. I told you weeks ago: 'The Rostislav-Ratsheskys are staying the night of the fund-raiser.' I distinct—"

"Then we're not," I announced flatly.

"Now don't be funny, Sam."

"Who's being funny? We've got tickets to the Dead. At the Garden. I told you, *weeks ago,* remember?"

"What about dinner? I'd like to know what arrangements you've made to give your guests a proper dinner."

I told her I had made arrangements.

"Well I want you to bring your guests to the party. Just for a few minutes, Sam. Things won't get started for another hour or so—the drummers are late—and then you can go to your concert."

Carelessly, I said: "Maybe we'll come down after."

"You will not, young man! You will come down *before* you go, having had a *proper* dinner—and please give your guests some *fresh* towels; the good ones, but not the white ones. And please bring down your c.v."

"My c.v.!"

"Yes. I'd like Dan Schmermer to see what you did in Paris last summer."

"Dan Schmermer could give a shit what I did in Paris last summer." I had lived with a French family and operated the Xerox machine in the library at UNESCO. My brother had lived with a separate French family. To retaliate, we had stolen ashtrays from cafés and ordered Orangina soft drinks by asking the waiters for "Orange vaginas."

115

"Nonsense," replied Muz. "Dan's perfectly interested in you—if only you'd ask his advice. . . . And Sam?"

"Yes, Muz?" (Gunning the door handle.)

"I won't have any shacking-up in this house—any toozling. The Mansfield sisters will take the spare room. Is that understood?"

Muz had nothing to fear for those smashing Mansfields. My well-laid toozling plan was unraveling by the minute, and Muz was the least of my marplots. When I emerged from the study, Hattie had vanished and Berry was in the living room with the tall tanned man who used to have something important to do.

"We know each other from N.H.!" Berry chirruped from across the room.

"Wintered for years at Cannon," I heard the tall tanned man telling someone as I went upstairs.

In Murray's room, where Hattie was now supposed to be meditating, there stood a kind of educational peasant tent, a small-scale yurt, assembled by Rudolph Rostislav-Ratshesky, courtesy of some international summer camp. Inside the yurt, sleeping bags had been rolled up, neat and spruce, and several tiny cones of turquoise-colored incense smoldered in the ashtrays I had specially set aside for Berry's and my post-coital cigarettes.

In my room, where Berry and I were now supposed to be popping the cork on the Cold Duck, there was an unbelievably bad smell. I recoiled at the stench—a clammy, clinging odor, like diarrhea. I was even more taken aback to find Hattie meditating in there. Sitting on my bed in the lotus position, eyeballs salaaming under pink-rimmed eyelids, a loopy smile floating on her lips, Hattie happily practiced the Vedic Sciences of His Holiness Maharishi Mahesh Yogi—as if devotees of higher states of consciousness judged not the vileness of loose stools. Maybe freethinking Hattie had reached Nirvana. Back here in the real world, my room stank sky-high, and I had just begun to search for the source when Berry marched in, holding her nose.

"It's under your bed," she said.

"What is? How do you know?"

"They just found out. Your mother told me. That Rodolpho kid fed your dog chocolate Ex-Lax. That Seth guy just took the dog to the vet. The parents are working the kid over in the study. I just heard him scream, the little jerk. Oh, and your mother wants you to give me your résumé and some clean towels."

By eight o'clock, Hattie still hadn't come out of her meditation. Downstairs, the party was in full swing; the beat of African drums thumped through the house. Berry and I were sitting on the floor in my room, staring obstinately at one another, my plan in full collapse. After cleaning up the mess, I had thrown open the windows and uncorked the bottle of Cold Duck, from which Berry had consented to take one sip. Then I'd rolled some joints; but, after taking a tiny, squinty-eyed puff to humor me, Berry claimed the stuff only gave her a headache. When I decided to risk everything and bring forth the tin of brownies from under the bed, Berry declined, and no matter what I did to prove that the brownies hadn't been contaminated by the dog, even eating a sample myself, Berry refused.

"You guys?" Hattie said at last, stirring slightly on my bed. "What *smells*?"

Neither of my guests, it turned out, cared a fig about going to a concert. Both preferred to stick around for my mother's party. And by the time we were scheduled to leave for the Garden, I was so fretful that no matter what I smoked, euphoria remained out of reach.

"I'm hung'y," said Hattie.

"Yah," Berry agreed. "When's supper?"

Ignoring all protests, I led my guests Indian file down the dark back stairway to the kitchen door. I figured we would grab something to eat before making our getaway, and I had just reached the door at the foot of the enclosed stairwell, groping in the pitch black for the handle, when my mother's beaming party face appeared in the gray gloom of the upstairs hall.

"Oh, Sam," she sang down, "I hope you'll come and talk to Dan Schmermer." Muz evidently couldn't see Berry and Hattie behind me in the stairwell, for in her best *toujours gai* Mehitabel voice, she coaxed, "I'm sure he'll tell you what's going on in Paris. He's just come back from the Peace Talks."

"Paris?" I called up tonelessly through the protective umbra of the stairwell.

"Yes, dear. Dan's just come back with Dr. Kissinger."

"I'm supposed to ask Daniel Schmermer what's going on in *Paris?*"

"Yes, in fact." She sounded affronted. "Dan would be *delighted,*" said Muz. "He would be *thrilled,*" she insisted, "to chat with someone as 'with it' as you."

My entire face and neck now reddened as my mother added: "Dan Schmermer does not suffer fools gladly!"

"Meaning what?" I suddenly shot back. "Meaning: Dan Schmermer is a big, pompous jerk who doesn't like the sound of any voice but his own!"

I had had no idea that I was going to show off. I remember that for the first time all evening a surge of power commensurate with the scope of my plans crackled along my spine.

"Shhh!" said Muz, ducking her head, and for a second I thought she was going to descend the stairs—and then what? Trembling with fury, she said: "You lower that voice and show some respect, young man. Dan Schmermer may not be overflowing with modesty, I'll grant you, but he's been having a fascinating time in Paris, he's an old, old friend of Henry's, he's terribly important in his own right, and I suggest you goddamn well drop this pose of intolerance and ask Dan a few questions about the way the world works.'' In a voice full of dignity and emotion, Muz concluded: ''Men like Daniel Schmermer know a side of life that you are not going to find in the Boston Garden.''

Then my mother said: ''Sam?'' And after a brief interval during which I struggled with an almost uncontrollable urge to giggle, I replied: ''Yes, Mother?''

''I have something for you and your guests.''

Now we all paused. In her low, chesty, everyday voice, Muz clarified: ''To have with your supper when you get home from the concert.''

Apparently she had this thing, whatever it was, right there with her on the landing.

''Shouldn't you give it to Sethna?'' I asked, fully renewing normal household protocol.

''He's still with the dog—at the vet's,'' she stage-whispered, ''and I'm afraid that when he gets back he won't have time to cook you anything.''

''That's O.K., Muz,'' I said, but she wasn't listening. She had stooped to rustle through an airline bag that had been marooned at the head of the back stairs since her last trip. From among newspapers and memoranda and a miscellany of junk, she plucked an aluminum-foil parcel and turned back the foil to take a sniff.

Berry and Hattie began to quake with laughter in the darkness beside me.

Upstairs, apparently satisfied that all was meet and right, Muz refolded the foil and then released the packet with no more care than the average sneakers-wearer allows when discharging his shoes at the end of a long day. Without further warning—without a word of any kind—the packet came shooting down the stairs, skipping past our ankles, skittering to rest on a lowly tread.

"Muz!" I yelped, and felt a strong stab of vertigo over the haphazard flight of our supper. "*Muz*, what the hell is that?"

"A lovely piece of filet of sole," she answered.

8. Brimstone

I look back on the rest of Switch Night like a spectator peeping into the innocent flickerings of early Edison filmstrips like *The John Rice–May Irwin Kiss* or *Fun in a Chinese Laundry*. The concert of course was a disaster. The scalpers' tickets seated us miles from the stage, up near the turdy rafters of the Garden. The warm-up band turned out to be a folk singer who more or less tuned his guitar for two hours. The Dead didn't show up until past eleven. Hattie meditated all the way through "Uncle John's Band" and "Sugar Magnolia." Berry fell fast asleep during "Dark Star," and I spent most of "Wharf Rat" and "Not Fade Away" standing on my seat, trying to persuade myself that I was very, very stoned, knowing full well that I'd been ripped off by the kid at Palfrey Street School.

We left early, though not before countless Dead Heads and chowderheads from Malden and Revere had come up to our seats to ask Berry for her "telephone numba."

"Down, boy—down, boy," Berry cheerfully told her fans, which only egged them on.

One bulky chowderhead, determined that Berry should know him best of all, lumbered past our seats repeatedly. All through "Bertha" this chowderhead kept rolling by, until finally he threw caution aside and sat down in Berry's lap.

"Dahlin', how-a'-ya?" he said, as if he'd been sitting there all evening. And before I could stand up to defend her, Berry, bored, said, "Move over, Rover," and shoved the chowderhead out of her lap, into the aisle, and onto his butt.

Somehow, we got home—Hattie in trance ("I'm s'eepy, you guys, I'm s'eepy"), Berry fending off Blue Line creeps ("Shove off, sailor!"), and I, glum and sober, toying with the Red Line platform in Park Street Under like a man on a ledge.

My mother's African Museum fund-raiser was in its dying phase when we limped through the front door. In the living room, a gang of drummers, outfitted in full tribal dress, were collecting their drums. A string of barefooted folk dancers threaded out through the hall. The sparkly-eyed guests, some of them still robed in their hand-dyed dashikis and authentic necklaces, were on the point of staying for "just one more *very short* Scotch."

Muz, resplendent with the success of her soiree, urged food and drink on Berry and Hattie, introducing them around as "those smashing Mansfield sisters." Hattie smiled wanly, and fled; Berry could not be torn away. She lingered in the hallway, openly impressed that Eugene McCarthy was standing around beside the coat closet handing out copies of a recent book of poems. I think the former presidential candidate even signed her flyleaf—with high hopes and very best wishes, "to Perry Mansfield."

In deep dudgeon, I stalked up the front stairs and slammed shut the door to my room. When Berry opened it, some ten or fifteen minutes later, she found this spectacle in the kennel-scented gloom: her best friend sound asleep in her Switch Night host's bed; a hungry, four-foot-long milk snake winding along the floor in search of mice and birds' eggs; the Switch Night host posed tragically at his desk, head in hands.

"Give me a break," said Berry. "What are you doing?"

"Rien," came the troubled reply.

"Bull, you're sitting in the dark feeling sorry for yourself."

"I am not."

"Are so—where are you going to sleep?"

I had decided to level with Berry—to come right out and tell her. But I couldn't think of what to say. I stared, confused, cheeks afire, at Hattie's lumpy shape in my bed. The glint of the streetlamp shone on her slightly waxen night-skin. Below, on the floor near the bed, the light picked up the dark smooth scales of the Rostislav-Ratsheskys' snake.

"Do you want me to get rid of this thing?" I asked Berry.

"I don't care," she said.

And with a great rush of breath, I blurted: *"Dornez avec moi."*

I even made a broad, open-handed pass through the air, as much as to say that anywhere Berry wished to *dornez*—the summit of Katahdin on the first freezing morn of the twenty-first century!—I would *dornez* there with her.

"Dormez," Berry corrected, amused, scornful, vaguely distracted. She had kneeled down to trap the snake behind my old green reading chair. "It's *dormir,* dummy. And anyway," she added briskly, "it's really *'Voulez-vous coucher avec moi?'* "

So saying, Berry seized the snake in an inexpert but competent grip. She marched to the door, flung it open, and released the writhing creature into the hall. Without another word, she leaned over, tossed her head twice, and began brushing her hair.

"Berry," I whispered, addressing her upside-down face.

"Yah?" she said, as though she had a mouth in the middle of her forehead.

"I love you."

No reply came from the creepy, inverted face.

"Really, I dream about you. I—"

"Down, boy," she broke in, blinking with mustachioed eyes.

"But I do, I—"

"Not tonight, Sambo," said the face, and I felt a pang of diminution, almost an ache, sink into my bones, like the first shiver of a fever. "O.K.?" she said, firmly, flipping her head up in a decided way. She regarded me with flushed, shining eyes.

I refused to look at her.

"You jerk," she said.

But I would not meet her eyes. Like a seasick passenger, I concentrated on the one good thing I knew: staying in one place with my head down.

Meantime, she busied herself with the things in her overnight bag. Then I felt her warm fingertips rumpling my hair— the way you would rumple a boy's head. My eyes smarted at the lightness of her touch. For a second I was afraid she might also chuck me under the chin, and I braced myself. But all at once, she squeezed into my clenched fist something of apparent importance, something small and smooth and cool—a stone of some kind.

"I want you to have that," said Berry, "and I want to be your friend."

The illusion that I was ten years old seemed sealed when she bent down to explain: "It's brimstone. From Maine. If you rub it hard, it'll bring luck."

I began rubbing instantly; then, just as quickly, burning with self-consciousness, I quit.

Downstairs, one of the phlegmier grown-ups was chortling in farewell, and the open front door let a draft up the stairs and into my room. The wafting night air, the parting laugh, the shutting door—all demonstrated something that I had been too foolish to see: Berry wasn't leaving. My mother's guests had gone, but *Berry Mansfield wasn't leaving*. She wasn't going anywhere. She was here. In my room.

Slowly, I looked up and peered around, absorbing through clear eyes this information: that it was fairly late at night—and a school night, at that—and of all the houses in the world where Berry Mansfield could have gone to sleep on this night of nights, she had chosen my house. And she was here in *my* room, in the fullness of *my* things, and now that I thought about it, I swelled a little: Berry Mansfield. In *my* house. Planning to spend the night in *my* room.

I looked at her carefully. Her hair, charged with electricity, had begun its gradual descent, folding in like wings behind her shoulders. I fingered the brimstone. "O.K.," I conceded, and my voice relaxed for the first time all night, "but what about us? What about Mount Katahdin?"

Standing there beside my desk, looking down at me, steady, untroubled, smiling gently—a figure of such indescribable beauty I felt light-headed at the folly of my longing—Berry spoke cautiously, as though afraid she would injure me with her lips, her tongue, her low, sweet voice:

"*Peut-être* another time, Sambo. *Peut-être* next week, *peut-être* next year, *peut-être jamais*—I don't know." She inhaled, skeptically. "I think I love you, but probably not the way you want me to love you. *Je ne sais pas*."

She smiled, not unlovingly. "Maybe someday," she offered, "I'll look in your ear and see what's there."

"My ear?"

She reached over and poked her finger into my right ear. Inside me, she gave a humorous, a strangely pleasing, little wriggle, and I felt myself make a sound, a sort of exultation of the throat, which emerged not so much as a groan but as a whimper. It sounded feminine, and I blushed.

Berry had the kindness, or the good sense, to ignore it. "Now scram," she said brightly, steering me to the door. Then, fully clothed, she jumped into bed with Hattie, pushed her long golden tresses into a careless pile above her head, and rolled over.

9. A Birthday

"Pitiful," said Danny.

"It's brimstone."

"*This?* That's all you got?"

"If you rub it hard it brings luck."

"That's not the only thing you're going to have to rub to get hard."

"It's *brimstone,* man."

"You got hosed," said Danny.

The thank-you note Berry pinned to my cubby, with its affectionate message and luxurious penmanship, seemed to suggest otherwise. But Poopsy Winslow warned me not to take cubby notes too seriously:

"Hattie leaves them in my cubby all the time. They're incredibly cute and absurdly well written, but what, finally, do they *mean?* Does Hattie Bancroft *rebeeleebee libike meebee?*"

Murray, the first Little boy to be taken home by a Little girl, had spent a frustrating Switch Night in Manchester, on Hilary Fraser's parents' king-size bed. Reading aloud from *Winnie the Pooh* and subsisting on Underwood deviled ham and Triscuits, Murray had for twelve hours been in bed with five girls, yet never long enough individually to start anything with any one of them.

"They kept getting up to take bubble baths together," Murray reported.

Wentworth, though baffled by the bubble baths, had a theory about why the smartest, best-looking girls in the school all had the same handwriting—that loopy, slantless half-print, half-cursive in which all the stemmed letters looked like tulips cut out by Matisse.

"Take a look," Wenty Bird urged me one afternoon as we watched Berry straddle a drawing bench in Mr. Vitarelli's figure study class.

"So?"

"Look what she's doing with the piece of paper."

"So?"

"She's a lefty, you fool—a Leonardo lefty."

And sure enough: Left-handed Berry Mansfield knuckled down to her drawing not with the cramped, smudgy fist of a Dark Ages scribe, but (she had *adjusted the angle of the paper itself!*) with the open-armed sensuousness of the enlightened Leonardesque lefty.

"So what does that prove?" I asked.

"Don't you see, *Dummkopf*? They're *all* lefties. All the smartest, best-looking, artistic-spiritualist girls at this school are lefties."

"Is that how they do it?" I was impressed.

"No, stupid, they take bubble baths together to make their handwriting look alike—how should I know?"

The real truth, we all knew, lay concealed inside those India-inked cubby notes (with their misleading O's and X's marking unclaimed hugs and kisses). For autumn was almost over. The first harsh winter would soon be on us. And I—we all—had yet to get one single kiss out of Miss Little's tribe.

The Friday before Halloween—a sharp, bundling after-noon at the peak of scarf season—we celebrated Hattie's six-

teenth birthday at a surprise party in Louisa Little's chapel. We
were all there for the ambush, all of us, that is, except Armbrister
and Crocker who said they had better things to do on a Friday
evening than *bobobbibing* for *apapples* with the Mansfields.

After sports, Berry, shushing and whispering, herded us
into the chapel and directed us to hide between the first and
second rows of pews. Behind us, the altar overflowed. There
were pumpkins and gourds and jugs of sweet cider and an
abundance of local apples—crispy Macouns, tangy Empires,
fat, hard Granny Smiths. There were brimming bowls of popcorn and carameled McIntoshes and Halloween candy and
Halloween cupcakes, with Hattie's birthday cake elevated into
the cornucopian center of it all, four layers high and frosted
with Ducky Wigglesworth's special pink icing.

Above the altar, the stilted, archaic *-eth* words of First
Corinthians, hand-carved into large rosewood panels—carved
and oiled by Miss Little and her pigtailed helpers—spoke to the
absent school in monumental letters that seemed somehow
more conversational than wooden. To the side, on the rim of
the pulpit, two quarts of grape Kool-Aid filled the preacher's
pitcher, flanked by a salver of Sally Ann's sugar doughnuts, and
a basket of tart wild apples from a secret place Emma Mansfield
knew in the Estabrook woods. To this day I cannot partake of
the flesh of the apple, or the sugar of the doughnut, or the
grape of the Kool-Aid, without hearing once more Hattie's
doleful footsteps, without waiting once again as they ring acous-
tically along the chapel's creaky, uneven floor planks.

We sprang from the pews, chorusing "Happy Birthday" in
glad, goofy voices; and that lurching, pathetic anthem, with all
its history of caring and neglect, caught Hattie full in the face,
and she sat down in the aisle, legs spread out childishly, eyes
rucked with tears.

"You guys," she gasped out, sobbing freely into her muffler.

Efficient and maternal, Berry lighted the candles on the birthday cake. Glassy-eyed, Hattie blew them out. The rest of us gorged ourselves, and each in turn mounted the pulpit, partly in tribute to Hattie, partly in parody of the earnest, revelatory talks seniors took turns giving in morning chapel.

Wenty Bird, our funny man, went first, and though he refrained from telling us how he'd discovered the meaning of life by building a dulcimer in his "year off," he did stand on his head and use his duck-billed boots as pulpit puppets to sing alternating verses of "John Henry." Gussie followed, taking off her shoes and socks to show and tell about her actual webbed toes. (It amazed me that for two months you could know a girl like Hannah Gustin and then one afternoon learn that she had webbed toes.) Poopsy Winslow opened his mouth—first to show us his vestigial baby tooth, then to sing "You Must Have Been A Beautiful Baby" to Hattie. Emma exhibited the double and triple joints in the marbled knuckles of her artistic hands. Lili, it turned out, had a near-perfect German accent in which she sang the lullabies of her earliest nanny. Murray and I revealed constellations of identical birthmarks and other incunabular phenomena.

Berry refused to rise. She sat in her pew, straight-backed, squinty-eyed, predicting our futures. A shaft of rosy, late-afternoon light beamed into the room, falling from the west, striking the pair of white birches outside the opposite window. I remember I didn't want to listen to Berry's fortunes, so strong was my own conviction that Poopsy Winslow would be President of the United States—not an *actor;* Emma, a struggling artist—not an *art-gallery owner;* Berry, a Supreme Court Justice *and* a mother of five. I listened, but mostly I watched the pinkening birches through the mullions of the tall meetinghouse windows; and I remember the gusts of curled, russet leaves sweeping past the tinted trees, down across the yellowing fields, and the big feeling of life beyond—out there, waiting for us.

Inside the chapel, the old, oiled pews, warmed by our bodies, smelled sweet as toffee, and as Hattie rose to take the pulpit, I found myself in the most fantastic mood, and I can't tell you why. I only know that at that moment, in that chapel, on that afternoon, I was as close to bliss as I had ever been.

"Golly! Good morning, girls!" Hattie began in a crisp, genteel voice, lifting her chin and squaring her shoulders. "My name, for you girls who don't know, is Louisa Little-Did-You-Know, and, as most of you do know, I *love* surprises but I *hate* to read prayers! So I decided, rather suddenly, this morning in the tub while I was soaping up the old flab, to talk to you girls about wholeness. Not just the wholeness you get from your local dairy or Mrs. Cleveland Swimm's buttermilk flapjacks, or from an outing on the river or a day in the sun. But the wholeness of life! The wholeness of *everything*. . . ."

Hattie paused, having sensed props at her elbow. From the pulpit salver she selected one sugar doughnut, daintily raising it to her lips, then cramming the whole thing into her mouth before resuming:

"Truth be told, girls: Now and then we *all* get cross with ourselves for being *too* whole! Why, just yesterday I learned that over the holiday some members of our community, like myself, became vulgarly overweight no matter how sensibly they tried to eat, so if you'll just excuse me—and golly! I hope you will!—I'll just go right ahead and eat like mad. . . ."

We applauded and Hattie continued, the parody receding by degrees, her own homiletic voice taking over as she covered her pet topics—courtly love, chivalry, beauty—all the while devouring doughnuts and announcing her lifelong aspiration to become a "principessa," or, failing that, a "lovelorn abbess in charge of the bakery at a French convent." Then, as she pledged her allegiance to Charles I and the Confederacy, Marcel Proust and Monty Hall, her delivery slowed, her lips curled into a ghoulish grin, color drained from her face, and in the end we could actually see her skin go white.

Hattie threw up all over the pulpit. She tried to be polite about it, bending decorously at the waist and puking *into* the pulpit as if it were a bedside pail, but there was too much solid, upcoming material to be mannerly about it. The doughnuts, the cupcakes, the birthday cake with the pink icing, the Kool-Aid, the Halloween candy—it all came back as orange and yellow froth.

Berry took charge, dispatching Gussie and Lili to find a mop and bucket, ordering the boys to make a fireman's seat on which to escort Hattie back to Hoare; and with Emma leading the procession and Berry bringing up the rear, across the immaculate lawn of Senior Garden we hustled. Inside the house, we made quickly for the stairs, suddenly passing all previously known boundaries, rising up through the carpeted stairwell into a moist, aromatic world in which nightgowns seemed to hang everywhere, like wind-stirred Spanish moss. Girls scurried to and fro, and a shrill, avian cry pierced the air, warning of our presence.

We stretched Hattie out among the love-worn teddy bears on her bed. Ducky Wigglesworth materialized with a pleasant greeting for everyone and a steamer blanket for the patient. But as soon as Hattie was plumped up with pillows and tucked under the rug, she had to throw up again.

"It's *way* down the hall!" Emma warned, and we all pressed together in the general dash to the toilet, crouching and running as though advancing on goal.

This time, she made it. Kneeling beside the bowl, her

shoulder blades skating up a storm, Hattie held Berry's hand through several yawing turns. Emma, calm and reverent, pinned back Hattie's spattered hair. Ducky Wigglesworth pressed to Hattie's rhubarb-red forehead cool compresses soaked in iced tea.

"Not to mind, dear," Ducky kept murmuring. "You go right ahead and have another upchuck."

The boys, technically useless, stood around bobbing our heads, while Hattie delivered herself of what must have been her hundredth kernel of undigested candy corn.

"How do you feel?" said Berry, opening the bathroom window, letting in the night air.

"Crampy," Hattie answered, wiping her chin.

"Green-apple cramps, no doubt," said Ducky.

"Where does it hurt worst?" said Emma.

"All over," said Hattie. "Now I know what a bathtub feels like when it overflows."

"Accidents may happen," Ducky Wigglesworth stated in her clear, cool voice. "Accidents may happen in the most orderly of houses, and to the nicest of girls—pray, who found the ring in her slice of cake?"

All at once the girls exchanged hurried, excited glances. Emma bit her lip. Berry, at the window, smiled her crafty smile and, with a twinkle in her eye, showed us the back of her hand, giving her fourth finger a wiggle. A homemade gold foil ring caught the light from the window.

"First to marry!" sang Ducky (at precisely the moment when I decided that I was the man for the job).

The dinner bell had begun to toll across campus, and although none of us wanted food, we excused ourselves and trooped down the carpeted stairs. Girls' voices escorted us out into the fresh, quiet evening: "Bye, you guys!"—"Thanks!"—

"Bye . . . Bye!"—"They're so cute . . ."—"Bye! . . . Bye! . . . Bye! . . ."

I wasn't sure whether to try for a train to Cambridge, or to stay and have dinner with the boarders. The sun had just gone down. Bars of blue and gold light lingered over the western horizon. Like four cowled friars we drifted along Elm Street, speechless, our breath emerging in short, frosty puffs, and even Wentworth, for whom breaking wind had become a morale-boosting trademark, was silenced by the consensus of content-ment. We could rest now. We had been somewhere. Something had happened. We had seen things. We knew secrets. We had kept the feast—Myrrh, Poopsy, Wenty Bird, and I.

At the front door of Brewster House (still no one had broken the spell), I shot a long look back up the darkened street toward Hoare—a kind of postmeridian sighting from which, that autumn, I frequently plotted, wherever I happened to land at nightfall, the surest, swiftest course back to my cardinal point. I still retain the clear image of that evening's pavonine sky fanning out behind the cloak-black roofs of the Little houses, and I can picture now the preposterous face of Fred Harr's jack-o'-lantern, round and glowing, perched beside the front door of the headmaster's house, leering on into night.

Inside Brewster, wisps of shower steam crept down the front stairs. From the common room came the dizzying per-fume of cher-bidi cigarettes and the pounding chords of Danny Armbrister muscling his way through "Glad" on the Brewster upright piano. Still spellbound, we homed on the music, saun-tering into the common room with nail-chewed thumbs hooked into trouser pockets. Wavering awkwardly, we formed a loose semicircle around the piano. Danny raised his square chin and pointed it at us.

"So. Where did you dickless wonders go for cupcakes?"

Someone—I think Poopsy—told him. Danny tugged at his mustache. "The chapel," he said, grinning a little, interested: "What could you do with chicks in the *chapel*?"

There was no answer save the steady hiss of the shower upstairs, then the flushing of the toilet, followed shortly by the howl of the scalded shower-taker (LaFarge) and the sadistic snickering of the toilet-flusher (Hemmerdinger).

"Wait a minute," said Danny, eyes flashing across our mute faces. "Whoa. *Whoa.* Are you dinks telling me that nobody did anything?"

The enormous silence now begged for Wentworth's all-purpose, all-weather answer. But Wentworth's career as a wind-breaker seemed finished, and our disappointing male lexicon supplied no ready description of the idiosyncratic, apple-green passions of that afternoon and evening. We just stood there, as we had stood in the girls' bathroom—supernumeraries—nodding our heads, each with his Kool-Aid mustache, each with his sugar-doughnut whiskers.

10. Mansfield Blue

I was the first Little boy to spend the weekend at the Mansfields'. Their place at Prides Crossing—a massive homestead, built in the Shingle style, with bulky gambrel roofs, irregular gables, rioting dormers, and chubby triple chimney stacks—sat high on the lip of a wooded scarp overlooking the rock-ribbed coastline of Boston's North Shore.

When we arrived from school that weekend, the enormous shingled house seemed idle, like a rustic summer lodge in the off-season. Mr. and Mrs. Mansfield had taken the three Mansfield boys, ages nine to twelve, along with the Blanchards, the nearest neighbors, and the Blanchards' youngest sons, for a weekend hike in the White Mountains. The third Mansfield sister, Lindy, thirteen, a raven-haired beauty whom Berry and Emma had often billed as the one for whom I'd really flip, was, to my regret, grounded for the weekend at Milton Academy. The youngest of them all, Amy, a smart, sunny toddler aged two-and-a-half (I grasped immediately the lifelong potential for romance in that evergreen house), had been left at home, in care of her sitter, a freckly girl who vanished the instant Berry and Emma returned to roost.

Berry had done the shopping at a small, cardboard-smelling, charge-accounty sort of store called Henry's Market. Gussie and Hattie and I unloaded the groceries from the rear of the station wagon. Emma thinned the overstocked kitchen cupboards; Berry supervised the distribution of supplies to the butler's pantry, the cold-larder, and a gleaming, industrial-sized stainless steel refrigerator the likes of which I had seen in no family house I'd ever visited. At the counter, Berry diced, Emma chopped; Hattie made ratatouille. The aproned sisters smoked each other's cigarettes, which Berry had filched from their father's carton of Larks.

Toward the end of the afternoon, Emma guided Amy into a bib and high chair. Berry told the yawning child to keep her hair out of her mouth. Emma served the soft food silently. Berry identified each of the colorless lumps by name, sweetly asking Amy to ape her in reply. Emma called for the dogs out the back door. Berry swatted the oldest dog on the nose, upbraiding the bitch, a big, chunky Labrador, for leading the others into the Blanchards' pergola to pee. Emma fed the dogs. Sun rays convened on the kitchen table, and the sisters smoked through the smiling, copper light. Neither girl was ever far from a baking potato or the sizzling, gamy scent of the oven-roast.

Superfluous, I orbited the house, passing by chilled pantries and cold brick fireplaces redolent of apples and woodsmoke and Hu-Kwa tea. I wandered through spacious, shadowy halls with lofty ceilings and Oriental rugs and hip-high Nanking vases. Upstairs, I glimpsed the parents' bed, a fantastic slab, and paused briefly to measure myself at a bathroom doorjamb, whose pencil-scored indices marked the relative annual heights of all Mansfields. (Well pleased was I at seeing myself a head taller than Lindy at thirteen, Emma at fourteen, and Berry at twelve.)

Impudent as Goldilocks, I stole into tidy bedrooms and tried out beds. None of them felt just right. Each came equipped with lace-trimmed sheets, a baby-blue puff, a bedside crucifix, and a little silver stoup in which consecrated water hung suspended alongside the switchplate, ever ready to anoint Mansfields and their communicants in the dark of night.

I continued on, passing through wainscoted back hallways where old tin laundry chutes plunged down to cellar laundry rooms, and dark, spicy stairways climbed up to ancient attics that smelled of snuff and roof tar.

Somehow, no matter where I went, the house was always giving onto a porch. The place was promiscuous with porches. There were broad outdoor porches, cool with shade and lazy with hammocks; deep indoor porches, done up as sitting rooms; wide-open sun porches with belvederes between gables; screened-in sleeping porches with smelly canvas cots; and forgotten porches stacked with birch logs and ice skates and outgrown skis for snow and water.

On the main veranda—facing the sea—a curious chandelier, formed of several interwoven racks of antlers, dangled from the cantilevered ceiling, creaking in the wind. Straight ahead, over the shingled balustrade and a border of shrubs, the well-tended lawn spread wide, abutting the escarpment. At the lawn's ferny lip, a green garden hose lay coiled beneath an old wind-bent apple tree. The ground dropped away sharply there, and in the distance, beyond rocky offshore islands, the ocean met the sky at an unyielding horizon. Boston existed somewhere off to the right, down the craggy shore, below Salem and Marblehead. Otherwise, all familiar reference points were gone.

"You could lose," I said to myself, "a *million* virginities on these porches."

Even inside the house, the air carried the salty, summery tang of sex. Every bed had a view of the sea. Every view was hallowed. The Mansfields might as well have placed embroidered church kneelers beneath every porch railing and windowsill. To lift up one's heart to sky and sea was a daily household custom, but whether visitors stood, sat, or kneeled, it hardly mattered: To Mansfield eyes the holy sea beckoned; in Mansfield ears reverberated the antiphonal roar of tidal surf pounding distant rocks.

The ocean's horizon, a steely blue line in the fading afternoon, followed me around. It must have bumped into the tranquil silhouette of a black cat at least as often as I did. The Mansfields had thirteen cats and every single one of them was black as coal. If you were superstitious about such things, you were in trouble, for Mansfield cats dwelt chiefly on thresholds and windowsills, and they were like leeches; you hardly knew they were on you until they were on you. Hattie loved to chant their names until her eyes watered: "Blue . . . Catch . . . Grizel-Greedigut . . . Hephzibah . . . Hardname . . . Pluck . . . Grimalkin . . . Goody Good . . . Tituba . . . First Smack . . . Second Smack . . . Third Smack . . . 'Emma's Cat' " (which had a secret, fourteen-syllable name that everyone knew but which nobody but Emma bothered to pronounce).

They gave me the creeps, those cats. I blundered on, looking for signs of man—a footprint larger than size seven, a clay pipe, a silk bathrobe. Except for the lacquered, old-fashioned sportsman's chandelier on the main veranda, boys and men seemed invisible, or extinct.

At the Mansfields', I later learned, you seldom saw or heard from the spear side of the family. Even when father and sons were at home, they were like Jovian moons; you had to send out distant signals to know they were really there. Mr. Mansfield, a Boston banker, tended to revolve around the first floor, sweeping its outskirts in a dodgy path that took him through five distinct phases: pruning the roses, playing the harpsichord, mixing the martini, carving the roast, and tapping the barometer with a sticky onion-dip finger.

Mansfield boys were usually away at a hockey game, or lurking in the back part of the house; I almost never went back there—guests rarely did. The rear wing, though somewhat newer and brighter than the rest of the house, was nevertheless a scary place, dense with the dignified dust of Mr. Mansfield's Yankee past. The back halls were cold and cheerless, heaped with rolled rugs and brittle furniture whose naturalistically carved arms and legs invariably ended with raptorial claws holding glass balls or ersatz pearls in their scaly clutches.

Girls alone stood sure-footed. In those years, when Hattie, Gussie, Lili, Tizzy, Hilary, and a host of others inhabited Mansfield rooms as auxiliary sisters, leaving their toothbrushes in silver Mansfield christening cups and folding their nightgowns under downy Mansfield pillows, the house served them as a vast girls' dormitory—an informal seaside priory for rest and meditation. And as I circulated through those constant, faithful rooms that first afternoon, I noticed a certain color common to every knickknack I perused. It was a deep, faded blue, so characteristic of the house and its occupants that it dawned on me for the first time that its persistence might not be random.

I had of course seen the color all that fall, at school, mixed into the daily wardrobe and cubby notes and chummy presents and watercolors of the Mansfields and their magic circle. Again and again, I had seen but not recognized the sacred cup of bluish water, the small dry wafers of paint. But now, in the Mansfield homestead, I caught glimpses of framed Mother's Day cards, cat-clawed sofa cushions, children's watercolors of the ocean view, and I began to understand why these girls and their friends had a special name for that shade of blue; I remembered their intense doctrinal debates over its essential blueness:

"Mansfield Blue is a middle-range blue, like the middle part of a mussel shell," Berry believed.

Emma: "It's more the hazy blue of mountaintops in Maine and of beaches in August."

Lili: "Purply blue, like cornflowers and morning glories."

Gussie: "All I know is, it's got some red in it."

Hattie: "Either the creamy blue of Canton china, or the velvety blue of a blueberry before the bloom gets rubbed off."

To me, it seemed just one more uncanny thread fastening me to the Mansfields: Blue—any damn blue—was my favorite color.

At sunset, Hattie came and found me in the main living room. I was lying supine under bars of fading light, listening to Grateful Dead records and keeping my eye on an upright chair whose legs terminated in the horny, ball-clutching talons of a dragon. The last of the shadow-branches had not quite left the ceiling. Outdoors, the leafless trees, framed by the veranda's ogee arches, stood eerily calm, hooded in violet. A train rattled over the Boston & Maine railroad tracks in the woods behind the house.

"It's strange, no?" said Hattie.

I nodded agreement, glad that Hattie was here, glad I wasn't the only foreign body hurtling through the Mansfield universe. Without the sun, a suspenseful, vesperal feeling had settled over the house and its chilly, darkened halls.

"It's weird," I remarked in an overawed, campfire voice.

"Want to know why?" Hattie's face, I noticed, was blanched of its usual high color—the pious left side especially—and her skin was cold to the touch when she came over and took my hand.

She urged me to kneel with her at the hearth—beside a large copper tray which brimmed with small, smooth black stones. I recognized immediately the mother lode from which Berry had made her Switch Night offering. A cool draft stirred the ashes in the fireplace, scattering gossamer particles. Hattie plucked a stone from the tray. She blew away the ashy film and held the stone aloft.

"Look," she whispered, and rubbed the matte-black surface of the stone against the wing of her nose. Copying, I drew one of the stones across my nose and cheek. Hattie's stone came away with a high gloss into which she peered and darkly murmured a sort of incantation. I looked into the polished patch of my stone, but all I came up with was the oily glimmering of my next zits.

"You know," said Hattie, fixing me with ecstatic, shiny eyes, "Mrs. Mansfield's a witch."

"What kind of witch?"

"A good witch."

11. Eskimo Sisters

Just before dinner, which they called supper, Emma took my fingers off the rosewood keys of her father's coffin-shaped harpsichord. She led me by the hand into the television room. She curled up on the couch and patted the blue slipcovered place beside her, beckoning me to come sit; I sat.

Ahead of us, an old color television stood inside a wide wooden console. It was the kind of set that was always on but never watched. Behind us, on the wall above the sofa, there were so many framed family photographs you could hardly see the blue-striped wallpaper.

"That's Berry on Singing Beach," Emma narrated for me. "That's Mum and Berry on the tender in Maine; that's after Berry won the Mill River Race, in her first two-piece—flashy, huh? That's after Lindy's first Communion; that's me in the graveyard, with the boys; that was in Rome, outside the Vatican."

"What happened to Berry's hair?"

"Mum made her wear it under a baseball cap so that Italian men would stop following us around, calling her a madonna and stuff. So one night, Berry stayed in the hotel and cut it all off."

I hurried on to the next picture.

"Dad," said Emma. "Can you believe it? On Soldiers Field. Isn't his helmet weird? He was halfback, All-American, in, like, 1948."

The pictures dazzled me. They portrayed a family and a life that was larger than life, certainly larger and more demanding—more fun—than any family life I knew anything about. In black-and-white and color, the Mansfields combined the familiar physical properties of home with the boundless dimensions of school. They had institutional allure. They seemed not just a family, but a grand, well-regulated enterprise, and I wanted to be part of it.

"That's Mum," continued Emma. "On their honeymoon. On the *Lizzie,* on her first transatlantic. Mum wasn't the beauty of her family, but she was the smartest."

"What's *that* thing?"

"The sextant? She's shooting the sun."

But the "thing" I had meant, on closer inspection, turned out to be a ring, an enormous engagement ring on Mrs. Mansfield's sun-shooting finger.

"Sapphires," said Emma, when she saw what I was studying. "Three sapphires, 'cause Mum was one of three sisters."

"And seven diamonds," I said, counting the smaller stones.

"Yah, Mum knew," Emma said in a semimystical quaver. "Mum knew. Even before we were born. Can you believe it? She always knew she was going to have seven kids."

Mrs. Mansfield appeared the same way in all the pictures: attentive, blond, pigtailed, dowdily suburban. Here she was at a school field-hockey game, and there she was in the ski-lodge cafeteria, wrapped always in the same duffel coat and surrounded always by the same adoring, pink-cheeked girls. She didn't look as though she would have the heart, let alone the time, to bewitch anyone except her children. So far as I could see, the only thing that made Mrs. Mansfield different from any of our mothers was that she'd gotten pregnant so many times it had become a profession. Also, her first husband was still her one and only husband, and her daughters (following their mother's lead?) treated their father as a matter of blood relationship to an amusing, slightly foolish man with quaint, old-fashioned habits: just one more guy orbiting the house.

"And that's J.J., our littlest brother," Emma was saying. Gussie and Berry had come into the TV room for a preprandial cigarette, and Gussie flopped down on the couch beside Emma and me.

"What's he trying to do with that boat?" I asked Emma.

"The dinghy," corrected Gussie.

"O.K., the *dinghy*."

"Cleat the painter," Emma and Berry answered at almost the same instant.

"Em," said Berry, "are you going to turn the roast?" And when her sister didn't reply, Berry said: "So who's going to turn the roast?"

"Not me, said the blind man," said Gussie.

"Is this guy *related* to you?" I prompted, trying to get Emma to stay with me by drawing her attention to a photograph of what looked like a coeducational sailing class, though at the Mansfields', it might just as easily have been the family Christmas card.

"Who?" said Berry, testing her clairvoyance. "Towny Lee?"

"I don't know who—this guy. Over here. *Way* over here—Mr. Tennis Tan."

"Don't put your fingers on the glass, hon'," whispered Emma.

"That's not Towny Lee," said Berry. "It's Cotty Woodward, and he's a lush."

"Cotty Woodward," echoed Gussie: "Cotty Woodward was the first guy I made out with."

"Cotty Woodward!" Berry crowed, triumphant.

"Summer after eighth grade—at 'Sconset," reported Gussie.

"Yup, yup," said Berry, as if telepathic channels had already filled her in. "You and Emma are Eskimo sisters," she boasted, enormously pleased. "Em made out with Cotty Woodward—in the Whaler, on Little Misery, right, Em?"

Emma didn't answer.

"Right, Em?"

Indulging the delay, Emma gazed, grimacing, at the ceiling. She appeared to fight for control of her voice before answering, "And so are we Eskimo sisters, Bear."

At supper, the sisters quarreled about whether seven was the correct number of pups whelped in their summer caretaker's last litter of Labradors. The argument volleyed up and down the long refectory table. Berry had claimed her father's place, at the foot, and Emma, with Amy in her lap, occupied Mrs. Mansfield's chair at the head. I sat with Gussie and Hattie on the side—dazzled. I had never heard the Mansfields—I'd never heard *any* family—get so wound up about puppies.

"It's hardly valid," Emma kept saying from behind pinched brows. "I mean, is this what we're *thinking* about?"

"I think they're nice," Berry returned, cool and composed. "They're nicer than those fluffy dogs the Blanchards breed on Vinal Haven."

" 'Nice?' " said Emma. "Nice, *how*?"

"I'm just saying that Lab litters are usually nice, O.K., Emma?"

Scolding, Emma said, "What about the Laotians?"

"What about them?" snapped Berry.

"Just: What do we think?—What about My Lai?"

These questions, it turned out, were rhetorical, for, having raised the spectre of refugees and massacres, Emma seemed to have qualms about offering any thoughts of her own on either subject. In her wise, wobbly voice, all she could finally bring to her lips was: "I'm just puzzling this out, you guys: I mean—God!—*My Lai? Lab litters?*"

When no one spoke, Emma lifted her hand to her brow and sighed, sinking back into her mother's chair, exhausted apparently by her pharisaic sympathies.

In the silence that followed, the backbeat of the Rolling Stones cut across the grain of the parquet floor. Under the table, cats swished up against everyone's legs, and I jumped half out of my skin every time I felt an inviting flick of fur. Berry, impatient for a cigarette, brushed the cats away as if they were flaky skin. Emma hooked them from under the table, landing them in her lap. She spoke to each black blob by name, making a point of her patience. Then, with magical ease, she fed the animals their worm pills, and the cats, one after another, wandered away as though hypnotized, knocking into walls and table legs.

"Is everyone finished with the cow?" Emma then asked, removing the main dish.

During dessert, boys appeared. North Shore boys seemed to know intuitively, without telephoning in advance or ringing a doorbell, the look of a house in which the parents were away, the bar open, the dessert served. No one needed an invitation. Boys simply attended the Mansfields' as if by subscription.

"Ripper!"

"Boy-Boy!"

"Nibs!"

Emma greeted each visitor with a big personal hello. She wasn't afraid to double them up either. When Ripper Blackwell hiked into the dining room, tall and stiff-legged, Emma slipped her hands through his long dangling arms, embracing his trunk. Then she stepped back and looked him over, marveling, squeezing his fingers, holding his knuckles; and when Ripper's older brother, John, pet-named "Boy-Boy," happened to come over just then, Emma took Boy-Boy's fingers too. Then she kissed them both, starting with the older.

When Emma kissed a boy hello, her eyelids lowered, her wrists rotated like weathercocks, and her fingers, all aflutter, flew cheekward, alighting on either side of the boy's mouth, first gently, then clamping down, as if she were going to have to pry open the boy's mouth to give him his kiss. But each time—it never failed—the boy's lips would part by themselves, and Emma would feed him his kiss, and the boy would wander away, knocking into walls and table legs.

With Berry, it was different. She handled boys with a light, dry touch. Brusque and unflappable during activities such as table-clearing and candle-extinguishing, she cut an almost impersonal path as she scuttered through the front hall, a busy body, with time only for rapid, cheery, information-gathering greetings. Her at-home style was hit-and-run; Berry seldom came to what Mr. McCloskey, our driver's-ed teacher, liked to call "a full and complete stop." She hated to be detained or cuddled—simply would not permit it—and only gave you her hand to hold if she had something else to do (watch TV; talk to her friends) while you were holding it. Berry was never a Friday night hand-flirt, the way Emma was, and the boys who came to the Mansfields, starving for Berry, found themselves forever filling up on Emma.

12. Berry at the Beach

An overnight storm had rearranged the beach. "God," Berry accused, "it's all *changed*." A fresh tidal runnel stood between the breakers and the upper beach, and Berry rolled up her corduroys and waded into the new trough. She bent over, her hair and breasts obeying gravity, her hand plunging into the icy green water. From the washboard surface of the sandy bottom she salvaged the storm's castoffs, calling out the name of each shell: ". . . Smooth Whelk . . . Blue Mussel . . . Dwarf Cockle . . . Limpet . . . Winkle . . . Quahaug . . ." She knew them all.

"Mum taught them to us," Berry said, piously. "Mum taught us the names of all the organisms that live in tide pools."

Above a nearby shelf of sand, Emma had picked the place for the blanket and was now smoothing it out. Serene and watchful, bundled in sweaters, she regarded the sky with her lovely air of detachment, then found her place in *The Mayor of Casterbridge*. She looked up briefly to put in:

"Mum says cowrie shells bring luck with boys."

Berry's interests gradually crept up the beach, her gaze falling on the terraced lawns and shaggy herbaceous borders of the old summer estates fronting the ocean. Many of the wisteria-covered houses stood empty or subdivided, and Berry hinted at domestic scandals as she identified the old places and named the organisms who had once lived within:

". . . Edgewater: Lymans . . . Fayreweather: Gales . . .

Greengate: Frosts . . . Seacliff: Thaws . . . Rockhurst: Hathaways
. . . Brightside: Forbishers . . . Moorings: Aspinwalls . . .

"George Aspinwall is still in New Haven," Berry reported, parenthetically, to her sister.

"Doing what—bartending?"

A long, detailed account of alcoholism among Aspinwalls unfolded, and as each sister jealously added episodes to the family chronicle, the deserted summer estates came alive: One after another the sozzled Aspinwalls staggered through the decades—sinking on the *Titanic,* tanking up for War, bootlegging in the Boom, liquidating in the Crash, getting bombed for the Duration. The Mansfields' thirst for 100-proof puke stories was unquenchable, and since I had no history with which to slake them, they carried on as if I were no longer on the beach.

"Anyway," said Berry, concluding the Aspinwall saga, "*George* got fired out of Yale."

"Figures," said Emma.

"Yah, but goll'," said Berry.

"But goll', *what*?" Emma took up sharply. "Mum says all George ever does is drink like a fish."

"Look," said Berry, "*I* went out with the guy; Mum didn't." And that settled that. For at least fifteen seconds the reputation of one modern Aspinwall rested secure in our time.

"I mean," Berry resumed, a fraction of a second before the body turned cold, "the guy *drank,* but he never booted in the house or anything."

Whenever the older sister paused to take sun, or to sing a burst of lyrics from a top-forty WRKO song, the younger sister reopened the Baedeker of local barflies, the village roster of lost lads. Emma, in a studied voice, liked to point out the sights almost as much as her slangy older sister did. Calling my attention to a tawny-colored pile of uninhabited offshore rock,

147

Emma recited: "That's Misery Island, where we used to make out with boys from Brookwood."

"Emma let Nibs Knowles put his tongue in her ear," Berry related, "but then she wouldn't put *her* tongue in *his* ear."

"He had wax," said Emma.

"Well, I Frenched with Bobby Strayer and he had grinder-breath."

"That's where our crazy grandmother lives," continued Emma, gesturing vaguely to the west.

"Where?"

"Right out *there,* on the point," she said, not unkindly but stubbornly, as though there were no other point in the world. "Stuffy—that's Dad's mother's name—" Emma narrated, "lives out there with Dad's older sister, who's about one hundred years older than Dad, by Stuff's first husband, and since Stuff's so sick, Dad's sister'll get everything. That's what Mum says. Mum says we stand to inherit the wind when Stuff dies."

"Mum's older sister almost married President Kennedy," Berry put in. "They were sweethearts before World War Two. They first met in dancing school."

"Nutkin was the oldest of the three 'honey-haired Shanahan sisters,' " said Emma.

"She was the beauty," Berry added.

"Nutty Nutkin," Emma mused admiringly. "She hasn't washed her hair in eight years."

"Get out," I said.

"It's true: eight years this November. And she's had five husbands, one of whom she—"

"When did Mum say that?" Berry cut in.

"About Stuff? She told me."

"Yah, Emma, I know—*when?*" The sound of injury was strange and clumsy on Berry's tongue.

"Whenever she told me, I don't remember the exact

millisecond— There's the Crockers'," Emma announced, and without waiting for me to request a compass heading, she took my head with both hands and rotated it into a new quarter.

To the east, a pinkie finger of land extended prettily into the sea. There, atop a bulwark of stone, stood a tremendous house—a castle, really—with conical roofs and turrets and terraced lawns falling away to the cold waters by way of blond, pebbly pathways cut into the rock. In the damp yellow grass, benches—mossy stone benches and blackened teak benches—had sprouted like toadstools.

"That's where Charlie Crocker lives," said Berry, and I whistled, because I was supposed to, and because it was an astonishing place.

"Oh, it's not so much," Emma said reprovingly.

"They have three living rooms and two Monets," Berry informed.

"But once," took up Emma, "after the Yale game, Dad was helping Mr. Crocker light the fire in the windward living room, and Dad sneezed and he didn't get his handkerchief out in time, and this big gob of phlegm rocketed out of his mouth, and the phlegm landed on the good Monet, right in the foreground—on one of the haystacks—and no one ever said a word about it, but they all knew it happened."

"Danny Armbrister's over there with Charlie this weekend," Berry reported.

"Oh, yah," confirmed Emma.

"But supposedly the parents are away and they got Hovey and Scott to sneak up for the weekend. Ducky told me Lizzie and Sherry got pink slips approved for the Scotts' New York apartment."

"Sherry Scott is the richest girl in the senior class," Emma annotated for me.

"In the school," Berry pronounced.

"Senior class," Emma insisted.

"I bet money," Berry challenged, shooting out her hand. But Emma would not bet, and something menacing jumped into the older sister's eyes when she now played this card: "Towny Lee's home this weekend."

And something defiant pulled Emma's lips over her teeth when, after a moment, she replied: "Mum says Towny may get kicked out of Groton, and if he is, Miss Little's is going to take him because Miss Little's wants more boys from real boys' schools."

I asked who "Tommy Lee" was.

"*Towny*," Emma stated, leveling her stern gaze at a point on the horizon just over her sister's shoulder, "Henry Townsend Lee."

"Cuppy Cabot and he are sharing a study this year," Berry told her.

"A cell," amended Emma.

"You know they got in trouble *together*," said Berry, leaning forward excitedly. I had no idea what they were talking about, but to me it sounded daring and glamorous: "When they got back from the treehouse," continued Berry, "Towny was the one who threw up onto Mr. Gerard, but Cuppy was the one who told about the treehouse in the first place."

"Where you spent the night," Emma reminded her sister.

Emphatically, Berry replied, "I did not."

"Uh-huh," said Emma.

"I did not!" Berry exploded, starting up suddenly, wild with outrage. Within seconds, however, she'd subsided, and though two carmine bruises remained on her cheeks, she quickly ducked behind a smile, took a deep breath, and mock-innocently sang out, "*Anyway!*"

Emma seemed reluctant to resume normal relations. The pinched look now stole over her lips, but then she gave way, drawing her knees up to her chin and confiding to her kneecap the tragical news: "Mum said he took Fluffy Blanchard to Tuckerman's."

"You love it," said Berry.

Back at full strength, the older sister leaned over, and, more for Emma than for me, lingered at my ear with exaggerated, artificial leisure. I could feel puffs of warm breath on my throat and knew that the Argus-eyed Mansfield sisters were having a war of eyeballs over my shoulder.

Cupping her hands, using them as cement, Berry fastened her face to my ear: "This weekend," she whispered, and I throbbed like a needle in a gauge.

"What—?" I squawked, having of course heard and understood every single secret syllable. Berry was an accomplished whisperer, a pro. She never spat into your ear, never blew on it as if it were a stubborn dinner candle, never made a cheap and easy show of how hot and sexy her breath could be. She simply let you feel and hear the cool unconcern in her bravura whisper.

"*This weekend,*" she repeated, enunciating: "*Emma still likes you. She wants to lose her virginity with you this weekend.*"

"What—?"

"Yah, *what?*" said Emma.

"You'll see," Berry told her sister. To me she snapped: "You heard, I know you did."

I protested that I had not.

Unmoved, Berry shot back: "Solly, Cholly."

"Wasn't loud enough," I nagged, and probably I whined as I begged her, unable to stop myself, "Just whisper it once more."

151

13. Another View of Berry

"Are you all right, hon'?" Emma asked when we walked into the kitchen—always the first port of call at the Mansfields'. "Do you want something to eat?"

Emma fixed me eggs. I sulked about Berry. I did not sit in Amy's high chair nor did I wear Amy's bib, but I sat at the kitchen table, and I sulked, and when Emma carefully placed a plate of steaming scrambled eggs in front of me, I looked up at her in infantile wonder.

"Oh, it's nothing, hon'," she said.

Emma's cat, the one with the secret fourteen-syllable name, lay curled on the sideboard, beside some green Coke bottles, staring at me with its unblinking yellow eyes.

After I'd had my feeding, Emma removed the plate to the sink and stood there, looking out the window.

"It's strange out," she observed.

Mansfields were at all times aware of unusual atmospheric occurrences. Weather-wise, they nodded knowingly at forked lightning, stable fog, giant clouds, moon halos. They had a word or two handy for every harbinger ("odd" . . . "queer" . . . "strange" . . . "cool" . . .), and at times the weather seemed a natural extension of Emma and Berry, and of their family's orphic mysteries. Mainly, though, their comments served only to make bland, ordinary phenomena seem overly sinister. After all, if you look hard enough at anything north of Boston, you can find the Devil in it.

"Walk?" Emma now suggested, and she slid over and gave

the back of my neck an encouraging rub. "Let's take a walk," she said, "in the graveyard."

Not far from the house, set back from the escarpment in an overgrown coppice, a burying ground had been flowering for three and a half centuries. As Emma led me out there that afternoon, the sky in the east, above the ocean's horizon, swelled with dark, dense, anvil-shaped clouds.

"Weird," Emma noted.

In fact, the clouds had formed a fairly normal thunderhead. At most, if pressed, you could have termed them threatening. All the same, the instant Emma divined ill omens in those clouds, my eyes began to moisten, and soon, to water.

"Bizarre," she gasped out.

"No way," I warbled, wishing like hell I'd stayed at the house and listened to some cheerful Grateful Dead records.

"Oh, yes, hon'," she said.

In the rising wind, we came abreast of the graveyard's mossy stone wall and its rusty, scrolled iron gateway. I hesitated. The old burying ground brimmed with lapidary hourglasses and winged skulls, and as I followed Emma into that lonesome acre, the black boughs of old horse chestnuts and yellow-leaved lindens creaked like planks in a hove-to hull. I was certain that a piece of pizzicato music had followed us out from the house, joining us, cuing our stately procession. *"This weekend,"* a cool voice breathed in my ear.

Emma threaded her arm through mine and drew me down the first aisle. Her brow darkened and her long-lashed eyelids descended to half-staff as she nodded her head from side to side, solemnly reading aloud the names of the dead, just as her sister had called out the names of departed mollusks and Manchesterites. The ground was packed with Emma's paternal ancestors and their good neighbors, all those pitiless East India traders and China-trade merchants—the powerful, whale-bellied men who today would have been kept out of the way, pruning their rose bushes, practicing their harpsichords, carving their roasts, sipping their martinis, and tapping their aneroid barometers with inglorious sticky fingers.

In silence, Emma and I continued along between weed-choked gravestones, examining the dates of once-proud Mansfield men. Emma paused occasionally to acknowledge the despair of it all. (How I admired her gloom that day—her expertise in woe!) Now and then she nestled her head into my arm, just below the shoulder, and from this vantage point, she raised her large, humorless eyes to give me her look of apprehension and misgiving. And though our arm-in-arm status qualified us for nothing more specific than a vague, huggy friendliness, we had nevertheless reached a kind of *potential* pre-make-out stage, when every exchange builds either toward the first signs of a kiss or to a silence longer and more complex than the one before it.

In the farthest, oldest, creepiest corner of the graveyard, Emma steered me toward some graves that had been flung willy-nilly beside the stone wall. Wiry vines and intertwined climbing plants strangled this forlorn plot, marked only by seven faceless slates, five of which were not much bigger or thicker than the shingles that covered the Mansfields' house.

"We think the two big ones were maybe witches, we're not sure," Emma narrated in a low, but lively voice. "Mum says they were originally just plain ordinary goodwives, but then, when their babies started to get sick and die, the Puritan fathers started to think their babies were dying because the mothers weren't feeding them."

Emma knelt down, sympathetic and understanding, as if she intended to lay a bunch of posies before the godforsaken goodwife graves. "Mum said that the fathers believed that their wives had an extra tit, and that instead of nursing their own babies, they were using their extra tits to suckle little imps who were children of the Devil."

"You're kidding," I said, and, meaning to divert if not change the subject, I asked in a rather practical voice: "How big were they supposedly?"

"Their tits?" Emma gave me a reproving look: Silly boy with silly thoughts.

"No, no! The *imps*," I protested, flushing, temples knocking, horrified that breasts—my inescapable theme—were so thickly in the air. "No," I replied, starting fresh: "How big— how *tall*—were the imps?"

And Emma said, "A little shorter than me, I imagine." And to demonstrate the height of imps she flattened her hand at earlobe level. At that moment, her body looked so frail and small, so very imp-like, I found it hard to believe that she was Berry's sister, or that Berry was *her* sister—I was no longer sure how I was oriented.

Emma quit the goodwife graves and sat down on the low stone wall, sighing sadly. Not wanting to press myself on her in her unhappy mood, I sat a stone or two away. She surprised me by narrowing the distance with a few short wiggles of her behind. We pressed against each other at the shoulder, and I remembered the gentle night at Punkatasset when Emma and I had lain in the leaves and she had pointed the way to true north and to magnetic north. How clear had been my conviction that Emma would be my true course!

Now, on the roughhewn wall of the graveyard, still magnetized by Berry and her lodestones, yet somehow also still on the verge of Emma and of a silence longer, more complex, than any we had yet known, I slipped my arm around Emma. I squeezed her shoulder. I paused, stomach churning, and turned my head—I was just beginning to draw Emma closer—when into my burning red ears rushed the statement: "Everything this weekend sucks."

"What do you mean?" I stammered. "Why this weekend? What sucks?"

"*Everything* sucks," Emma insisted, shrugging, taking the whole cosmos into her affronted tone, and somehow shrugging my arm off her shoulder to boot.

"Yeah, well, sure," I agreed, wanting to be on her side (in case Emma had arrived at some profound, macrocosmic grave-yard truth, I figured I ought to be in position to share it with her), but mainly wanting my arm to be back on her shoulder.

"Just sucks," she mourned.

"Are you thinking of anything in particular?"

"Anything in particular?" she parroted, and gave me her despairing look, as much as to say that I was hopelessly, irredeemably foolish—a silly boy like me—too frivolous and faulty, all around, to understand and appreciate and share in the serious suckiness of life.

"Is it that guy?" I asked. "That Towny guy you and Berry were so weird about?"

No answer.

"What is it?" I said, spooked by her silence.

"Just, nothing," Emma whispered, sighing through her nose. "Just sister stuff; sad stuff."

I told her I wanted to know what happened. She took out a cigarette and lighted it, and I could see that she was going to tell me; Emma loved to smoke and talk despairingly about things that sucked, and I loved to smoke and listen.

"That boy, Towny Lee, was the only boy I've loved," she said, dispassionately, emphasizing no one word more than another, but, for lack of emphasis, making whole sentences ring. "I loved Towny Lee so much, whenever I saw him, I could barely breathe," she continued, and I felt my own breathing quicken and my heart begin to clobber around in my chest.

"Towny was the coolest boy in Dark Harbor, and the coolest-looking. He had wild brown hair and dark brown eyes and a smooth brown chest, and we were the same age, and we were in seadogs together, and our boat was blue and it was the best seadog in the fleet because it was the oldest and the lightest, and I was in love with Towny Lee for—just, I don't know—three summers? *Four* summers? Who knows?

"Anyway, the summer I was twelve and Berry was thirteen, Towny Lee came up to me in this white dinner jacket at the awards dance after the Mill River Race. He usually had short hair, and when it got long, it sort of stood up—like Beethoven, only not as artistic, just wild—and that night it was really long, and I was looking at it when he came over and took me by the wrist.

"He didn't say anything. He just took my wrist—sort of circled it with his fingers—not hard, but not gentle either. And he wouldn't let go. He had me in this grip, and he wouldn't let go, and he wouldn't let anyone else see. And he took me outside real fast."

I had begun to blush, recalling my own clownish antics with Emma's wrist, but at the moment she seemed not to remember.

"Towny was wearing blue jeans," she continued, "which were against the rules, and this white dinner jacket, which he was supposed to wear, only he'd taken off his shirt and tie for some reason—I guess to look cool—and he was smiling, which he sort of never did with girls, only with his friends, only with boys. So when he took me outside, pulling me along by the wrist, it was weird that he was smiling—kind of making it look like we were just horsing around—but he wouldn't let go, and he wouldn't let go, and then we walked out along the trees, picking our way onto the big rock, and he still wouldn't let go. And I'm thinking—wait, are we going to fool around? But then, right away, before anything, he bends down, and really slowly, four times, twice on the bones and twice on the skin, he kisses my wrist. Then he looked up at me, and that was it, we—''

''Emma!'' I broke in.

''What?'' she said, startled.

I looked at her fixedly, but she seemed not to connect her story with me and with the afternoon I had foolishly kissed the back of her hand in the beech tree down by the river.

''What—?'' said Emma, frowning.

''Nothing,'' I said.

Emma ground out her cigarette in a cleft in the wall and hooked one flank of hair behind her ear. She looked determined to go on, so I held my tongue, but I didn't understand—I just didn't get it at all. Why hadn't I aroused Emma's passion with *my* wrist-grip? Should I have kissed her on the bones? On the skin? Should I perhaps have shown my seadog smile?

''Anyway,'' said Emma, ''we were in love for all of Labor Day weekend. And even though I wanted him to love me for more than just fooling around, and even though he still wanted to do more stuff—he was always going for me, reaching under my shirt—I wouldn't let him. But it was O.K.: we were still in love, and we made out a lot, I remember, 'cause it was the first time I had chapped lips in the summer. And on Saturday night, we took out our blue seadog and sailed out into the moonpath, and he held me really close and made me promise that when I was ready, I would lose my virginity with him, and I almost said, yes, now, here, but I wanted to wait, I wanted it to be just, I don't know, just . . .''

''So what happened?''

''Well, everything would have kept going, I guess, except

Berry dropped Wicksie Lyman on Sunday morning—'cause she, quote-unquote, wanted to be in love; as much in love, quote-unquote, as I was—and she called up Wicksie after breakfast, dropped him, and then around lunchtime decided she wanted Towny Lee.''

''You're kidding,'' I said, or, rather, that is what I meant to say, but instead blurted, ''You're kissing,'' a muddle that set us back a few seconds and made us both lift to our lips phantom cigarettes we'd already finished smoking.

I begged Emma to go on.

''Well, Berry got him,'' Emma replied anticlimactically.

''What do you mean—'got him'?''

''Just, got him, is all. Story of my life: Berry wants him, she gets him; just takes my Towny Lee.''

''Hold on,'' I said, seesawing nervously between commiserative sympathy and prurient interest, and hoping the low end didn't show in my face. ''Got him? Got him *how*?''

''It's mean.''

''Nah,'' I said, and pressed with my shoulder against Emma's shoulder, ''it's fine.''

''No, it is *not* fine,'' Emma returned sharply, drawing away, and I thought all was lost. But then, impiously, she lighted a fresh cigarette and, after taking a few experimental drags, she leaned back against my shoulder and said: ''Do you swear, if I tell, you'll never tell Berry I told you? You've got to *swear*.''

''I swear.''

''Do you *swear*?'' She rubbed the fresh cigarette ash into the thigh of her blue jeans.

''I swear!'' I hung my head solemnly—so solemnly I could have been knighted on the spot—and swore and swore. When I looked sideways and caught her eye, Emma said:

''Berry let him have her breasts.''

She tossed it away, as if the sentence itself were grammatically weightless, a bit of fluff, as if a world in which such things happened deserved no structure, no rules, no apparatus for belief.

The words shook me. The marrow seemed to drain from my bones, and I felt weak and stricken, as though I could literally be knocked down with a feather. Berry? *My* Berry Mansfield: Bostonian in the parlor, French in the bedroom? My knees trembled. A ragged line of sweat broke out across my forehead. It seemed important to keep the conversation going, however inane, and through ringing ears I heard myself say, "Wait, *what* happened?"

"That's it, that's the whole thing," said Emma. "We had to get on the five-something ferry, and she seduced him. Berry'd never once let any boy under her shirt, but she wanted to get Towny Lee so badly that three hours before we had to get on that ferry, she just took off her bathing suit top in one of the catboats, and that was it. That's all it took."

"And Towny Lee? What did he do?"

"What do you mean—'what did he do?' " Emma laughed mirthlessly. "What do you *think* he did? He went cuckoo. As Hattie says, he went cuckoo for cocoa puffs. He went, just, crazy. He *loved* Berry's body. He was obsessed with her breasts. I heard him, afterwards, telling Cuppy Cabot: 'They're the biggest tits I've ever, ever felt.' "

Just then, the sun found a cut in the clouds, and a burning golden blade pierced through. We both looked away and studied the effect. It seemed the ideal atmosphere for me: purple, broken, overwrought. But of course I was wrong. "Trite," Emma decided.

"The thing is," she continued, lowering her voice, "Towny Lee didn't even *like* Berry. He always said how much he *disliked* her bossy personality and her games and the way she couldn't sit still. But he loved her boobs.''

Emma paused, frowned, then breathed deeply through her nose, filling her lungs, and pressing her palms together in a satisfied, isometric, moral-of-the-story sort of way. She seemed to feel better for it all, and after lighting cigarettes for both of us, she rubbed up against my shoulder and said, ''Why?''— resuming the discussion on a philosophic plane—''What would you do?''

''What would I do what?''

''—If you had been Towny Lee?''

''If I had been Towny Lee, when—in the catboat?''

''Yah.''

All around us, cones of cinnamon light fell through the lindens. (''. . . Cézanne-ish,'' Emma noted.) Colors sharpened, intensified, faded, sharpened again. The memento *But he loved her boobs* appeared all of a sudden deeply chiseled into every man's headstone. I shaded my eyes and peered into the shadowy acre and felt a kind of panic unknown to me since deepest childhood: I fully expected, at any second, a tribunal of sour-faced Puritan elders, white-ruffed and black-frocked, to spring from the soil and lock me headfirst into the village pillory.

''What would you do, hon'?'' Emma insisted pleasantly.

What was I supposed to say? What could I say to a moralist for whom no sin was more cardinal—yea, and what was more: even unoriginal—than the sin of preferring, in lust, her sister and her sister's big, bared boobs: *''I confess, Goody Mansfield! From these stocks of shame, I, Goodman Simon, confess the truth! Given half a chance—Heaven grant me strength!—I, too, would have felt up thine own sister in thine Dark Harbor catboat!''*

But in reply, I only stared with downcast eyes and fiery cheeks—pilloried, open-mouthed, sick with desire and self-disgust—and when at last I lifted my head into the light and saw Emma's weather-eye trained on me, I could almost hear her deciding on the one word with which to describe for the tribunal my natural fate: "Doomed."

14. Coat and Tie

After the Mansfield weekend—there were eventually too many Mansfield weekends to qualify any but the first with the definite article—I resumed the life of a freshman. My unstarted, unfinished romance with Emma, as well as the botch I'd made of the weekend, now granted me liberty to love Berry, while Berry's more or less continuous rebuffs conferred upon me the right to sorrow over Emma. And a week away at Walden Pond—for Freshman Class "ecology workshops"—furnished me the ideal setting for solitary lamentation, to say nothing of bellyaching.

When the class returned to school at week's end, I sat brooding on the bus. It was the last snowless Sunday before Thanksgiving. The air was sharp and clear, and in the leafless quiet over Elm Street I could hear Honoria's honking in the Hoare House barn. Chaste, snug fumes curlicued out of Little chimneys. Somebody in one of the houses was baking bread, and I could almost feel the lumps of new dough rising in my heart. The week away had sharpened my appetite and quickened my senses, and at the first glimpse of the Great Elm's bald November dome, with here and there a hanging yellow leaf, I looked down into my shirt and saw the skin below my left nipple convulse like the head of a drum. I was back.

I was back, and everything around me looked so fresh and unaffected I could scarcely believe that this was school. Every last evergreen shrub and shutter stood out in glamorous detail. Each path went its worn and well-known way. Elm Street swelled under my feet with that solid flush of familiarity that welcomes us back to a place the first time we are no longer new.

Berry, too, had never looked more unadorned, more radiant. I'd hardly had a chance to buckle on my armor. Within seconds of stepping off the bus, knapsack in hand, heart in mouth, I found her, or maybe she found me; I'm not sure. I remember the rapidly declining sunrays best of all—the way they dropped down between the bare branches, like gonfalons with golden streamers, heralding the arrival of a queen.

From downtown she came, gliding along Elm, her stride as sure as ever. When she saw me, her mouth buckled, the thick, striated lips suddenly pinching with the strain of keeping buttoned up. Berry Mansfield had news to tell—big news. She could barely contain herself; parturition might happen on the sidewalk, in the street, anywhere. Berry Mansfield was bursting.

She broke silence at twenty paces. "She did it," Berry called out.

I spotted the hard, torn look in her eye, and guessed right away who it was for, and felt such a heart-constricting surge of envy, I simply stopped breathing and shut up.

"Emma lost her virginity," Berry announced, not without a touch of pride, as though she herself had somehow gotten into the act. "They went to the Crockers' for the weekend, and Charlie Crocker tried with Lili Hooper, and Lili wouldn't let him, but Emma and Danny Armbrister went to the beach, and she said she didn't even know it was happening until it happened—can you believe it? It was yesterday, on Crane's."

Berry paused, conscious that I had said nothing. She stuck

163

me with a frown before going on to recite, with almanac-like comprehensiveness, the times and tides and moons and stars that had attended the great event on the beach to the north. But she also continued to pause at intervals, and I, immured in muteness, continued to answer each fact with a sullen, ever-widening moat of silence.

Irritably, Berry cut short her report and said: "So what's your problem, Thoreau? No action at Walden?"

We locked eyes for a split second, and I said, "Wazoo," and Berry said, "Wazoo to you, too, Hank," and I turned and stalked away in vast, overdramatic strides, limping a little. I made straight for the Great Elm and climbed its sheltering boughs, pressing my face into the softness of moss. I inhaled deeply the dank, boletic smell around the woody fungus. I shinnied up to my usual spot, but I was restless and cross and everything around me—trees, fields, chapel, river—looked dark and mean and wrecked.

I had some pot left over from Walden, and I smoked half a joint, thinking it would bring all my anger and frustration into a fine pitch of rebelliousness. The pot did nothing but make me feel grotesque and ignorant, clownish and incompetent. All my shortcomings seemed pinned to my clothing, like excuses from home. Desperate to regain poise, I rifled my pockets and found a slender package of Old Golds. These I smoked, eight in all, one after another, tearing off the filters and sucking them down to fingernail-scorching stubs.

It was getting late. I felt queasy and cold. I needed to talk to someone, and as I ran through the checklist of possible confidants, I was startled but relieved to find that Murray Simon was the only person on the planet I could face right now. I climbed down out of the tree and went off in search of my brother. He wasn't in his room, or at supper, or in study hall.

He wasn't flipping a toggle on anyone. Eventually, I narrowed down all possibilities to one.

I sneaked into the bluish amphitheater and crept into the senior section. In Berry Mansfield's alphabetically ordained place, between Lisa Mackay and Jane Melniker, I slouched down, owlish and stoned. No one had heard me come in.

Down below, on the semicircular thrust stage, a crew of techies manipulated scenery and lights for the fall play. The girls and the boys were uniformly dressed in painter's pants and work shirts. I didn't know any of them well; I had always thought that Trinka van Winkle and Pinky Thaarup and Tipsy Twistleton—an identifiable clique of wholesome sophomores—were either too giddy or too sensible. Jim Shea and Matt Taylor, a pair of sophomore day students, went all but unrecognized outside of sports, and roundheaded Tad Gillespie had faded into mild obscurity after his brief notoriety as the Boy Who Talks To His Sandwiches.

But now, here on the floodlighted stage, they all sparkled, they were all popular, they all glowed in the reflection of each other's goodwill and high spirits. Pinky and Trinka and Tipsy hoisted sheets of plywood and drove nails ringingly. The boys, high atop a tubular aluminum scaffold, hung fresnel lights from a grid of black pipes above the stage. Whenever anyone needed instructions, or encouragement, or praise, he or she turned to the rear of the auditorium—to the shadows of the glassed-in projection booth.

"Do you want bastard-amber gels in *all* these?" Tad Gillespie shouted from the scaffold, enjoying the sound of his big, swearing voice as it carried over the empty rows of the school.

"Or just in number four?" Matt Taylor added in a clatter of fresnel frames.

By and by, my brother emerged from the booth, unfollowed, unopposed—in charge. He was dressed in clothes I had never

165

seen him wear before, and on his belt there hung a bunch of keys that might have opened any door in the school. In pressed chinos and clunky workman's boots, he mounted the stage with a savvy, surefooted hop, directing his crew to "slide the bastards into the frezzies on five." Then on second thought he paused—the highest authority in the room, he wanted to be careful about this—and changed his mind, issuing a new order and returning to the booth to test it out on the many-dimmered, many-toggled, professional lighting board. He stopped along the way to apply various mock wrestling holds—in no particular order and in no particular rush—to his favorite girls.

"Almost time for the Myrrh Man's neckrub," proclaimed Pinky Thaarup.

"I dibs doing him next."

"Does anyone want another doughnut?"

"Is someone sitting back there in seniors?"

"Hello—?"

But the techies didn't see me right away, and neither did Murray, and neither did Mr. Harr, who happened to be passing along on the way to supper in a loden-green duffel coat. The headmaster stuck his face into the amphitheater, and just this once, instead of leering, Fred Harr smiled. It was a normal, equable smile, full of approval, and he smiled it at everyone on the stage. To my brother he called out: "Now this, let me say, is quite an improvement! I like the way you're running the show, Murray Simon!"

"Thanks," said Murray.

"Thank you," said the headmaster.

When Harr was gone, the girls flocked ecstatically to my brother, and he obliged each of them with a full nelson and some low-voltage torture. At about the same moment, over in the senior section, I got sick—at last I puked, and without gagging!—and like that other great former virgin, Emma Mansfield, I didn't even know it was happening until it happened:

I was looking into the big blue volume of air above the amphitheater seats, and smelling faintly the lingering perfumes of morning assembly. It had been three months since I'd first drawn a breath in this world, and the conviction that I had failed—that nobody with a penis had ever been as lucky and unlucky as I had been in this place—vibrated in my stomach, in the aromatic, tidal soup where real nausea begins. So I leaned over the arm of Berry's chair, and all at once I was vomiting—puking into Jane Melniker's seat—and Tad Gillespie, congratulating my brother on the headmaster's praise, was calling out across the seats, "Way to go, man!"

Murray waited with me outside Brewster House.

Blotchy-faced, bawling confessions and apologies into the frosty air, I sat shivering on the cold stone bench under the hemlock branches. Every twenty seconds Murray stood, looked at his wristwatch, peered out into the street.

"Where is Mom?" Murray asked the carless street.

"I think I'm having a breakdown," I said seriously.

"You're just high," said Murray, dropping his voice.

"I suck."

"You're high, is all."

"I suck. My whole life is a failure."

"Listen," said Murray, "Emma Mansfield lost her virginity to Armbrister. You lost lunch. They're just a couple of steps ahead of you. You're making progress. You're progressing."

"I'm a fool," I snarled.

"You are a fool. I hope you know, you're going to be kicked out if you don't clean up your act. Half the school knows you tried to feed hash brownies to Berry Mansfield on Switch Night—even the teachers. They talked about you in Faculty Meeting."

The chapel bell, sounding the last of the evening's summonses, tolled across campus like a warning. Lights snapped off along Elm Street, first in the common rooms, then ascending through the warm upper stories of Buttrick, Oldham, Ordway, Brewster, Hoare, Hooker, and Walton.

"Where *is* she?" said Murray, stepping out onto the road.

"Bet she forgot."

"Typical," said Murray, giving the back of his head a vicious scratch.

"Murray?"

". . . Just *typical*."

"You're great," I told my brother. "I love you, Murray."

"Very touching, Pieman, very touching."

"No, you are. You really are."

"Yeah, well, you're a nut, an absolute nut. I can't believe you—I can't believe *Mom*. Where is she?"

She didn't appear until nearly midnight, and by then Murray was seething and I was punchy. Muz pulled the car over and rolled down her window, calling out, "Chauffeur service!" Murray hustled me over to the car. I could smell Muz's perfume, warm and indelible, wafting from her window, and when she peered out and saw Murray guiding me over—"*What's happened?*" she said—I began to laugh hysterically.

Muz began to cry. "What's happened?" she gasped out. "What's happened to my boys?"

"Don't ask me," said Murray.

Muz's eyes turned silver with tears, and her sinuses filled up so quickly that when she spoke now—"Oh, Murray, tell me, tell me what's *happened*?"—she chortled over the words, as if with pleasure.

"It's nothing, Muz," said Murray, holding me by the shoulders because I was laughing so hard. "He's just a nut. Come on, Pieman—time to go."

*   *   *

Early the next morning, though I would be late for school, I paid a visit to Keezer's, the camphorated used-clothes emporium where Max Keezer recycled the tweeds and flannels of the Cantabridgian community. For less than twenty dollars, I reassembled my Ruxton School uniform. After an over-the-ears haircut at the LaFlamme barbershop on Dunster Street, I hurried home to dress.

Once more I donned the blue oxcloth shirt, the cuffed gray flannels, the navy blue blazer with the Ruxton School patch. Once more I polished the cordovan loafers (front and back) and stood before the mirror in my mother's dressing room, knotting the old school tie. There, in the oval glass—and later that morning in the oval-mouthed faces that greeted me on Little School pathways—I glimpsed a familiar figure:

"Oh, thank God," said my mother, getting dressed to take me back out to school. "It's you again!"

"Queer," said Sara Samperton.

"What a relief," said Dean Brickley.

"Ew," said Lili Hooper.

"I *like* it," said Gussie, who thought that I was a new boy, until Lili corrected her.

"Are you sure, hon'?" said Emma, her correcting hand fluttering upward to arrange, in vain, the shorn locks.

"You could always hang yourself," said Poopsy Winslow.

"Wow," said Starry Knight, "did you get into an accident?"

"Dashing," said Ducky Wigglesworth.

"Very Mr. Chips," said Mr. Coy, my French teacher.

"Hey," said Wentworth, "you got a haircut."

"Pieman, you look like you got struck by lightning."

"What are you—dead, or something?" Danny flung at me, loudly, before hurrying off, muttering, "You've got to drop this clean-cut, conservative shit right away, man."

I didn't see Berry until late afternoon, and by then she was in the middle of a field hockey scrimmage and could only toss me a perfunctory, rubber-faced expression of astonishment.

At dusk, in the barn, I learned from Hattie that on account of my *scapapalping* I was no longer considered *"veberibee cubute."* In fact, a quorum in the Hoare common room had that afternoon voted me *"rebeleebee ubugleebee."*

"But it doesn't matter," Hattie decided. "I still love you, Nomis—we all do. It was nice when you were a golden boy with long golden hair, but this new you may prove even better, and wiser, although at the moment you happen to look cuckoo."

"I guess there's no chance now with Berry, is there?"

Hattie regarded me gravely, then smiled her gummy smile. "It doesn't *always* have to be sex, you know, Nomis. Sex isn't the vital thing. Up on the Big Board, it's more than just a question of who rumpled the sheets with who—with *whom*? Is it *who* or *whom*?"

I told her I didn't have the faintest idea.

"But, Nomis?" she said in her flattering, wheedling, *But, you guys?* voice: "There's no sense in your being mad at Berry. You're not the first boy she hasn't slept with, and you won't be the last, I dare say. You've got to remember, Nomis: She really loves you, and by itself that's a pretty big thing."

"Oh, come on—"

"She *does,* and it *is* a big thing. It started in the twelfth century, you know, the realization that when man left behind bearskins and wolf teeth and caves and clubs, something ennobling began to go on between men and women."

"Oh, great. So now, maybe once every couple of centuries, guys get laid?"

"Stop it, Nomis— Crikey! You are such a *boy,* you even look like one now."

"Well, what do you want?"

"No!" Hattie cried, "don't change! Now I can study you every day to see what makes you go to ballparks and eat wienies and spend all your time dreaming of girls with 'stacked chests' and 'big jugs' and all those other things you call them. You are funny that way, you know.

"But," said Hattie, peeking out the wide barn doors, apple-cheeked and innocent in the sharp night air, "I don't blame you. You're probably tired of us now and want to go back."

"No," I said, but the more I sat there in the red wheelbar-row, fingering the four-in-hand knot in my needless necktie, the more it seemed graspable again—that old Roman world that Hattie knew was back there still—back behind the trim Little houses and the dome of the Great Elm, behind Main Street and Walden Pond and the Boston & Maine railroad tracks. It was way back there, that acrid, ancient, ever-westering world, but it didn't seem far away at all.

15. Esposito's Night

Then one frigid night before Christmas vacation, warmed by a host of angelic voices, we were corralled into the Buttrick barn, and there, by candlelight, in the custody of older girls, we sleepy-faced Little boys received the last part of our initiation into the world of Little women.

It was a pearly gray December eve, with several days' worth of snow already drifted up beside the pathway duck-boards. As soon as school let out, I made spry snow angels and earthy snowpersons with Poopsy and Wenty Bird and most of the Hoares. In the darkening afternoon, everyone hiked down to the river for cider and cigarettes, and I missed train after train.

Who wanted to go home? I wanted to be with my friends. I wanted one last look at the school before 1972. And with new-falling snow fast piling up excuses on unplowed roads, Murray persuaded his houseparents to let me spend the night in the window seat of Armbrister and Crocker's room in Brewster. The Worrells assented unwittingly; it was their first Christmas at school, and of course ours too, so none of us had any idea what was coming. We knew only that senior boarders were traditionally allowed to make merry in the Buttrick Butt Room, staying up all night if they cared to. Next morning, everyone would go home for the holidays.

After some halfhearted caroling around the common room piano, the men of Brewster prepared for bed as usual: Albert Ackerman got into bed with a rolled bath towel wrapped around his neck; my brother sprayed Lysol into Poopsy Winslow's boots; Poopsy Winslow pulled on his black silk eyeshade and kneaded his gummy French earplugs; Tad Gillespie stockpiled flashlights; Sergei LaFarge lurked in his closet; Wentworth and Purvis quarreled; Armbrister and Crocker slipped out onto the widow's walk and smoked a joint.

Ackerman, the most articulate boy in the house, had all his life suspected that a green-gowned surgical team would operate on his vocal cords while he slept, and he used the rolled bath towel as a kind of throat cosy—for protection, and warmth. My brother, on the other hand, still hadn't found a foolproof defense against *his* main bedtime fear: One night in childhood, soon after Dad moved out and Murray and I got separate rooms, Murray claimed that Ulysses S. Grant personally materialized, in uniform, at the foot of Murray's bed. The Blue General had not been unfriendly to Murray, but he touched my brother's pillow with "a greenish-looking hand," and he

172

"reeked of cigars and gangrene," and Murray had ever after worried that Grant would again appear to him in the middle of the night. At home he had tried batteries of floodlights and smoke alarms, hooked up to his bedside control panel, but at school, no matter what he did, the gangrene and cigar fantasy was nightly refreshed by the harsh stench of Poopsy Winslow's feet.

Foul-footed Poopsy, meanwhile, slept with the *Oxford English Dictionary* fortifying his side of the room: Every night, Poopsy shaded his eyes and stoppled his ears, convinced that unless he fell sound asleep within ten minutes, insomnia would quickly lead to "questions," then to "doubts," then to "madness," and finally, "into the void"—from which, as we all knew, only the *OED* in twelve volumes, plus supplements, with a half-million entries, could vouchsafe Poopsy's safe passage to morning.

Across the hall, Tad Gillespie, a genuine nyctophobe with the nyctophobe's morbid fear of the dark, lay wide awake, eyes peeled, armed with a collection of quartz-halogen flash-lights whose total candlepower could have lighted the Washington Monument. On the other side of the room, Sergei LaFarge, who lived in dread of one thing—that other boys would spot his undescended testicle—cloaked himself in darkness. Bony as a bat, Sergei had spent his whole life at school ducking into darkened places to change clothes, and sleeping always in his tight underpants, a pair of stringy bikini briefs, which, as far as anyone knew, Sergei had never changed. At lights out, the Gillespie–LaFarge room resembled a kind of avant-garde ballet, with as many as six of Gillespie's quartz-halogen beams crisscrossing the dark floor, scissoring the prancing, wraithlike figure of LaFarge as he sprang, seminude, from the security of his closet to the cover of his comforter.

One flight up, Wentworth and Purvis, sharing Brewster's

narrowest double, climbed into their squeaky, iron-frame bunk bed. Wentworth, on top, wearing expensive orthodontic headgear, fell instantly asleep, and no more than a minute later began grinding his teeth. Purvis, below, turned up the volume on "Sleep-O," a bedside sleep-sound generator with which the city boy had slept every night of his metropolitan life, but which here at school, for all its gentle soughing sounds, hardly put a dent in Wentworth's continuous metallic grinding.

Meantime, across the hall, Danny and Betty Crocker and I settled down to the main business of the night, as Danny saw it: getting wrecked while we waited for some seniors to "come over from Buttrick to ball us."

"Listen to that," Danny urged, crouching in the windowseat, his ear bent to the chaste, white campus. Lizzie Hovey had told Danny that something "really wonderful" would take place the night before Christmas vacation, and though Danny's interpretation gave me, I have to admit, a certain mistletoey tingle, I was the first to lose heart:

"To what? Listen to what?"

"To *that*"—as over the snow and up to our window floated the faintest, faraway giggle.

Around midnight, when the slutty wassailers still hadn't turned up, we began trading half-hour watches, and I remember stirring from a stoned doze during one of my watches, noting the hour, and thinking that even when my brother and I had once stayed up to see if Santa Claus *and* Ulysses S. Grant would show up in uniform on the same night, I hadn't made it past two.

"When do we think this is going to happen?" Crocker asked after three.

"Any time now," Danny promised alertly. He elbowed me. "Lizzie Hovey said she'd ball you, man, so in case she's not on the Pill, I hope you've got a rubber."

"I don't—I haven't got anything."
"Then you better hope she'll go down."

Four-thirty in the morning. A low, herdlike rumble—felt, more than heard. Then an all-penetrating screech, swelling, rushing out of every corner of the universe, speeding across the snow, crashing into the house. Then, on each floor, in every room, a systematic pattern of rushing and screeching, pausing and glory-whooping. Then trumpetings of fear, incomprehension. Pitiful cries: "Sleep-O! Where the fuck is Sleep-O?"—"What? Wait!"—"Someone's got Sleep-O!"—"Oh, God . . ."—"Help!"

Sandy and Wendy Worrell, on the first floor, were yelling loudest of all. Awakened by the din, the houseparents had immediately determined that a pack of roving townies had gone on a drunken rampage. Dressed in their matching plaid nightshirts, the Worrells crept to the wide Dutch door that partitioned their apartment from the rest of Brewster, bolted themselves in, and hollered out warnings to the effect that, by God, they were telephoning the police.

On the second floor, Poopsy Winslow may have presented the eeriest face to the raiders: Wide awake at the moment of attack, Poopsy lay huddled behind his bedside dictionary—liverish, haggard, pasty with insomnia—reading aloud the *OED*'s thirty-two definitions for "water," while my brother, squirming to avoid the gangrenous hands of U. S. Grant, had activated every toggle on his bedside control panel, flooding the room with light and sound and alarm.

Ninety seconds after it began, the raid had reached the third floor. At the sound of footsteps approaching the door, Danny unbuckled his belt gravely. "They're here," he announced, and added, with emotion: "Thank God I woke up with a rod."

Just then, Starry Knight, disguised as an Indian, burst into

175

the room, whooping, "Get up! Get up! Get up!" Berry rushed in next, and at first I didn't recognize her. She was wrapped in a blanket; her face was stained a dark, angry, cordovan red, with green poster-paint blazes; her hair hung in braids, embroidered with feathers. The effect was obviously supposed to be bellicose, but Berry didn't have it in her to pull it off. It was one of my heroine's peculiar limitations: she was not equipped to play anyone but herself. In the role of Tea Party Indian, her eyes gave her away, and as she flew at me in the window seat, screeching her part, those Mansfield eyes, blinking and bright and merry, semaphored insistently.

"Let's go, Sambo," said Berry. "I know you know it's me."

One senior after another crashed up the stairs, red-faced, braided, blanketed. Each Indian had her own method of capture, each her own quarry. Penny Lane, across the hall, advised Wentworth not to worry about getting dressed. Starry Knight shrieked at Betty Crocker to get up, and when Crocker refused to budge, Starry Knight got into bed and hugged him. With me, Berry didn't fuss. She simply hauled me out of the window seat, wrapped me in her body-warmed blanket, and spun me, an armless papoose, toward the door. I remember the almost dirty, childlike thrill of being completely in her power.

Shivering, swaddled in blankets, bunched into groggy, subdued groups of two and three, we marched down the brittle wooden staircase, out the wide front door, and into the frosty hush of night. The snow had stopped. Elm Street had vanished. The world lay snowbound. And there, in the gelid stillness of the early hour, pure and clear, as only something seen at five in the morning can be completely pure and clear, the school stood arrayed along the downy, hidden street.

There they all were, each with a candle, framed by halos,

176

linked to one another in luminous, unlikely strands, the way they always appear in my dreams: the Wigglesworths with Ray Roy; Gussie beside Sara Samperton and the school nurse, Retha Batcheller; Topsy Johnson and Lili and Emma and Mr. Coy; the Waffles, Hattie, Pinky Thaarup, Mr. Sugarman, and Hilary Fraser with a dog; Mrs. Cleveland Swimm, the dessert lady in the kitchen, Dean Brickley, and Tizzy Tucker; Dr. Cox, Miss Pregnall, Trinka van Winkle, Tipsy Twistleton, and dozens of others—all of them sleepy-lidded and following in the footprints of clear-eyed, red-faced seniors, many of whose names I haven't once mentioned but who that night came forth to embrace us with a kind of willingness and joy that went beyond parental, beyond pastoral, and into a realm of affection which might have been love itself, the heart of it, First Corinthians sprung to life.

Brewster had been the last house captured. Even the Worrells emerged at last, shaken, still nettled, and as each prisoner was marched out the front door, all the wind-rouged faces turned to us with jolly eyes and small O-shaped mouths—they were singing. It seemed incredible: teachers with their hair afrazzle; teachers' pets with sweaters turned backwards over wrinkled nightgowns; team captains with tongue-wagging boots trailing laces behind sockless ankles—as if an earthquake had shaken them all out of bed.

They were singing "Good King Wenceslas," and with Berry as my sachem, I joined the tribe, trying to remember the hymn's male verses; but the bass parts, sung now by sopranos, had already lifted up over Elm Street, lighter than air, up over sagging fir boughs and frosted chimneys and the crests of gingerbread-fragrant houses.

The single file procession, dotted by disks of yellow light, advanced toward the darkened village. Through the column passed intoxicating news: In accordance with local history and school custom, we were off to rouse the citizens of Concord. But first, to fortify the coldest of the choristers for the hours of caroling ahead, cocoa would be served.

We turned off Elm Street and crunched along toward the rimy windows of Buttrick Barn. Inside, tapers flickered in coffee-can sconces along the rough, sable-colored walls. A pair of tractors stood off to the left, wearing stiff yellow snowplows under their bright red chins. The main floor had been cleared of maintenance equipment, and toward the rear waited a holly-decked refectory table loaded with silver urns of cocoa and salvers piled high with warm, raisin-eyed gingerbread men and women.

We entered reverently. A sort of mystic speechlessness settled over the scene. Bunched in groups, everyone heeled at the side of his or her sachem, and without a word we all sat down on the pitted, grainy floorboards. In euphoric, clannish silence everyone stared at everyone else. The cold air smelled of sawdust and oil and lumber, and it vibrated with a high holy hush—all things in their places, all things snug, and the snow packed tight over the sill, insulating the cellar, muffling sound.

In the mounting silence, Berry sat calmly, occasionally shushing some tyro tending toward giggles. Once or twice she slipped me a foxy look, but with Dean Brickley and Mr. Sugarman and my brother in our group, Berry would not wink at me; instead, she glittered all over, like new-fallen snow.

"See," her sharp eyes commanded, luxuriating in the mystery, "these are the real secrets, dummy: Love, sex, chastity, these three; but the greatest of these—"

From up in the maintenance men's hayloft came a quick, knowing voice: "Ho-ho-ho," it called down. "Ho-ho-ho!"

Dean Brickley turned to my brother and me, and smiled. "Well, boys," she whispered, "now you're one of us."

In the next instant, there appeared in our midst a familiar figure: Dressed from head to foot in a red flannel suit, pillowed at the belly, he was dimpleless and beardless (chinless, too, come to think of it); and if his overall aspect was rather more stalky, like celery, than rounded and quivery, like a bowl full of jelly, then all right. But no one could object to the spectacular bundle he'd shouldered.

"*Phew,*" he exclaimed, sagging at the knees as he set down his great load. He pulled off his eyeglasses and wiped them clean. Then, reaching randomly into his sprawling bundle, this goggle-eyed St. Nick brought out into the light a lavishly decorated Christmas stocking stuffed with loot.

Examining the name embroidered onto the stocking, merry old Santa called out, "Tad Gillespie!" and passed off the stocking to a helper who turned it over to Janet Daley who delivered it to the astonished boy's hands.

". . . Tipsy Twistleton!" continued St. Nick, and in the next half-hour passed on more than a hundred and fifty crackling Christmas stockings, one for every member of the boarding community, each of whom, weeks earlier, had perhaps noted a missing sock, invariably one in a pair of favorite knee socks, and now greeted with oohs and ahs and screeches of pleasure its unexpected return—swollen, sequined, stuffed beyond recognition.

One after another the stockings came out of the bag, bulky with trinkets and toys and candy and nonsense. Some emerged in pairs, fastened to their mate by kilt-pins and strands of popcorn and cranberries; or in nylon tights, stabilized by clove-studded oranges in the toes; or, as in Paul Winslow's case (no one could bring herself to touch Poopsy's socks, even the clean

179

ones), in cotton long johns tied off at the feet. Even I, a day-tripper, rated a stocking—stuffed by Berry—and I can still feel, as if it were one of my first Christmases, my tactile delight at holding and unwrapping that irregular, last-minute knee sock.

"When Esposito has a good night, you have a good night," Mr. Sugarman, a Bruins fan, commented, smiling at me as I brought forth my treasures: a Friendly's gift certificate, a rubber snake, a watercolor set with sable brushes, a passel of Matisse postcards, a clove-studded orange, an enormous box of Toblerone, a carton of Old Golds. . . .

What my memory dwells on most, though, is a handmade article that emerged that morning from my brother's stocking: Dylan Thomas's *A Child's Christmas in Wales*, every single word of which Berry Mansfield had copied out into a blank book. No cut-and-paste job, this—Berry had painstakingly calligraphed onto the stiff white pages every last comma, every last serif of the poet's three-thousand-word work. She had also designed a frontispiece and twelve illustrations which she'd reproduced alongside the text by cutting, inking, and imprinting with a dozen homemade potato stamps. What was more, she had needlepointed, over the course of a month, a jacket for the book, stitching the owner's name into the lower righthand corner.

Today, I marvel at this thing. Whenever I'm over at my brother's apartment, I rediscover this artifact, this edition of one, which Murray still keeps in his sock drawer, as though it had been given to him by his first lover (people always think it was). I look at the stitching of his school nickname—and there it is, white on green, as though freshly carved into the bole of an ancient tree: *Myrrh Man*. If the month is December I slip a peaceable hand into my brother's sock drawer and lift the book out into the air.

At first, I have to admit, it sometimes seems a little silly: "God, look at this," I call to Murray, pretending to thumb the book—this trifle, this sappy keepsake.

"Pieman!" Murray protests, shrilly. "My book!"

"My God," I muse, "my God, will you look at this! Berry Mansfield must have spent two whole days on the India ink alone! Can you imagine—*Berry Mansfield?*"

Murray shrugs. He loves to lord over me his ownership of a book made personally for him by Berry Mansfield. He says: "When Esposito has a good night, you have a good night." Then he puts out his hand. "My book," he insists.

I hand it over. He holds it. He palms the cover, opens the book, inclines his head—he's pretending he's reading his book. At once, I ask to see it again.

"I'm reading," says Murray, his eyeballs following Berry Mansfield's voluptuous, lefthanded penmanship.

"Just for a sec'."

"Why—Berry Mansfield never let you into her pants; why should I let you into her book?"

"You never had sex with her either," I remind him, as if he needs reminding, and we both grin: It was the first thing Murray's college roommate asked when he saw the little needlepointed book: "Never—?" Murray's roommate bellowed, assuming, naturally, that only Murray's grandmother or Murray's sweetheart would labor so exhaustively over a present: "—You *never* had sex with this babe?"

Tired of our ritual, Murray stops reading, relaxes his hold on the book. He allows me, delicately, to lift it from his hands.

This time, I cup the spine. I finger the pages. On my lips a tiny smile spreads ever wider. I can hardly believe there once existed a girl—O.K., O.K.: a woman—who had this grace, this crafty hand. For I, as a boy, was blind to Berry Mansfield's labor of love. I took for granted that little handmade book. I only dimly understood the essential fact of the transaction, the distinguishing idea that forever divided us from the Roman world in which girls were body parts after which boys lusted.

Now I sneak my nose into the crease of the spine, and then I can literally smell that morning—I can smell it for good: the cold barn air warmed by our body heat, the spicy redolence of chocolate and ginger and clove-studded oranges. I can see the hoarfrost melting on the windowpanes, the first violet paleness of day staining the glass. Then I can hear Fred Harr wishing us all a merry Christmas. Then Dean Brickley announcing the morning trains to Boston. And then we run out laughing into that pure white world, the dean's brisk voice carrying over the deep, drifted snow: "Now dash away! Dash away! Dash away—all!"

Then I shut the book. Casually, almost forgetfully, I scratch my nose with the nubbly green cover. But really, as I am doing this, I kiss the book. On my lips, I retrace the stitching of Berry Mansfield's friendship sampler. I taste once more the orange and the clove. I picture the way the world looked that griefless December morning, and I think of this girl—this chief of my tribe—this woman for whom only our mothers had prepared us.

PART THREE

THE LAST LITTLE GIRLS

There was a little girl
Who had a little curl
Right in the middle of her forehead;
And when she was good
She was very, very good,
But when she was bad she was horrid.

—Longfellow

1. Trader Vic's

On the last day of December, 1971, I caught the Yankee Clipper at Back Bay station in Boston. It became a school-year tradition—to roll down to New York for New Year's Eve. The train, poky and overheated, each year limped into Pennsylvania Station two hours late, then inched to a halt. Each year the New York passengers flocked to the ends of the coach and stood with fuming faces, shoulders hunched, absorbed already in the vast importance of their city. Each year the conductor alone remained boyish and gauche, cracking jokes, playing with the controls at the door; and when at last he stepped aside, I followed the New Yorkers, stepping lively. But I always paused at the threshold, relishing the moment when, with the steamy perfume in my nostrils and the sooty roar in my ears, I would announce to myself the arrival of myself. Then, hoisting my bag, I would run.

Framed by the rear window of a Checker cab, the city on

those New Year's Eve afternoons had a bluish tint, like hand-colored Currier and Ives winterscapes. It had always just rained, and if there were time for the museum, there would be a walk afterwards in the park—blue and smudgy, chill and damp—with the smelly tang of the rivers and, on the West Side, the surprising scent of the sea. Sunset gleamed like bullion in a thousand windows.

At dusk came the impatience for nightfall, and at nightfall, the rendezvous with "a whole bunch of people" at someone's grandmother's apartment up Fifth Avenue. The grandmother's building, color of bone, stiff with the spinal formality of the avenue, braced itself at our approach. The old woman herself had flown to Palm Beach; her fine brittle furniture cowered under dust-shrouds, and the more we noisemakers crossed her marble threshold, the more the great lady's heirs invoked her pet name—"Furfur" or "Gaga" or "Mormor"—as password and warning. But the evening would never really begin until someone had smashed Furfur's or Gaga's or Mormor's Murano chandelier, and someone else had left his drugs on her Louis XVI poudreuse, and some other Samaritan had thrown up onto the Sarūk runner in the gallery.

Fidgety, overexcited, everybody would go down and wait for cabs under the gull-gray canopy. When none came, we would set out on foot. Down the avenue we'd march, beside the guttered, glittering Christmas trees, beneath the rain-blackened ranks of oak and maple, down into a veil of mist, out of which rose, layer upon lofty layer, impossibly vertical, like an Oriental scroll piled high with velvety vapors and isolated, plunging peaks—the looming towers, the remote fastnesses of the fabulous, gilded city.

The Plaza claimed us first, luminous under its verdigris roof and the blazer-blue sky. In we'd go, we rubes from Boston, past the ersatz Easter Island statues, and down the festive stairway to the bamboo-ribbed corridor, where sat marooned the unmanned outrigger canoe—fifty-foot, two-ton vessel for hurriedly parked wads of chewing gum, unfinished road cocktails, teen vomit. Then the bamboo reservations desk, lashed with thongs of bark, and then the maître d'hôtel, the one who supposedly resembled the dictator of the Philippines (only he didn't really), and then the vain, sardonic Dalton kid who'd just strolled in without coat or tie, promising to wear some long-bounced barfly's forgotten sport coat (only he didn't finally: the lapels were too wide and it was the one with the soiled smell).

Beyond, in the jungly dimness to the left, the bar beckoned, cunningly thatched with long palmetto leaves and clotted with congenerous, half-familiar faces. A flock of vacation-tanned Brearley girls preened beside the tribal masks and tapa-covered walls, penned in by twenty head of Grotties. And over there, in the lamplight, leaning back from the kidney-shaped luau table— wasn't that Towny Lee? Wait a minute: there was Bobby Reilly. . . . And here was Woodie Codman, Buddy Hayes, and Cotty Woodward. . . . Whoa, here was Purvis!

Astonished, gleeful, all fetched up in coat and tie, each man strode forward carrying a rum drink the size of a soup tureen. Each faction of revelers seemed to present itself in random sequence, as if each encounter were the greatest coincidence the world had ever known. In fact the tribe was only signaling, not yet revealing, the immediate presence of its crucial, linking figure. But there she was—in the fan-backed wicker throne—and she was always there, always in the middle of it, always encircled by boys at the beginning and end of every new year: our Eve of eves, our girl of girls, our Berry Mansfield, who had knitted us together, then and for all time.

From that point on, only the night itself could unravel—at Woodward's house, or Codman's, or at Purvis's stepfather's in

187

River House, or Towny Lee's grandmother's out at Peacock Point. It was like living in an empire. Wherever we were, wherever we went, one of us had a house there, and we could always call, and we could always go, and Berry Mansfield was sure to be at one of them; Berry Mansfield was sure to be at all of them. None of us would need the directions, none of us would need the number. By heart we knew each other's telephone numbers; by heart we knew the way. In our young republic, the numbers never changed, the households never moved, nobody ever died, someone was always there.

2. A Mixer

Exams began three weeks after Christmas. The first bright morning of January's study-and-review week dawned bitter cold. The next day brought lowering skies, clanging radiators, some flurries. But the real snow didn't appear until late Friday afternoon, when liberty was more or less superfluous, and then it came on teasingly, the big, fat flakes dropping in under cover of darkness, snugly over-spreading woods and fields and the first black ice on the river.

By suppertime, the smaller pines and hemlock shrubs had begun to sag, crushed by the weight of the plastering snow. Under pathway lamps, in each brand-new layer, fresh tracks could be identified: squirrels, dogs, cross-country skis, tractor treads, crutch tips—these were the marks of elementary winter trail-craft. But on weekend nights, when yellow buses departed Main Gate for a mixer at Groton or Middlesex or Milton, a cotillion of footprints stayed behind: crazy conga lines, *pas de deux*, tangos of indecision.

By the middle of January, I had developed such a practiced eye, had studied so exhaustively the stealthy pattern of Mansfield tracks, that I would often follow along the paths of departure, inanely thinking I had picked out, from among all the dances modeled in the snows of Saturday night, the waffle-patterned quickstep of Berry's winter boots.

I was a boarder now—thanks be to Dad—though to be a boy boarder in the winter of 1972 no longer guaranteed widespread fame, much less backrubs, fresh baked goods, and breakfast in bed. My increased height of five feet seven inches had scarcely improved my stature among the Mansfield sisters. A second wave of Little boys had brought several new six-footers to Brewster House and, altogether, fifteen male newcomers to the school, three of them in the junior class. We now had our first Afro-American Little boy, our first Asian-Americans, and, unfortunately, our first rivals. An experiment in coordinated classes with nearby, all-male Estabrook Academy had begun for spring semester. Yellow buses now shuttled between the two campuses, snatching up Little girls after morning chapel, and planting within our gates, well into evening study hall, great furry hordes of Estabrook boys.

In a word, we'd been eclipsed. The glory days of discovery—and hugging—were over. The dreary, unromantic work of settlement had begun.

Danny and Poopsy and Betty Crocker and Wenty Bird and I roomed in a two-room, blanket-partitioned Brewster suite, with the Myrrh Man on intercom in the single next door. Our prestige, dimmed by exams, diluted by newer boys, expired for good the morning Dean Brickley announced in assembly that Estabrook Academy had invited the Little School—"boys and all"—to a Saturday night mixer. The answering "Yeas" rang out joyously.

189

Outside, afterwards, Poopsy glumly said: "Maybe we should just go."

"To a *mixer?*"

"We could go late."

"We could go in costume."

"I dibs Batman," said Wenty Bird.

"Not me," said Betty Crocker, who had spent his last four weekends in Vermont, making hand-pressed sweet cider and sleeping in a converted sugarhouse with Julia Haizlip, a senior whose full-credit, semester-long study of apples had been titled "Caring, Sharing, and Paring."

"Me neither," said Danny, who claimed to have a pink slip in for a massage-therapy workshop sponsored by Lizzie Hovey in Cambridge.

"What about Myrrh Man?" said Poopsy.

"Annie Johnston," one of us answered, and all of us groaned.

Annie Johnston, a chummy, irrepressibly cheerful day student from Carlisle, had become my brother's main—his only—social life. But what a life! Murray now wore on his belt the keys to every room in the school; he had officially been named technical director of the Lively Arts Center, and around Thanksgiving had begun locking himself and his beloved into the amphitheater for private screenings of *Butch Cassidy and the Sundance Kid*. My brother and Annie were both virgins, but by Christmas, with much talk of "saving it for each other," Annie had decided to go on the Pill. Now, three weeks into the "cycle," the responsible couple was going to be rewarded.

"Maybe we should put in pink slips for the Lively Arts Center," proposed Wenty Bird. "We could get bleacher seats and beer—and watch."

"Maybe we should hang ourselves," suggested Poopsy.

*　　*　　*

Caught in the shuttle bus headlights, Estabrook Academy's tall, black wrought-iron gateway bared a set of fanglike shadows. Halfway up the school's snowy, sand-speckled drive, yellow lights began to twinkle through the flanking fir boughs. Then dormitories blazed into view—Kentish manor house replicas, with dormered slate roofs and frosted windows casting broad yellow swaths over the blue, snow-packed grounds. Massed along opposite knolls, the red brick dorms gave the campus the solid, wolf-proof look of something built by the third of the Three Little Pigs.

Farther along, after a dip and a rise in the road, Estabrook's central organizing circle presented a clean-edged, almost childlike picture of order and reason. Stout brick buildings and tall pleasant trees were spaced evenly around the circle's wide Roman circumference. A massive, cupolaed academy building and a square white chapel with a storybook steeple faced one another in the cold brightness.

The Little buses rattled up the long drive. We had just entered the circle when raucous welcoming cries spouted from dorm windows. Tocsins sounded, sashes shuddered. Overaimed snowballs flew over the buses. Dark, hollering figures tumbled hatless out of entryways and sprinted shoeless in the snow, while far across the circle, out past the athletic fields, somewhere in the woods beyond, a hoarse voice shouted out: "They're here! McVee, man! They're here! Seriously! The pump buses are *here!*"

It had been a long time since I had been back to a boys' school. Only now, if I wasn't officially a girl, then I wasn't exactly a schoolboy anymore either. Male, yes, but only in the wispiest sense. For as Poopsy and Wenty Bird and I filed out of the bus, cutting mouth farts, rabbit punching each other's kidneys, and distributing wedgies among the newer Little boys, we no longer sounded even remotely like the real thing: When

Wentworth and I wedgied Jeremy Harkness—hoisting the fresh-man by the waistband of his briefs—Poopsy begged us to put Jeremy down, and we obeyed as Poopsy chanted, "Careful, you guys, careful: he might get ruptured!"

Our bus had arrived at an important-looking portico where we were released into the jurisdiction of a curt, courteous master. Bespectacled, with alert brown eyes and a rubicund nose, the supervising master stood alongside the balustrade wearing a six-foot crimson and black scarf over a tweedy coat and brick-red corduroys. He smiled pleasantly as we milled around stamping our boots. Then, jerked like a puppet, he toddled over to the parked buses.

The Mansfields and their retinue had lit up cigarettes the minute they'd set foot on campus. They smoked openly but discreetly, their quick, confident exhalations emerging from behind the buses. When the supervising master rounded the rear of the first bus, Berry stepped up to greet him:

"Mr. Apthorp, nice to see you!"

Pleased to be recognized, Apthorp beamed.

"Gosh! Hi! Look at you! Gosh!" Berry continued, ditching her cigarette as she stepped forward, buzzing, smiling, gush-ing, goshing.

Apthorp, for his part, could not seem to stop from beam-ing. He beamed from his balding crown to his bobbing Adam's apple. He beamed from one lobster-red ear to the other. He beamed so brightly he seemed to be saying something.

"I like your muffler," remarked Berry, taking between her fingers one end of the supervising master's Harvard College "six-footer."

"*Très* spiffy," Emma put in from the sidelines. "Dad's got one just like it."

"We heard Boy-Boy's in the infirmary," Berry took up offhandedly. Then, still wielding Apthorp's scarf, she leaned in and smiled, one grown-up to another: "Of course we all know he's faking."

As long as Berry kept hold of the man's scarf, he seemed not to know what to do with his hands. Apthorp jammed them into his trousers, gave his pocket change a vigorous stir, and dryly agreed that John Blackwell was quite the actor.

"We just wanted to visit him for a sec'," said Berry, giving the scarf a barely perceptible tug.

"Running bed-check, eh?" said Apthorp.

Emma now materialized at the other end of the master's scarf: "Yah," Emma offered in her hushed, bedside voice, "we'd be right back."

The pocket change stirred.

"Yah," agreed Berry, angel of mercy.

The pocket change jingled.

"Yah," chimed Emma, and then, all at once, as Apthorp himself responded with an antiphonal "Yah," something seemed to explode in the man's pants pocket.

Silver and copper coins suddenly cascaded from the bottom of Apthorp's trouser leg, spurting, rolling, wobbling across the icy ground. From nowhere, underclassmen appeared, urchins crabbing along on all fours, returning each coin with a croaky-voiced, "Here, sir." Apthorp flushed the color of freshly steeped tea.

Without another word, he waved the Mansfields on to the infirmary.

The rest of us were supposed to follow the senior prefect into the academy building, and as the serious, well-mannered boy held the door for us—"boys and all"—I turned away in embarrassment and glimpsed Berry out in the circle, skipping across the duckboards. I had never seen her look so completely at home, never heard her sound so much the oldest child. Apthorp was calling after her, "Ah-a-a, Estabrook seniors only!

Around the circle, please," and Berry soothed him—she cooled the tea-colored man—with but a toss of honey-thick hair, a peal of creamy laughter, a throaty "*Mais oui,* Mr. A!" as she continued directly across the privileged path.

Inside the academy building, everything looked jaundiced, every crack sealed tight by decades of yellow varnish. Up and down the darkened corridors, padlocked lockers stood in somber ranks divided by windowless bays of wainscoting, with here and there, in dimly lighted trophy cases, the ancient shine of silver. The smell of hot cast iron, stifling and melancholy, lingered in the air. Every particle of oxygen seemed to have been sucked out of this unventilated place.

Only beneath our boots did life seem still to pulse. Strange spasms of sound rose from deep within the building's core, spreading out along the black seams of floorboards. Escorted by the prefect, we trooped down to the basement and into a long, slender corridor, which was damp and cold and smelled of fish sticks. At the far end stood a double set of doors, which were closed and guarded by the members of the Mixer Committee. More than eighty-odd boys had been quarantined in this chute—waiting for girls to arrive, for the doors to open, for the band to start, for something to happen. But for a long time we all just stood there in the damp, fish-sticky passage, without anyone's saying much of anything. I kept looking around for Berry and Emma and the others. But nobody came, and nothing happened, and the double doors remained closed, and for a while the sole diversion was a humorless French teacher who spoke only at the top of his voice, only in terms of expulsion, and only to a poorly postured, muddy boy who was always, always, called McVee, even when he wasn't.

Finally, the closed doors throbbed with the vibrations of a huge amplifier. An introductory phrase leaked out: seven bold, clear, electrified notes, repeated once, then again, swelling in volume.

Zapped into action by the music, everyone pushed ahead. The important doorway remained shut. Puzzled, protesting voices called up and down the airless corridor. Then came a lull, then a burst of drumming, a splash of cymbals. And then, with an ominous scurrying underfoot, as though a stampede of cattle were flinging itself against an electrified fence, the herd pressed dumbly forward. The double doors gave way, bursting open, and the air filled with howls and screams as a dazzling electronic explosion rocked the building, crashing out into the corridor, sucking everyone forward into a fire storm of sound.

The band, it turned out, had launched into "Layla." The mixer had begun.

By the time the Mansfields showed up, the electricity had failed twice, the band had taken four breaks, and at least seven boys named McVee had been expelled from school. When the girls stamped in, caked with snow, carrying the night air on their clothes, they never hesitated. Motown records had replaced the band, and the Mansfields flooded the floor, each of them stretching and practicing parodic warm-up moves while Berry formed the line, ordering Emma to go here, Lili there, Hattie there, Gussie next, then Tizzy and Hilary and whomever else dared fall in.

Their boyless dance was the Nine Step. At the ravenous sound of Martha and the Vandellas singing "Jimmy Mack," all seven girls swung their right legs forward, pointing their toes like man-hungry vamps. In steps Two and Three, the right legs passed and repassed, with a smooth, easy crossing of ankles on Four and Five, all these leggy preliminaries merely a tease for the main event: the heavenly pelvic undulations of Seven, Eight, and Nine.

195

But that night something happened during one of the nine-fold sequences—some signal, some exchange of nods between the Mansfields and a group of boys who showed their faces in the important doorway. To a man, they were tall and shaggy and pretty, and from the rapturous depths of the ninth step, Berry jerked her head toward the door.

All at once, the line of nine-steppers broke up, and into Lili Hooper's wonderful, wide stable seat came a walking wiggle I had never seen on any of those girls outside my own daydreams. Hannah Gustin, leaving the floor, curled her shoulders forward, producing, intentionally or not, a larger, even more ostentatious bust. Hattie charmingly bobbled her head, tousling her hair like a mopheaded Beatles fan. And Emma was suddenly all hips—rolling, undulating, roomy hips. She also tossed off little gestures of indecision and debate—those judicious hingings and unhingings of her wrists—but mainly it was the consenting hips and their unnatural rubberiness, almost as though there was something out of whack somewhere: either in her pelvis or my brain.

Near midnight, when only five Little girls remained at large, Dean Brickley promised the bus driver that we would wait exactly one more minute. The driver started the engine, turned on the headlights, and somewhat parsimoniously allowed a trickle of heat to circulate through the frozen vehicle. The dean, straddling the aisle, turned once more to eyeball her girls—those of us, at any rate, who had returned promptly to the bus and taken our seats so that our friend the driver could drive us home.

"Aldridge," the dean began for the second time.

"Here," came the tired, reproachful reply.

"Bancroft . . ."

No answer.

"Cardew?"

But before the roll could continue, Abby Aldridge called out: "There they are, Miss Brickley!"

The moon had risen high into the dome over the Estabrook circle, and in the sharp, flinty light, we could see a column of figures cutting straight across the forbidden rotunda—not so much five truant Little girls as ten deeply entwined people, arrayed in pairs.

Lili Hooper came first, draped loosely around Buddy Hayes, who was buffalo-shouldered and gypsylike, with a sly, charming smile and a gold stud in one ear and a red bandanna tied around his head. Next followed roguish, red-haired Billy Kirby, who had Gussie's head in a playful wrestling hold under his arm. And then long-eared Bobby Reilly, sockless in his loafers, holding hands with Hattie, their fingers stiff with cold.

Off to the side, rugged, powerful Boy-Boy Blackwell strode along like a lumberjack coming out of the big woods. He carried Berry Mansfield in his huge, valorous arms, and though his smile—illuminated by bright-white, perfectly formed teeth— looked a little loony, John Blackwell showed positively no signs of ill health; and Berry certainly wasn't faking.

Bringing up the rear, Emma seemed to be adorning Billy Sheets. Her arms muffled Billy's bare throat, her thighs and legs warmed Billy's belly, her wrists bounced against Billy's broad chest like the limbs of an extra sweater. Billy seemed hardly to know a girl was back there. But then, with or without clothes, Billy Sheets was beautiful, unbelievably beautiful, and I had the feeling that he daily brushed his teeth with all sorts of wonderful girls hanging all over him. Nonchalant, chatting with Blackwell, Sheets approached the bus at a princely stroll, his long, silky Jack-of-Hearts hair curling up on Emma's arms.

On the roadway, the truants sidled into the beams of the headlights. Then they turned, presenting themselves to us in company: Shiny-eyed, red-lipped, panting a little, they looked like the curtain call of a musical comedy. Thwarted by love's mix-ups and mistaken identities, they'd been joined at last in blissful, tidy pairings, and I had to admit, it would have been easy to applaud them. Never in my life had I seen ten prettier people.

Dean Brickley charged. But before she broke it up, I got one parting glimpse of Berry and Blackwell lingering with lowered eyelids over their good-nights: I could see Boy-Boy's hands inside Berry's coat, and I had a clear view of Berry's fingers creeping into Boy-Boy's loose, thick mane, her cheeks dimpling with delight over her newfound mastery of a young man's scalp and its wide-flung network of blood vessels and nerve endings.

I snorted out a laugh, and a second later, with the veins in my own scalp pulsing wildly, I hung my head. For as I followed Blackwell's hands, cupping and working inside Berry's coat, I suddenly felt, inside my gloves, so palpable I was on the point of tears, the size of her, the soft and fleshy way she would feel.

"Does none of you have a wristwatch?" Brickley puffed into the frozen air. "Have you all lost your minds?"

No one said a word. The boys appeared unable to unclench their jaws, or, if prepared to do so, uncertain about whether, and in what order, nouns, verbs, and prepositions should emerge. Billy Sheets, who had burped several times, was now holding Emma close, gently rocking her back and forth. His bright blue eyes and lovely mouth and bruisable Pre-Raphaelite skin glowed so splendidly in the bus headlights I thought I might be sick.

When finally the truants filed onto the bus—unpunished—I saw Berry heading for the empty seat in front of mine. Back she came, stooping to pantomime a half-dozen farewell kisses to her boyfriend. Long-faced, I turned away and looked out my window. For a second, I thought I must be hyperventilating: the cold glass misted over solidly. Then I shut my mouth and saw that *heat*, not breath, had clouded the window—body heat, heavy and crude, flowing off my forehead in such continuous, dense waves I had to keep wiping the glass with my gloves so that when the bus pulled away and Berry came to sit, I could pretend to be looking out.

Most of the dormitory lights were off now, and a wing of cloud had darkened the grounds. The tall pitch pines, black as bears, reached out, pawing at the bus windows as we rattled back down the drive. Behind us, a chapel bell tolled its cheerless midnight message, and from somewhere back in the whitened woods came the call: *"Pump? . . . Anyone want to pump?"*

"So, hi," said Berry, sitting down in front of me, tossing her hair to weed her earrings. "Did you guys have fun?"

3. Green Dreams

When the new semester began, I saw the Mansfields and their Estabrook boyfriends everywhere: foraging for food at Friendly's; traversing the monotonous gray wastes of Louisa Little's lower fields; trekking to the frozen river like some shaggy, nomadic Ice Age clan. The girls wore bulky sweaters adorned with images of reindeer and caribou; the boys were layered loosely in buckskin. They halted constantly, I noticed, to huddle for warmth.

Lovesick, failing math and science, I took refuge in the public library—a handsome brick building at the fork of Main

Street and Sudbury Road. The library shielded me from school, from girls, and eventually, from the winter of '72 itself. For there, on leaden afternoons, armored in an ambience of metal floors and basement pipes, I began reading F. Scott Fitzgerald.

At first I hardly noticed what was happening to me. I had read *The Great Gatsby* at Ruxton; but Jay Gatsby, in the hands of plodding Mr. DePinna, had seemed unapproachable, adult. Now, among the green cloth volumes shelved from Dewey Decimal Number 3740.356 to .369, I discovered stories about boys—precocious boys who had sprung full-blown from the brows of remarkable mothers and retiring fathers; "fresh" boys who had come East to school with dreams of glory, only to ace English and history while failing math and science. Washouts at football, they became their own heroes. Immodest, worldly, clearly marked for larger glories, Fitzgerald boys were never quite tall enough, never quite rich enough to win the most popular, most desirable girl. They led amorous but comfortingly sexless lives.

I seemed already to know Dexter Green and Basil Lee and *All the Sad Young Men*. Giddy with recognition, I gulped down *Tales of the Jazz Age*, lapped up *Flappers and Philosophers*. When I came upon the green cloth spine and gilt Roman lettering on *This Side of Paradise*, a jolt ran through me. My head tingled. I opened the book very carefully, slowly drinking in the eponymous Rupert Brooke epigraph. By the time I turned with trembling hands to Chapter One—"Amory, Son of Beatrice"— I was smashed.

For a week I closed down the library every night. Pie-eyed and reeling, I staggered back to my room and flopped into bed. Morning after morning I slept through the rising bell. I scarcely noticed my roommates, my clothes. Everything around me grew daily more abstract, superfluous. People seemed an imposition; food: irrelevant; sunlight: harsh. Classes loomed as empty spaces, yawning gaps, chores to be endured until I could get back into the library and down into the green books, the green world, the green dream.

Day after day, like a diver descending into the iridescent underwater world of a reef, I sank back into the stacks. Things I had always thought dull now shimmered brilliantly. Down there, everything shone, everything seemed to matter. Pierce-Arrow motor cars mattered. Stutz Bearcats and Blatz Wildcats. Biltmore tea dances and Hot Springs golf links. Midnight breakfasts, moonlit verandas. Belmont collars. French cuffs. Pleats. Dates.

Dates *mattered:* 1896, 1917, 1925, 1929. Places mattered, and their proper names: Black Bear Lake. Tuxedo Park. The Yale Club. The Plaza Red Room. The Ritz Bar. The Sherry Island Golf Club—fiction and fact merging so completely that even Fitzgerald's boys' schools—those lustrous academies of the East: St. Midas's, St. Regis's—glittered in my eyes like all the satrapies of Arabia.

My roommates thought me ridiculous. They were slow to catch on, for at first, embarrassed, I was secretive about the habit. Yet as my tolerance increased, so did the supply of Scribner's paperbacks I kept in the room, bookmarked for pick-me-ups: *The Basil and Josephine Stories* for nightcaps, *Taps at Reveille* for eye-openers.

From the bunk above mine, Poopsy Winslow viewed the books with the cucumber-cold stare of a Puritan deacon. Wentworth started calling me "Amory," then continued with "Fitz," then "Ritz," then "Cracker," then "Crackpot"—a passage of notes whose factual echoes, however unintentional on Wenty Bird's part, sounded one more rendition of taps, one more dirge linking me to the destiny of my hero.

One night when I sneaked back from the library after hours, Danny was staying up late, finishing a paper. I got ready for bed. I pulled on a bathrobe and slippers, and when I came back from the bathroom, I said, "Time to retire—don't you think, old sport?"

Danny uncoiled slowly. "What?" he said. "What did you just say?"

The others roused themselves and turned to look. Poopsy snapped on a light. I stood in the middle of the room, blinking at them through bloodshot eyes, a fourteen-year-old boy in a Brooks Brothers bathrobe.

"You're losing it, man," said Danny.

"Danny's right," said Poopsy. "You've changed: You've stopped listening to records, you don't wear blue jeans, you don't like James Taylor—"

"You're acting like somebody *old*," said Danny.

"It's about the slippers . . ." took up Wentworth.

"You're getting way too carried away with this Gatsby shit," said Danny.

"A Republican," said Poopsy. "That's what you're acting like: a Republican."

"You're trashing your life," said Danny, "your real life—with your friends. You're turning into a snob. You're committing suicide! You're *wearing a bathrobe*, man!"

Bullying, Danny forced me that night to read a hundred pages of Thomas Pynchon. And I read them—every single dull, punishing page—just to prove that I still had an open mind. But of course I didn't—how could I? How could a concrete place called "Lot 49" shine brighter than *Paradise*? What could outsparkle a "Diamond as Big as the Ritz"—*Gravity's Rainbow*?

Next day, to retaliate, I went on a bender. I didn't need bookmarks anymore; I reread *Gatsby* in one sitting. I skipped lunch and dinner, and for the rest of that week, I returned to the stacks every afternoon, euphoric if I could find some new phial of Fitzgerald, melancholy and bereft if I could not. I discovered that the longer I stayed immersed, the better I could see the "lazy" beauty of Amory Blaine's Princeton, the clearer I could hear the "sad" horns and "wailing" saxophones of Jay Gatsby's Jazz Age, the quicker I could get back into the dream.

"We think you should stop," Danny announced that Friday. My roommates and my brother had all gathered in the window seat of our room to explain that my behavior had grown bizarre, intolerable.

Danny delivered their ultimatum: "Stop reading F. Scott Fitzgerald, or move out of the room."

Poopsy mentioned Dr. Ditsky's name, supplying the school shrink's office hours on a sheet of notebook paper.

"Just cool it," my brother advised, looking faintly ashamed of me, "just cool it with the books."

Naturally I didn't tell any of them, but the books were drying up. Before my astonished eyes, the number of green volumes had dwindled almost to zero. *The Beautiful and Damned* had disappeared in three or four stiff rounds; I had polished off *Tender Is the Night* in one lost weekend. There were some letters, I knew, and some essays, and a comedy. But I had no need of letters or essays; I had no appetite for a "vegetable." I had to have the nectar of the gods, the real Fitzgerald, pure as moonshine.

The weekend of the Estabrook-Groton hockey game, I had my first blackout. I remember going to dinner Saturday night, alone. The buffeteria looked dull, lifeless, with sweaty vapor rising off creamed chipped beef and boiled spuds.

The hands of the broken wall-clock stood still, pointing forever and ever to ten past ten. My roommates had gone to the movies. My brother, the Lively Arts Center projectionist, would lock the door to the projection booth and make love to Annie Johnston between reel changes.

The Mansfields had flocked to the Estabrook rink to root for Boy-Boy Blackwell, Billy Sheets, and the rest of the burly boyfriends.

For dessert, Mrs. Cleveland Swimm had poured some viscous cherry goo onto dry yellow cake.

I skipped dinner and drifted up Main Street to the library. Before dropping down to my usual haunt, I treated myself to a little browsing in the stacks. Then, stepping up to the welcome wagon, I reached for Old Fitzgerald.

My shelf tilted, the stacks spun, my brow lathered. The books were gone. The green books had somehow been checked out. I pawed along the shelf, pushing volumes aside, lifting others to make sure none had fallen behind. This had never happened before. First I suspected vandals, then scholars. Then I decided it must have been my roommates—playing a practical joke. But why would they have left any of the titles behind? For here on the shelf (I as much as swooned to discover) remained two collections of the novelist's essays and the Modern Library edition of *The Great Gatsby*.

I snatched *Gatsby* and feverishly began reading over my favorite passages, almost as if I would now find something new there—a message, a sign—something concealed by the author expressly for me. But once again, the eyes of Dr. T. J. Eckleberg looked out unseeing over the Valley of Ashes. The green light still blinked at the end of Daisy's dock. Gatsby's guests showed up from East Egg one more time—those strange predatory creatures named Leech and Fishguard and Hammerhead. And the saxophones wailed, and the Leeches leeched, and Gatsby's boarder, Klipspringer, agile as an antelope, bounced through "Ain't We Got Fun?" while scary Meyer Wolfsheim, with his "human-molar" cuff links, brazenly went on looking for his "gonnegtion" . . . And the green light on Daisy's dock blinked on and off, on and off. . . .

I woke up drenched, suffocating, the weight of fathoms on my chest. Instantly alert, I knew only that the hour was late, the library closed, the stacks deserted.

The rows of shelves pulsated with a clear, almost a fragile, beauty. I felt calm, peaceful. I had been asleep, now I was awake. Everything was simple, all was pure. But what was this? Some strange thing in my hands: a book. A book? Why was I holding a *book*?

That night, the library security guard unlocked the staff door for me, and I slunk back to Brewster wondering whether I ought to be scared, whether I ought to stop. Though shaken, I didn't think I *could* stop. Anyhow, *why* stop? For Armbrister and those guys? I liked books. I liked to read. Since when was it a crime to read books? Besides, who was I without those books?

I was . . . *Amory, Son of Beatrice*. . . .

By the middle of February, I had switched rooms with my brother, opting for his single rather than give up Fitzgerald. Even so, all that now remained for me on the library shelf was *The Last Tycoon*—and it wasn't even finished. My hero, sunk in Hollywood, writing with his last breaths, had failed to complete the last novel. And if the master himself had run out of air, then what, I wondered, would become of a greenhorn like me?

I had to go beyond the books. I had to take the next step. When I reshelved the last of the green volumes, I realized I wouldn't need them anymore. There was now but one thing on my mind.

I needed long trousers. Whatever else I would require to turn boy-errant—straw headgear, bow ties, raccoon coat—I had to have my first long trousers. Never mind that since the third grade I had never worn anything *but* long trousers to

205

school; I had to have the sort of thing in which all the sad young men had come East: long white flannels, cuffed and pleated, creamy and swank. And never mind that I was already East, already *in* school; in long white flannels I could sally forth like Amory, I could saunter like Basil, I could reinvent myself, as Gatsby had—as simple as that.

But the early years of my own dreary denim decade would have challenged even the Freshest Boy. In the bell-bottomed winter of 1972, not one haberdashery in the Commonwealth of Massachusetts carried what I wanted (and they weren't called haberdasheries anymore, either). To my agitated disgust, even the redoubtable Brooks Brothers no longer stocked the genuine article, and at each of the pleatless gray flannels and "permanent-crease" khakis and sailcloth "slacks" brought forth by polite, quizzical clerks, I heard myself scoff (or did I only dream it?): "Good God, man, I said *pleats*! And hang the cost!"

"We're sorry, sir," came the infuriating, indifferent refrain, "we haven't seen anything like that in twenty years."

"It's a shame your grandfather gave away all *his* flannels," my mother offhandedly remarked after one of my trouser hunts.

"He—what?"

"When they sold the farm, your grandfather simply gave away all his old clothes. He had," she recalled, "a smashing pair of white ducks."

"He—gave them away?"

"Sam, I hardly think they would have fit."

"To *who*?"

I scoured every Goodwill in the Greater Boston Area. I tried the Salvation Army and Keezer's. Then one day, while rifling a pile of outdated stretch ski pants in the ladies' thrift shop in Concord, I found them: not my grandfather's long-lost flannels but a pair of hospital orderly's pants—white as a daisy.

On the spot I shucked my blue jeans, and there in the thrift shop aisle, trembling a little, I stepped into the white cotton pants. These were long trousers, all right: thirty-six-inch inseam and waist. Six sizes too big, but with all that extra material gathered at the waist, I had pleats at last.

"In your size," the saleslady began, "you might try—" But I never let her finish. I notched my belt three holes tighter—as tight as it would go—and stepped up to the nearest mirror.

The figure I faced charged me with readiness. I scarcely noticed the mildewed seams, the split in the seat, the five missing buttons from the five-button fly. I didn't stop to fuss over the dried bloodstains that had several times encrimsoned the hospital orderly's knees. Nor did I check to see why the folds of material bunched under my belt had already begun to chafe against my skin.

Hang the folds! Enfranchised with pleats, I approved the purchase at once, and, without further alterations, sallied forth.

On Main Street, outside Harvard Trust, I crossed paths with Hattie.

"Mas Nomis," she called, "where've you been all my life?"

"Hello, old girl."

"You look a little haggard—" Her eyes widened, taking in my new long trousers. "I *love* your pants. Hey, what are you doing?"

"Sallying forth."

"I *thought* you were sallying forth."

"Say, Hat—have a bite with me."

I must have known that Hattie would not desert me when we sat down at the counter in Brigham's and I ordered a "double chocolate jigger."

"A what?" said the high school boy who ran the counter.

"Double chocolate jigger."

"Is that ice cream?" he said.

207

"I'll say so!"

I must have known that Hattie could be trusted not to join the laughter when, deadly earnest, I instructed the counterman how to serve a double jigger: "See here, man—two ponies of chocolate sauce and a dash of whipped cream!"

But how did she keep a straight face when the store manager came over to see what the fuss was all about, and I grandly urged him to "go on—tell the lad to stick a meringue in it"?

Hattie giggled, it was true, but only when I egged on the bewildered counterman ("That's the ticket!") and when later I roared at the manager ("What the devil's happened to our man?") and again when it came time to "pony up" and Hattie, having just bounced a check, turned out to be "short," and I, in my new long trousers, had "airy pockets" myself. To Hattie, it was "the cat's pajamas." She joined me in "taking a powder."

Outside, on the sidewalk, Hattie abandoned herself, lighting up an Old Gold and tying her scarf through her hair. Boyish as a flapper, she dropped curtsies to men and bowed satirically to women. She charmed everyone on Main Street—me most of all. I, who wanted only for a romantic, zany girl (my madcap mate, my Zelda!) fell under Hattie's spell as never before. I could suddenly see our flaming youth, our early success, our wild parties, our sudden collapse, our slide into dissipation, our tragic early deaths—I could see it all, right there on Main Street, outside Sally Ann's Food Shop.

In a burst of exuberance, I vowed to burn myself out by study hall. And when Hattie danced ahead, turning a pirouette, I remember thinking to myself that this was it. This time I'd really found it: the girl on whom I could realistically throw my life away.

The treetops along Nashawtuc Hill were now hanging onto sunset until almost six. That evening, as I sauntered to supper, the lingering lavender light gave goose-down parkas the patina of coonskin coats. Inside the dining hall, silver chafing dishes glistened with "creamed oysters" and "julienne potatoes." For dessert, Mrs. Cleveland Swimm and her white-jacketed staff had served up "cherries jubilee."

Too excited to eat, I sauntered into the dining room and looked around for someone to sit with. Hattie had not yet come to dinner, and though faces everywhere sparkled I didn't seem to know anyone. At the back of the room, my debonair ex-roommates sat sipping milk highballs under the clock.

"What the hell is he doing?" said Armbrister.

"Are you operating tonight, old sport?" Winslow called to me, breaking into a smirk.

"Can't say that I—"

"Hospital pants," said Danny, enunciating. "Why in hell are you wearing *hospital pants?*"

"They happen," I told him, "to be white ducks."

"Hey, Crackup," said Wentworth. "Doesn't a straitjacket come with that outfit?"

Pretending to check the time, I turned away brusquely. The dining room clock was still broken, only now the hands, instead of pointing fixedly to ten past ten, showed no time at all. The hands were missing. I stood staring at the amputated clockface, not quite knowing what it meant. In truth, I was feeling a little dizzy. All around me people continued to talk and joke and laugh and eat, none of them the slightest bit concerned about the time. Everyone seemed to know something I didn't know, and it scared me. I turned to leave.

Across the room, Hattie and the Mansfields had just settled down with their boyfriends, clannishly crowding into one small table with their heaping trays of food. I had not taken more than two steps toward the door when an Estabrook boy, sitting between Hattie and Berry, broke off a loud belch and shouted out:

"Yo, F. Scott!"

He was snide and gummy, with an earring in one ear and a scruff of beard on his chin, and he seemed exhilarated, in his smirking way, about calling me by my hero's name. I had never seen the boy before and could easily have kept right on walking. But something told me to stop; something told me that Amory Blaine would have tested his mettle by facing the cad.

The tables around me hushed. With elbows squared and cutlery poised, people seemed eager for my riposte. But I couldn't think of what Amory would say. I didn't know my lines. Blood rushed to my face. I plucked helplessly at the pleats of my long trousers.

A volley of Estabrook voices now came broadside across the room: "Fitz! . . . Hey, Scotty! . . . Hey, F.! . . ." I could hear Hattie shushing the boys, and Berry defending them, insisting, "They're just joking!"

Paralyzed, I looked out over the tables and just then caught sight of my brother. He had come into the dining room only moments ago, and he didn't know what was happening. He was carrying his tray, looking for somewhere to sit. He saw his brother standing in the middle of the school, wearing a pair of bloodstained, clown-size hospital pants. He heard jests and catcalls—"Fitzy! . . . Ritzy! . . . Yo, Mr. Ritz!"—and for one brave second, he tried to smile, to go along, for my sake, with the joke he thought he had missed.

I burst into tears—and fled.

"Sam?" I heard my brother calling after me. "Sam, what happened? Are you all right?"

Dusk had fallen. I skipped study hall and made straight for the dorm. I was too upset to saunter; I walked, the frigid air drying my cheeks. For the first time since donning long trousers, I felt the sting of February through the thin cotton weave.

My single room stood silent. Drafts whistled at the fire

escape door. I undressed, got into bed, turned out the light, and lay there in the dark. But that seemed like a creepy thing to do, and I sat up. I turned on the light. I got out of bed and got dressed and peered into my apple crate of record albums. I still didn't want to listen to James Taylor.

I thought I might take a shower. But it was too cold to get wet, and also I didn't want to hear the spooky sound that one solitary shower makes in a dormitory at night. So, fully dressed, I got back in bed, and my eye fell on the Scribner's paperbacks proudly arranged on my bedside table.

Now I realized I had to face something I had known for about an hour: I was afraid of those books—scared to read them. Yet the idea of *not* reading them seemed terrifying. More than anything, I was nervous just being in the same room with the books, and for a while I lay there with closed eyes, unable to move, petrified by the thought that I had been possessed, or transmigrated, or transformed by my own egoism into the post-mortem receptacle of Scott Fitzgerald's unfinished soul.

When I opened my eyes, my body was still my own and Scott Fitzgerald's books were still in my room. I started up, thinking I would just put them out in the hall, or down in the common room, until it occurred to me that I wouldn't be fooling anyone. The whole dorm—hell, the whole *school*—knew about me and Scott Fitzgerald. Short of burning them, I couldn't very well just rid myself of the books. Besides, they were my books. And I liked books; I liked to read.

With a tremor in my hand, I reached for *Babylon Revisited*. I opened the book deliberately, daring anyone, friend or foe, flesh or spirit, to object. I had just begun to read, for perhaps the tenth time, the story of poor-boy Dexter Green's "Winter Dreams," when I felt the sensation of being watched. My skin tightened. The hair on the back of my neck stood up. My nose prickled, my eyes watered. A light-haired figure with a round pale face was standing outside on the fire escape.

He wore a tweed jacket and a pair of old-fashioned wire-rimmed spectacles, and at first I almost got up to greet him. Without a sound, he advanced, flattening his unearthly, bespectacled eyes up against the pane of glass in the fire escape door. Sickened, I turned away, remaining as calm as I could as long as I could, and then I did what I had to do. I looked the figure straight in the eye. I was shocked to see, behind the wire rims and tweed lapels, Poopsy Winslow.

Poopsy Winslow was standing out on the fire escape wearing Gillespie's reading glasses and Crocker's best tweed coat. I called to him; he wouldn't reply. What was spookier, he wouldn't move a muscle or change his wide, unblinking, all-seeing expression. He just kept staring at me from behind Gillespie's glasses, godlike, indifferent.

Now I really got scared. A shaky, faltering rendition of "Ain't We Got Fun?" filtered upstairs from the common room. Next, the hallway door creaked open, and when a dark silhouette appeared in my doorway, I lay rigid, feigning sleep. Sergei LaFarge, cloaked in his black opera cape and reeling from the push someone had just given him, staggered into my room. To my almost ecstatic relief, Sergei strutted around my bed for the next ten seconds, unaccountably mumbling, "Telephone for Mr. Gatsby, telephone for Mr. Gatsby." When I caught on that this was supposed to lure me out to the hallway pay phone, I felt very nearly rescued. I told Sergei to get lost, and Sergei, relieved, got lost.

Feeling much better, I rolled back into bed and snapped off the light. Though not exactly comfy (Poopsy's eerie impersonation of the eyes of Dr. T. J. Eckleberg continued out on the fire escape), I did fall into the beginnings of a turbulent sleep. In the background, out in the hallway, I was vaguely aware of "roaring" noises and snatches of "lyrical" narration. After about an hour, during which I slept through the better part of a sound-effects record that over and over popped a champagne cork, I suddenly lurched up to find a green spotlight flashing on and off at the foot of my bed.

My brother, I guessed right away; my brother had jerry-rigged the thing to my bed. I didn't know how to turn it off, and I let the light blink for a while, thinking I could ignore it and fall back asleep. Gradually, though, the greenness began to alarm me. There was something sinister in the repetitive, word-less blinking, and it quickened my breathing.

I broke out into a cold sweat. I felt feverish, fidgety. I tore off my clothes and threw them at the blinking light. My heart jumped and pounded, and as I lay there in the dark, listening to its repetitive, muscular thumping, I allowed the unreasonable, sinister feeling to expand in the stillness of the single room and the greenness of the light.

In seconds, my heartbeat and the blinking fresnel were throbbing at precisely the same suffocating rate. My eardrums also took up the beat, and even after I had thrust out my leg and kicked the tormenting green light crashing to the floor— and heard someone's terrified laughter out in the hallway—still I felt its thumping pulse.

My head and eyes now danced with weird, lurid names and glittering things, diabolic schemes and wild, infernal places. I could not stop from hearing inside my skull the words, "gonnegtion" and "Oggsford." I couldn't seem to shut out the crazily wailing saxophones, or to turn away the viperine East Egg party guests—the Leeches, the Fishguards, the Hammer-heads—but now also the Smirkes, the Chromes, S. W. Belcher, and fishy-sounding Beluga, and Beluga's egg-filled girls, as well as the Catlips and the Bembergs, and of course Klipspringer,

Gatsby's boarder, whom even Gatsby himself had been unable to get rid of.

All these phantoms were in my bed that night. Not quite asleep, I tossed and rolled for hours, fighting off Gibson Girls and heiresses and cloche-hatted flappers who chirped "By the sea! By the sea! By the beautiful sea!" At one point, the Mansfields and their Estabrook boyfriends, speeding along in a Pierce-Arrow, swerved to avoid a drunk in the road and instead ran over a man who kept saying he "just wanted to ask them for the time of day," and who, I realized, when I saw the bloodstains at his knees, was me, and that *this was the message I'd been looking for in the book*. . . . But when I jumped for safety into the white-marble fountain outside the Plaza, the fountain was dry, and the green statuesque lady who stood there couldn't save me, and I plunged headfirst into nothingness, awakening with a scream, dragging myself, suffocating, out of bed.

At the fire escape door, I stood on quaking legs. I could hear the regular ticking of a clock in another room, and upstairs the soughing sound of "Sleep-O," Purvis's sleep-sound generator. Outside, there was no moon. The wind beat against the windowpane and the heat from my brow frosted the glass. My teeth chattered, my body shook. I was fourteen years old. I had cried in front of the whole school. I was thirsty.

The next morning, in weak sunlight, I took my vow. Before my roommates and my brother, I swore I would never read another word of F. Scott Fitzgerald. I threw the bloodstained hospital orderly's pants into the common room fireplace, and Danny burned them. Wenty Bird proposed an inquisitional burning of my bedside books—the Scribner's paperbacks—but Poopsy was satisfied simply to confiscate them. Danny produced two pink weekend permission slips, and a pair of tickets to the James Taylor concert at the Orpheum in Boston. Then, each in turn, my roommates and my brother came forward, embraced me, welcomed me back to the room, the world.

That afternoon, I slept—a deep, drugged, dreamless sleep—and when I awoke, I remember that it was dusk, just dusk, colorless and gray.

4. First Thaw

We had clear black ice into the beginning of March. Afternoons, Danny and I skated the flooded frozen meadow across the river. The Mansfield clan was often out there, skating in a pack, the boys with hockey sticks, the girls gliding smoothly across the creaking ice. Berry sometimes blew me kisses as she wiggled by, quick as a fish, and Emma would occasionally skate over and plop down next to me on the ice. Taking our gloves off—feeling the delicious cold air between our sweaty, leather-smelling fingers—Emma and I would share a cigarette, now and then murmuring deep-felt but conventional things about art. We never spoke about romance, never alluded to the past.

Some afternoons I would just sit and watch Hattie as she rushed ahead of the others in reckless, passionate bursts. Hattie was mad for skating, for the measured, waltzing rhythms of the sport, but there always came a point when she lost patience, when she could stand no more of gracelessness. Chin tucked into scarlet muffler, mittened hands windmilling, ankles wobbling, she would suddenly slump down onto the ice, wherever she happened to have gotten, and there—invariably right in the middle of the boys' hockey game—she would have a ten-year-old's tantrum, complete with kicking feet and a runny nose. Then, pretending to be ashamed of herself, she would lie out all asprawl under the big forgiving sky.

Toward the end of the month, during the first major thaw, news came that Hattie's father had lung cancer. A tumor had been removed. Treatment would start. Mr. Bancroft, a Harvard-educated investment banker who in the early sixties had dropped out of Wall Street to become a society nightclub singer, might have six months to live.

For a couple of days, Hattie carried on as usual—doing her barn chores, going to classes, taking tea with the Wigglesworths. But then, almost constantly weepy, she left Hoare House and checked into the infirmary, where, to Ducky Wigglesworth's great outrage, Dr. Ditsky preferred to "keep an eye on her."

Within the week, all the Hoare common room regulars had come down with mysterious menstrual symptoms or "flu." Thanks to some high-powered Wigglesworth lobbying, they were allowed to join Hattie in the infirmary. Poopsy Winslow, who didn't think he had what it took to get a bed, settled on a dozen roses, sent them to Hattie, and said they were from all of us.

The thaw lasted through the week. Thick fogs blanketed the campus. Most of the bulky, dirt-encrusted snow mounds melted down to gray slush, which expanded from puddles to pools to ever-widening tarns that engulfed pathways and ran down Elm Street in splashy, gritty streams. On Sunday, at the height of the thaw—a nearly tropical day, with temperatures soaring into the sixties and water dripping from every stem, stalk, and leaf—I saw some daffodils and strawberries in the non-Sabbatarian section of Anderson's, and I bought a bunch and a basket and took them over to the infirmary.

The thaw had given the wintry corridors a placid, holiday atmosphere. Windows had been flung open to the balmy afternoon. In one of the rooms, a beam of sunlight must have been bearing down on some old, pink hot-water bottle, for the whole place exhaled a breath of summer—of rubber air-hoses and warmed-over swim floats and the cool, strong smell inside them.

Nurse Batcheller greeted me enthusiastically. She was so delighted to have a relatively unmuddy male visitor ("We've had pushy, weevily boys, all week, all hours") that she pointed the way to the girls' rooms as though urging me to join one of Louisa Little's Crane's Beach outings.

I crunched down the linoleum corridor, my footsteps echoing into the tranquil sick rooms. None of the stout doorways had doors. In the first room I passed, I could see Emma sleeping without a pillow: all bunched up in a tight, dry little ball, lips cracked and swollen, hand beside mouth, fingers curled like a thumb-sucking infant's. The next doorway framed a pair of dozing, golden-haired invalids, one of whom I recognized by the curve of her hips: Lili Hooper. When I came to Berry's doorway, I wasn't sorry to find her asleep under the covers; even uncontagious, Berry's body had the power to weaken any resistance I'd built up against it.

In Hattie's room the shades, translucent as peapods, were drawn against the equinoctial sun. The window sashes stood wide open, and the stiff green paper shades respired freely in the soft, sucking breeze. Sudden rays of light shot into the room, illuminating Hattie in all her stagy sickroom glory.

"Are you O.K.?" I said.

Hattie had shed some weight, and her hair had lost its gingery luster; it lay around her head in dull, dry, cracker-colored clumps. Her eyes were feverishly bright, set off by ever-widening rings of sleeplessness. Under the covers, the outline of her pelvis poked at the sheets like a rack of antlers.

"Largely, I'm constipated," she replied. "If I'm largely anything, that is."

I lifted my hand to her forehead. "You feel O.K."

"Do not. You lie, Nomis. I feel like a bunch of chicken parts spread around on butcher's paper. But it's sweet of you to lie on my account."

"What does Ditsky say you have?"

"He's a quack—Dr. Cox, too. Mainly, Nomis, I'm just sad. I wasn't at all surprised—when I first heard the news. Then I got despondent, which probably isn't even a valid emotion till I learn to spell it, and then I got numb, and now I'm in sackcloth and ashes, purifying my soul, you know?"

"What do you mean, you weren't at all surprised?"

"Daddy: Cancer. It's too perfect. And awful, of course. And yet: How typical of him. How exactly like the pathetic, blighted man he's decided to become."

"Your dad?"

"Oh, I know; I'm shocked at my own detachment. But I haven't seen my father since I was eleven, I don't understand the life he's chosen to lead, and I certainly don't understand how he can expect to—" Hattie was breathing hard through her nose, almost snorting. She fixed a stern eye on me: "Oh, Nomis, don't you see? How useless all this is without love! Don't you see?"

I saw that the veins at Hattie's throat were bulging.

"Without love?" she begged at the top of her voice—really shrieking it at me: *"Without love?"*

There was a stunned pause into which Hattie blurted: "Do you know what Bobby Reilly said to me on this subject?"

"I thought you'd decided you didn't really like Bobby Reilly."

"But then—*poof*—I did. That's the trouble with teen girls,

Nomis: one minute we're reserved and cautious, the next minute—Silly Putty."

"So what'd he say?"

"Bobby Reilly said he didn't care one way or the other whether he ever saw me dance 'Giselle,' but that he would do anything to do it with me?"

"So what's wrong with that?"

"But I misunderstood completely! I got cross, and I said, 'You can't! You can't *do* someone.' And he said, No, no, he didn't mean that—he wanted to do the *dance* with me, though he wouldn't mind also being boyfriend-and-girlfriend if I felt like it. And I said, 'It? Love? Love's an *it*? Without all the beauty and the bravery: the whole. . . .' And to think I really liked him. To think once more it all comes down to flesh, when I thought we had a unique rapport of souls.

"Anyhow," she concluded, suddenly pleased with a bowl of sunlight that had brimmed in the bedsheets. She dipped her fingertips, spilling the light. "Anyhow, thanks for my treats, Nomis—my strawb's, my daff's, my sad and beautiful roses. You guys are my heroes." She cocked her head to one side, then the other, hunting for Poopsy's roses. "Oh—look," she murmured, "they're unfurling.

"That's it!" Hattie cried, her eyebrows lifting. "That's the whole point, isn't it? That's what I'm doing here, isn't it, Nomis? I'm *unfurling*!"

On my way out, I stopped at the door to Berry's room. Hands behind my back, I pretended to peer interestedly at her nightstand, her chair, her bed, her covers. I couldn't bring myself to look directly at her while she slept.

I had not stood this close to Berry in five months. I listened for her breathing, and the sound of it rehabilitated my hopes: I knew it instantly—knew it as I knew the cracks of her voice, the step of her foot, the toss of her hair. More than anyone or anything I had ever known, with the possible exceptions of my mother and the Atlantic shoreline, Berry had that way of evoking herself, of simply *being* herself, so wholly, so authentically, that within seconds of reentering her systolic sounds, I was reacclimated, immersed, synchronized. I edged over to the bed.

Her hair had grown longer, thicker, more entangling than ever. Her lips remained full and rounded, saucy with defiance, and now, just barely, almost imperceptibly, they parted. Her breathing faltered. Her chin stiffened. Her eyelashes moistened, blinked once, then again, each time more competently, until her eyelids, like new wet wings, fluttered open.

"Sam," she said in a hoarse, chesty voice, and I bent down and kissed her—a hello kiss, but still: on the lips.

Her cheeks dimpled. Her eyes darted from one part of my face to another, as though scanning a smorgasbord of delights. Berry Mansfield was looking at me with a gaze I had never before seen in Berry Mansfield: The sea-blue eyes, at once affectionate and knowing and bright, favored me with a fixity of focus that seemed limitless, bottomless. She appeared to be thirsting for me.

"God, I'm glad you're here," she said huskily.

"You are?" I said.

In answer, a tender, confiding smile parted her lips. "Yah," she decided, as though just now remembering a decisive fragment from a fresh dream.

"Honestly?"

Her smile widened, spreading encouragement, and she looked all around—pleased and expectant—like a dreamer who, though awake, is still watching for the great white prow of a ship to come crashing through the bedroom wall.

Heart thumping, I leaned down to kiss her.

"You'll get my bug," she said, and checked me with a lifted hand.

"I want your bug."

"No you don't." She pushed against my chest. It felt as though we'd already been married and divorced and married again.

"I do. I want your bug."

"You do not," said Berry. "You dummy." And she lifted her head and gave me a loud, bugless "Mwaah" up the side of my ear. She subsided onto her pillow. Then, as though only just now coming to consciousness, she started over in a brisk, newsy voice:

"But wait. Did you hear about Emma?"

5. Emma's Eyebrow

Emma had shaved off one of her eyebrows.

At first, she wouldn't tell anyone why. A cold snap followed the thaw, and as the muddy ground froze back up, so did Emma. Dr. Ditsky, delighted to have a real case on his hands, begged Emma to "share" her pain, but Emma would only report that what she felt was sometimes in her colon, sometimes in her ovaries, sometimes in her "spleen." Sometimes, it was "just—the Cambodian situation" or "the slaughter of the whales," and sometimes it was simply "constipation." She languished in the infirmary, tantalizing Ditsky, through the first week of April. Hoare House rumored that Emma had stopped menstruating.

Emma's spring torments remained beyond the reach of

medical or psychiatric science, so she moved back to Hoare, a frail, joyless figure who looked as though she'd been through a car windshield. The absence of hair over one eye gave her a lopsided, maimed appearance, and though the reason for the shave was now rumored to have had something to do with art, Emma herself would only concede, in her stricken, anguished way, that it was "hard to explain."

Back in the house, Ducky Wigglesworth put Emma on a program of bed rest, bubble baths, and lemon verbena tea. I resumed my daily visits to the common room, where Emma spent her afternoons stretched out on the important sofa, being cheered up by her sister and friends.

"Look at this," Berry would command, holding up for all to admire one of the watercolors Emma had painted in the infirmary—a series of self-portraits *sans* eyebrow. "I think Emma's going to be a great artist," Berry would predict; and Emma, swaddled in black turtlenecks, her head in Gussie's lap, her lips dry and puffy, would roll away from the attention, then turn back, to-ing and fro-ing on the sofa until her knuckly fingers attached themselves to her stubbly brow. Then she'd turn to us with her wise and tragic eyes. Her lips would part:

"It's . . . it's . . . it's—so hard," she would tell us. "And my work's so—bad."

"But it's really good—it's cool," Gussie would rejoin, nodding her pleasure. "Look, everybody . . ."

And we would look, and we would praise, and Emma would try to tell us about "her work," and several Hoare House freshmen—aspiring poets and painters who had impulsively shaved off their eyebrows in homage to art and Emma—would exclaim "Wow" and "Whoa" and "Weird" between large pink gum bubbles.

One afternoon, the editors of the school literary magazine met in the Hoare House common room to consider submissions. The *Elm* had two editorial boards, and I, a candidate for the literary board, took my place with the "lit" editors. Emma, a full-fledged graphics editor, with the rest of the graphics board arrayed powerfully around her, lay recumbent on the important sofa, the illusion of her innocence preserved by invalidism.

Submissions to the *Elm* were considered anonymously, and the graphics board happened to have under "blind" discussion that afternoon a portrait of a nude figure who bore an uncanny resemblance to Boy-Boy Blackwell. The work—pen-and-ink on paper with "multi-media additions"—was in fact called *Boy-Boy*, and as discussion passed around the room, as one board member after another praised the piece, it emerged that no one knew what to do about the fact that the artist had used actual, shiny brown eyebrow hairs to represent the boy-figure's pubic hair.

"I think it needs clarification," Alice Cohen, a graphics editor, said finally.

The board sat speechless. Moments ticked by. Emma, with her hand at her brow and her chin sinking deep into her black turtleneck, gave a great anonymous sigh.

Kate Coffin, one of Emma's eyebrowless freshman followers, and a candidate for next year's graphics board, spoke up: "I think as art it's, like, so far *beyond* clarification, it's, like, almost an insult to the artist to ask for clarification."

"I don't think that's valid—or helpful," said Alice Cohen.

The room fell silent once more. Libby Munro, a freshman trying out for the literary board, had been fidgeting ever since the graphics editor had put *Boy-Boy* up for discussion. She gave a shy little wave, no more than a flutter of her fingers, and Alice Cohen invited her "unofficial" opinion.

"I'm not sure," began Libby Munro, "but I think it's really a waste of a perfectly good line drawing." The freshman took a deep breath, blushing furiously. Alice Cohen asked her to clarify her objection.

"Well, the pen-and-ink details are fine—they're lovely," said Libby, "but the rest of it . . . it's just a stunt, a gimmick to catch your eye and make you think you're seeing something new and important."

But how could Libby Munro have known? How could she have guessed that in almost no time at all (only ten years, and still all dressed in black) Emma would become the most publicized "new and important" artist in New York's East Village, selling to international collectors and museums such lavishly praised, highly priced works of art as *This Boy, Bob, He Drank Scotch, I Don't Know Why* and *Bob Got Bombed, We Had No Sex, He Threw Up, All Over Me*, as well as the companion portraits: *Dad Got Drunk, Don't Ask Me Why, I Have No Clue*, and of course *I Went Home, Dad Was Drunk, He Blew Lunch, All Over Me*, and the record-setting, highest-priced work of art ever sold in a downtown gallery, which we all read about on the front page of *The New York Times: Look At Dad, Dad Is Bombed, Dad Is Bad*.

When the vote was taken that afternoon in Hoare, *Boy-Boy* was accepted for publication by a vote of eight yeas, zero nays, and one abstention.

6. Independence

On April fifteenth, after chapel, a pall fell over the senior class. By recess, most of the girls had drifted over to Hoare House to be within earshot of the mailroom. In the common room, where the menacing date was marked on a Sierra Club wall-calendar, no one spoke above a whisper; girls who never smoked, smoked.

When the mailbags arrived, seniors bunched together, squeezed each other's shoulders. In small, imperiled clusters they advanced to the back hallway, closing ranks for one last embrace. Then, with tears already brightening the rims of their eyes, they separated, entering the chilly room Indian file.

Shortly after eleven, the first screeches sounded. Jubilant cries rolled out of the mailroom, followed by hysterical, unbelieving young women clutching fat envelopes stuffed full of welcoming papers and important forms from Yale and Harvard and Stanford and Brown and Princeton and Vassar. Berry, I heard, had gotten into Harvard. I didn't hang around to watch her open her mail. Like the seniors with skinny envelopes, I hurried away, talked with no one, and gave serious consideration to living in Alaska the rest of my life.

Berry Mansfield had been admitted everywhere she'd applied—an embarrassment of fat envelopes—but to her father's alma mater she would go, and my reaction (not that anyone was interested in my reaction) was fear and joy. On the one hand, since I knew it was only a matter of time before Berry and I started our affair, I took it as an omen that she had selected my hometown for college. On the other hand, the marriage of Berry and Harvard thrust me into an agony of envy for which I had barely begun to prepare myself.

In the widening world of that spring, I had begun on weekends to hang around the crossroads of Cambridge: the Forum of Harvard Square, Upstairs at Casablanca, the Fly Club garden party. I had observed that wherever there were college men, even as far south as the Acropolis of Morningside Heights, there was talk of Berry Mansfield. Harvard men especially—all those overconfident favorite sons—loved to welter in the cleavage of her name, always eliding *Berry* and *Mansfield*, always gliding through the name continuously and with a certain fatuity, like reporters covering the long-running trial of an axe-murderess. That spring I was always coming face to face with guys who'd say: "You go to Miss Little's? You asshole—do you know Berry Mansfield?"

One night at dinner, Berry sat down with me to discuss her "summer sitch." The temperature that day had spurted to 70° and a freak April snowstorm had fallen—all in the space of six hours—and to me Berry seemed very grown-up to be planning for summer, and beyond.

She was going to major in art history at Harvard, she said, and a summer job had been offered to her by a family friend at the Fogg Museum. The commute into Cambridge from the Mansfields' house on the North Shore, while not unbearable, would be, she guessed, "kind of a pain."

"I mean," said Berry, nosing in over my chicken croquettes to confide: "I don't mind the commute—Dad commutes—I just thought the living situation ought to be fun. . . ."

I agreed with her completely.

"But, listen," she continued on a defensive note: "If you

226

or your mum thought for one second that in any way I'd be asking out of convenience, as a *use* . . ."

I told her that even for a fraction of a second nothing like that would ever occur to *us*.

"Because," said Berry, "there're other options—I guess."

I said that if I were her, I wouldn't give any other option a second thought.

"You see, the job's only through the beginning of August . . . and it starts in June, so . . ."

I as much as swore I would have a spare set of house keys made for her immediately.

"So it's O.K.?" she pursued, her voice charming and husky, with a little scratch in it: "Could I, *peut-être,* stay at your house?"

"Oh, sure," I told her, "no problem. We actually haven't got any plans."

In June and July, my mother, I knew, expected to be away in Sri Lanka on a film. Sethna would be returning to see his family in India. Murray and I were scheduled to go back to France on the Experiment in International Living. For August, Danny and I had planned to meet in Paris and then travel around—mostly to Scandinavian countries—on Eurail passes. The Experiment fees had been paid, the special student-rate Eurail passes bought.

"Are you sure?" said Berry. "I thought you were going to Europe with Danny Armbrister."

"Oh, yeah—but no. That got changed. I'm actually going nowhere this summer."

"Great!" she agreed, and we both got so excited about going nowhere together we had to go outside and smoke a cigarette about it.

"All I'd need," she ventured, "is a bed—a cot, is all—in the attic or the cellar, or out on the porch—"

I told her that that was nonsense; she could stay in my bed.

"No, really," Berry insisted, swept up in the soundness of the plan: "All I need is a cot, and I could cook, clean, do bathrooms—anything."

I telephoned my mother during study hall.

"She says she'll do bathtubs," I whispered, as soon as I'd broached the worst of it.

And Muz put up a good fight, I have to admit. She countered my initial proposal ("Berry says she'll sleep on the porch") with a rather cool, headmistressy, "Certainly not, under any circumstances." She parried my next thrust ("I'll take a course at the Fogg") with "Maybe another summer, Sam," and caved in only under ceaseless battering ("All Berry needs is a cot!"), and then only when she had won the right to impose on the arrangement a house-sitting linguist from Mali, as well as concessions for mail-forwarding, message-taking, and no less than two informative personal letters per week.

As a final consideration, Muz added: "I would warn you, however, to think very carefully."

"What do you mean?" I was so elated at the prospect of playing house with Berry Mansfield I couldn't bear to stay on the telephone another second.

"It's all very well," said Muz, "for the smashing Berry Mansfield to want to stay here with you while she puts in a summer's work at the Fogg, but I wouldn't be flattered too easily if I were you."

"Muz, what are you talking about?"

"You act, Sam, as if it were *she* who was doing the favor."

Louisa Little had always relaxed household rules for April Eighteenth—the evening before Patriot's Day, Concord's annual celebration of the Fight for Independence. It was a windy night that year, and a large crowd had assembled in Monument Square to await the post-midnight appearance of Dr. Samuel Prescott, the patriotic messenger who on horseback had first brought the warning from Lexington nearly two centuries earlier.

Townspeople milled around the green in loose, vapor-clouded groups. Estabrook boys and Little girls and boys, free to roam the town, were scattered around the square, overflowing into the trees beside the Wright Tavern. High-school boys were headquartered up the dark, slate-ridden slope of Old Hill Burying Ground, their horselaughs rising from among the graves of British and Concord war dead.

Primed by a can of Maximus Super, loosened by the rampant feeling of the night, I made a full confession to Danny.

"Get out," he said, a touch of awe in his voice. At first I couldn't tell whether he was impressed at my summer of domestic bliss with Berry Mansfield, or angry that our trip in Europe would be called off.

"You can't," he snapped.

"I'm sorry," I offered lamely.

"When are you going to get real, Sam?"

"I'm sorry. I know."

"You know nothing! You're telling me you're going to pass up all the babes of Europe . . . for Berry Mansfield?"

I told him I was as sorry as I could be.

"Don't be sorry for me, Blue Balls. I'm the guy who's going to be getting his wick wet all over Denmark and Sweden while Stud-boy Blackwell is pumping the custard out of Mama Mansfield and you're standing around the hallway, waiting for them to finish so you can lick the bathtub clean."

"No one's cleaning anybody's bathtub."

"You will be, man. If you don't start getting strong—" Danny broke off here to punch me in the arm "—you're going

229

to be lapping up Berry Mansfield's bathwater the rest of your life."

Cantering hooves had raised cheers from the crowd, and everyone pressed forward to have a look. Horse and rider blazed under a streetlamp down the Lexington Road, flashed past us, and rode to a prancing stop in the square. Prescott, short and swarthy—the Lexington High School's machine shop teacher in his present-day life—pulled hard at his reins, frisking all over the square.

"The regulars are out! The regulars are out!" we heard him bawl in a rough, eager voice: "Revere has been taken and held in Lexington! Dawes has turned back to Boston! The Lexington company has mustered on the green!"

I hurried away to find Berry. We had urgent matters to settle (for instance, where *was* Boy-Boy Blackwell planning to spend the summer?), but when I let myself into Hoare House, no one was around, and the sign-out book had the Mansfields and their gang down for "Prescott/ North Bridge/ Pancake Breakfast @ Monument Hall."

The common room slumbered, quieter than the streets in town. The shadowy sofas wafted to me a complex, adult perfume—rank with smoke, suffused by a rotting, fruity fragrance and the wet cellar smell of the cold spring night. I was all at once ashamed by the vastness of my immaturity and the truth of my slavishness. Anxious that something look the way it always looked, I flicked the wall switch.

The overhead light brought the room back to normal. Then a creature of denim limbs, with a woman's head, a man's body, a baggy, unbuttoned shirt, and masses of soft, uncut hair, emerged from the cushions of the big sofa.

"Sam?" said a throaty Mansfield voice.

The other half of the beast stirred, raised an eye-shielding hand, and Billy Sheets said, "Hey, man."

"*Sam*," said Emma, beckoning me over to the sofa with an outstretched hand and her warmest, soulful smile.

"Whoa," said Billy Sheets, who smelled of nighttime and leather and woody, watery places outdoors.

I stood by the door, eyes on the rug. Billy Sheets had one hand up the front of Emma's shirt and no plans, evidently, to make adjustments on my account.

"Oh, Sam," Emma chimed piteously, "no one's here."

"Down watching Revere roll into town," said Billy.

"It's not Revere," Emma noted. "It's Prescott—Doctor *Sam* Prescott," she emphasized, and rewarded me with her smile, as though I, Sam Simon, man of the hour, knew something that silly Billy did not.

"Whatever," said Billy, unhurt.

"Whatever," Emma agreed, sitting up in a preening, yoga-ish way. She lifted a hand to Billy's hair.

Billy let Emma baby him, then gave her a townward toss of the head, resuming an apparently unfinished discussion.

"Do you think?" Emma replied, doubtfully.

"Frappe la rue," said Billy, jaunty and proud. "Want to come, Mister Simon—dip at Punk?"

"But it's illegal, hon'," said Emma.

"Give me a break," said Billy.

Straightening her spine, Emma pressed her flattened palms together isometrically, and Billy's hand came tumbling out of Emma's shirt. We all understood that the time for frivolousness had now come to an end.

"What've you got against a dip?" Billy complained, rubbing the detached, cancelled hand into his gut, as though maybe it might belong *there*.

"I haven't got anything," Emma answered gravely, searching Billy's face, then mine, with her worried gray eyes.

"We've got the Two-Thousand-Two," Billy reminded.

"Oh, in that case," said Emma.

"Let's cruise," said Billy, unaware or unconcerned that he had been condescended to.

"Gas?" said Emma.

"What about it?" said Billy.

"Gas costs money," said Emma. "Gas pollutes."

"Whoa," said Billy.

"The en-vi-ron-ment?" Emma asked, as though the situation needed to be spelled out for a child. She placed a fluttery hand on Billy's head and gave his scalp a searching stroke.

Billy drew away sharply. "Give me a break," he said. "Like what—like you never drive? Like you didn't drive all over the country last summer, all the way to freaking Oregon with Gus and Lili?"

Emma's hands fluttered questioningly, alighting on Billy's jaw, then his cheeks, his shoulders, his arms. Wherever they landed, they unmanned him, and he shrank from them.

"Em, I just want to cruise," stated Billy, pulling himself off the sofa. "I just want to cruise to Punkatasset Pond for a midnight dip."

Emma turned her decided, stoic eyes to me, but this time I dropped her gaze.

In the morning, I set out for Old North Bridge alone. Fog hung everywhere. It trailed along the roads and lingered in coils in the corners of orchards, the vapor so thick and elemental a dinosaur might have lumbered out of Walden Pond and marched down Main Street without causing much of a stir.

The sun came up. The early-world gases burned off. Centuries ticked away in seconds. All along Monument Street, small, red-streaked windowpanes peeped from barns like tiny bloodshot eyes. Hawthorne's Old Manse, melancholy as a bison, stood brown and bearded beside the slumbering river.

In the parking lot across from the famous bridge, tourists with Styrofoam cups of coffee and loud, carrying voices tumbled out of overheated buses into the cool morning. The citizens of Concord, calm and seasoned, gathered on the Manse grounds. Across the crude wooden bridge, a detachment of British regulars, red-coated and bristling with musketry, formed a solid red bridgehead to guard Captain Parson's retreat from Colonel Barrett's house. Above the line of lobsterbacks, Daniel Chester French's armed Yankee farmer came striding out of the meadow mist with head held high and shirtsleeves rolled.

Boy-Boy Blackwell, with Berry under his large, leathery arm, drew ever nearer to the spectacle, leading an antic group of Estabrook boys through the bulrushes. Berry went as far as the water's edge, then pulled back, yelping in protest as Blackwell plunged ahead, blundering into the cold river with Sheets and Reilly and the others in tow.

Unhurried, soaked to the thighs, Blackwell strode mightily along the margin of the Concord, showing his teeth, laughing his loony laugh, calling for Berry to follow. Ducking his head in the water, flinging back his dark wet hair with its silvery cockade of river water, Blackwell began to peel off his shirt.

"What are you doing?" I heard Berry whine at him from the riverbank.

A hush had fallen over the bridgehead. Modern men, stiff with the sound of old-fashioned labials and fricatives in their throats, hurled wooden commands up the river and across the meadow. The skirling of fife and drum stirred the crowd, as up along the dewy hillside, lines of minutemen and militia, in tricornered hats and moth-eaten brown breeches, with our own Mr. Laidlaw at arms, came marching two by two down upon the heavily defended bridge. Major Buttrick's orders to desist broke across the quiet morning, answered by the rattle of British musketry. Then, with the first puffs of battle smoke

233·

slanting against the pale blue sky, and Major Buttrick's hoarse command to fire, the fabled shot once more rang out across the bridge.

Down below, like trolls in the shallows, Blackwell and the Estabrook boys, buck naked, stepping high, advanced across the river. With the butts of their hands, they dispatched a volley of inflated brown paper bags, drawing hoots and titters from the tourists, and, from local patriots, orders to "knock it off!" But Berry's voice rang out above all:

"What is your problem?" she cried. Then she told Boy-Boy, with a sneer I'll never forget, "You smoke too much, you drink too much; you're just like my father."

7. Queen of the May

May burst into Old School Building in one sudden, superabundant gush of lilac and azalea. Spring, late that year, had also been abbreviated by the spirit of the age: I had only myself and my unisex generation to blame for missing the sights and sounds of Berry singing May songs with milkmaids and morris men; Berry romping around the Maypole with pastel cloth streamers of apple-green and apricot-yellow and damson-plum; Berry crowned as May Queen, with May-dew moistening her cheeks, and blue and yellow flowers set upon her honeyed head.

Final exams began after Memorial Day weekend, and for several suffocating days the chapel bell slowed in its circadian cycle, the morning hours measured only by a succession of Blue Books and the non-stop flight of Rapidograph pens. On the last afternoon of exam week, the bell simply ceased to toll. The whole school paused, suspended in the far-off drone of tractor mowers. Summer waited outside examination room windows and along the buttercup-studded lawns. Yellow jackets hummed around the hive holes in the chapel steeple. After-noon lingered, itchy, warm, without end.

Dogs barked. Bells pealed. Teachers grinned. Suddenly we were free. The yearbooks, already signed, were signed again, and there was singing and laughter from the bubble-filled bathtubs of Senior House all through Friday night. Over the weekend, white-haired women from the Alumnae Associa-tion would braid circlets of flowers for the heads of graduating girls. Knob-shouldered gardeners would work overtime prepar-ing Senior Garden for Monday morning's commencement exercises.

I could think of nothing but Monday night: Muz would be winging toward Sri Lanka, Sethna toward Bombay, Murray (with Annie Johnston and a guided group of cyclists) toward Ireland. The house would be empty, the keys would be mine, and Berry Mansfield would at long last be my . . . would be my what? My lover? My roommate? My pretend sister? My surrogate mother? My resident Eve? My live-in sphinx? My house witch? My—*what*? What *was* Berry Mansfield?

I couldn't get a word out of her about Blackwell. There were rumors that Berry had broken up with Boy-Boy, but also counter-rumors that Boy-Boy had done the breaking up be-cause Berry wouldn't sleep with him. Hattie refused to com-ment. She had begun attending church on Sundays—dressing up in one of Mrs. Mansfield's tailored suits and going off to Mass—and whenever I asked Hattie about the status of Berry's virginity, Hattie said that she was shocked at how little I, of all people, seemed to have learned about faith, hope, and charity.

A wild panic seized me when exams ended and Berry, her

manner varying each time we spoke, continued to insist that all she would need for accommodations was "a bed in the attic" or "a cot in the cellar." She grew increasingly evasive about her job at the Fogg. One day, cleaning out her cubby in Senior Cloakroom, she wheeled around to tell me, point-blank, that she would be "spending every weekend out at Singing Beach anyway."

The night after her last exam, she packed up some things in her room and let me take home to Cambridge a duffel bag full of her summer clothes. Now she spoke gaily of the summer meals we would cook and the parties we would give and the fun we would have. Consoled, I began to relax, and when I went home after my last exam, I stashed Berry's bulky duffel in the back of Muz's closet and swaggered around the master bedroom, conjuring at certain key sites (the master bed, with its firm mattress; the master bath, with its Marimeko shower curtain that, when wet, became translucent) visions of our forthcoming domestic idyll.

Then on Friday, when the close June night thickened with lilac and fireflies, I unzipped the duffel. Like a truffle-crazed pig, I plunged in my snout and withdrew with Berry's blue bikini between my teeth. After I had filled a pair of pendulous water balloons to within an ounce of perfection, and after I had implanted those warm, bouncy bazooms in the bikini's top piece, I then undressed and lay down in the darkness with my sleazy mock-mermaid, believing with all my heart that I was doomed to die—and to die soon—if I did not make love to the real girl.

Saturday evening, in a convoy of cars, we all drove up to the North Shore for Berry's black-tie graduation party. The Myopia Hunt Club's front gate, marked by a sign so unobtrusive we overshot the entrance twice, invited us to turn onto a long, rustling driveway that swept past weedless polo fields and over a small stone bridge, given in memory of golden lads fallen in France.

Flanked by a golf course, the clubhouse turned out to be a recreational, inland version of the Mansfields' house. Bright yellow Myopia, though smooth-skinned with clapboards, had the same well-fed look, the same gambrel roofs and shabby-genteel furnishings, the same rambling, splintery verandas—only at home, *chez* Mansfield, the porches, though pillared and furnished, had not been pitted by the fangs of a thousand cleated golf shoes.

Berry's party drew us out onto a sort of fantail porch, capped by a striped yellow tent-top, facing the eighteenth hole and the receding, rolling sea of green. Berry's rich aunt Nutkin, with Berry's parents as honorary hosts, had agreed to give her an informal dinner-dance in lieu of a coming-out cotillion. Flower-decked tables had been arranged with place cards and dinner settings all around a polished oval dance floor. White-gloved, white-haired waiters stood planted at the edges of mallard-green carpets and beside oxblood chairs, their trim silver trays shimmering with glasses of champagne.

Rich aunt Nutkin had also sprung for a twelve-piece jazz orchestra. And an open bar, lined with liquors. And little bundles of fresh, filterless cigarettes standing in silver cups. But the orchestra is what I remember most vividly—those fancy swallow-tailed figures with their gleaming yellow horns. For as we Little boys paraded in our Keezer's tuxedos, the summery scent of sweet clover breezed in off the practice tee, the jazz-men struck up "The Girl From Ipanema," and the pleasure my brother and my roommates took in the whole elegant setup seemed at last to vindicate my winter's greenest dreams. Only the girl herself had yet to make her appearance.

The first grown-up guests had begun to arrive—grandfathers,

237

gaunt as bishops; horsy aunts; bashful, big-eared uncles. Berry, gowned in something sleek and strapless and black, huddled with her sisters and Hattie on an adjacent porch. She seemed to have done something to her voice: combed out every blunt and slangy snarl, leaving behind womanly softness, smoothness, shine. And she wore some makeup and some lipstick, but not much of either. Her hair had been brushed to a fine, feathery goldness, then spun into waves and coiled back with some white flowers to reveal her graduation present: a string of pearls with matching earrings.

I had never seen her so beautiful—or so befuddled. Over and over, she kept marveling that all this had been done for her. She would not stop thanking Hattie for coming to the party, or apologizing to her sisters for how nice and correct and overadult everything looked. And she wouldn't budge: All agog, she stood off to the side, hiding behind a porch pillar, and it was touching, somehow, the way she kept peeking and pointing, amazing herself with the fantastic scene of her own party.

8. The Alumni Association

It was going to be a big party. But because it was Berry's, no one could be sure how big. It didn't seem to matter that individual invitations had been sent to individual guests. Invited or not, boys just showed up, in pairs and by the pack. From Estabrook, in black tie and Converse high-tops, came Boy-Boy Blackwell, Billy Sheets, Buddy Hayes, Billy Kirby, and Bobby Reilly, who had all eaten Frank Purvis's psilocybin mushrooms and were now filled with such joy and dread they knew not what to do but stand around the eighteenth hole, shirts untucked, smirking into the cup, spraying their mouths with Binaca.

Wicks Lyman, home from St. Mark's, so loose-limbed and lanky he appeared to have just come into his bones, had brought along his lanky cousin Digger, Digger's lanky Yale roommates, Laddy, Roddy, Jeffrey, and Joey—all oarsmen on their way to row at Henley—and a tight-lipped friend of Joey's called Skiddy, who was a Hornblower, I remember Emma telling me in the embarrassed, hesitant voice she used whenever she wished to release herself from her caste.

From Groton—detached and diffident, with strange, secret smiles that tugged at wholesome faces—Cuppy Cabot, Cully Cutler, Cuff Chandler, and Cotty Woodward, who were all related, though none of them could ever explain, to the full satisfaction of the others, the full extent of their kinship—except to insist, frequently, if vaguely, that they all shared a certain great-grandfather named "Scuppy," who was either *the* Scupper Woodward, or his son, I can't remember.

Peter Gale, home from St. Paul's, bearded, faintly crazy— "the fastest skater in SPS history," Emma informed me—loped in, took one turn under the tent, then loped out, looking for his sidekick, Bradshaw, who had a joint.

From Milton, in an open Jeep sprinkled with hay and grass and clumps of dried seaweed, came Woody "Wupper" Codman, "Whoop" Hallowell, "Limbo" Ames, and "Gooner" Loring— red-eyed boys whose grandfathers' dinner jackets tonight smelled not only of camphor but of field, forest, and wetland.

From Berry's Misery Island days came the make-out artists, Teddy and Nibs Knowles and their step-brother Bobby Strayer, the first boy who'd ever French-kissed Berry Mansfield, and from dancing school, Nick Oberpacker, Will Sears, and Georgie Aspinwall. And from Maine, Joe Shoat and the Schadler brothers—red-bearded mountain climbers, friends of Emma's,

239

on their way out to Oregon. Though Harvard had not yet claimed Berry, her admirers that night were already varsity—Mike Magnoli, Frank Pennoyer, Johnny Wenzell—hockey stars, mostly, with a few steeplechasers, racquets champions, and a miscellany of clean-cut, cologned men whose knotty, hard limbs came in odd lengths, like lumber.

From Dark Harbor they came, and from Aiken, from up and down the East Coast—a Schuyler from New York, a Grayson from Virginia, a du Pont from Delaware, a Morrison from New Jersey, a Carroll from Maryland, a Cadwalader from Pennsylvania—a congress of adolescence. All told, some fivescore men and two dozen women from thirteen states turned out to honor Berry, with Danny, Betty Crocker, Poopsy, Wenty Bird, the Myrrh Man, and I representing the androgynous state customarily reserved for Little boys. Even Purvis eventually turned up from Manhattan, just in time to resupply the Estabrook boys with enough magic mushrooms to cover eighteen holes of "night golf."

I guess that night we all rededicated ourselves to the pursuit of Berry. For as each man stood at dinner to give his toast, there circulated for the first time among us a powerful, nearly a ludicrous, sense of group recognition: We were all in love with the same girl.

We all carried in our pants pockets the smooth black Mansfield stones. We all knew which blue was our Blue, and we had each had our minds read and our fortunes told and our ears whispered into. We had all fallen for the line (not realizing that it *was* a line, and innocent of its contempt) about Berry knowing us better than our wives would ever know us. We had each felt the surpassing sweetness of unfulfillment. In the heart of every Mansfield alumnus—starting back with Bobby Strayer, vintage of '67—had lingered, or would linger, the imprecise, unspoken suspicion that somehow, somewhere, in some other room, on some distant porch, some other guy was being given the love.

That night I was just thankful I had the girl's duffel bag in my house. Throughout dinner, Berry kept slipping away and reappearing, and whenever she was forced to pass my table she would flash me her characteristic occulting smile: Y–O–U. If she saw that I had been looking for her—to dance, to talk about our summer plans—she would toss her head, smile her special sibylline smile, and maneuver around me at oblique angles, as though I were a squash opponent. If talking to me proved unavoidable, she would flit by, saying, "I'm still here, I'm still here. . . ."

"Where were you?" I asked after Berry had stolen onto the golf course with Digger Lyman's lanky Yale roommates and returned, barefooted, with Skiddy Hornblower.

"Over there, but I'm here," was the answer.

"Over *there*?" I persisted, trying to sound funny and charming, as Berry paused to periscope over my shoulder at some distant object of her desire.

"Yup . . ."

"There, by the practice tee?"

". . . Yup, yup . . ."

"There, where that spaceship just landed and those Martians got out?"

Before tripping away again, she tossed me a backward glance over her bare shoulder—the glance Mansfield sisters reflexively gave to Little boys at a certain point in the evening: the unseeing, unthinking glance you give to something that's been sitting in your freezer too long, bearded with crystals, frosted over beyond recognition.

"But wait," I called after her each time she rushed off. "Come back—I need to talk to you."

"I'm back," she insisted, moving each time farther away from me, "I'm back."

I had just resolved to call off our summer of homesteading (I would mail back Berry's duffel bag from Alaska) when an amazingly good-looking boy strolled off the golf course, stepping into the tent. He wasn't dressed for the party—just khakis and a polo shirt—yet everyone seemed to know him, and everyone was ecstatic about his arrival. Mrs. Mansfield hugged and kissed him like a son; Mr. Mansfield, hearty as a vestryman, patted his back, offered a drink. Girls turned lighthearted and trusting when he approached. Boys lunged forward to greet him at the bar, brimming with a sort of pure athletic pride as they bear-hugged their hellos, bugled their tantaras:

"Towny! *Dude!* How the hell are you?"

He stood a couple of inches over six feet and wore his thick, unruly chestnut hair unfashionably short. Most of his height and splendor radiated from long, sinewy legs and high, equine hips. He had a whiskerless chin and girlish cheeks and heavy-lidded brown eyes with long curly lashes. Yet for all the obviousness of his beauty, he traded less on looks than on some inborn facility for clannishness and idiom.

Henry Townsend Lee had barely set foot under that tent and already he was dealing in nicknames, retailing in-jokes, trading inside information. For every man, woman, child, and dog who greeted him, he was ready with a secret grip—a private, semi-jesting clasp of the wrist, the elbow, the shoulder, the neck, even the knee. Often, the person gripped would countergrip, and then a whole series of dexterous clasps would entwine the parties into further intimacies.

Within sixty seconds, everything he said sounded funny. By the time I wandered over he had a good crowd around him—an audience so hot for cool Towny Lee that he could

have casually dropped in their midst almost any word or phrase—
let us say, for example, *bird turd*—and everyone would have
ignited, exploding with pleasure. He seemed to take everyone
and everything in his stride.

At the bar, with a foot up on the rail, the Mansfields'
standout boy soberly drank in the fellowship of fathers, the
admiration of mothers, the homage of sons, the laughter of
daughters, and the eyes of younger sisters. Emma, I noticed,
was the only one in Towny Lee's entourage not laughing.

Emma looked weirdly spinsterish in a stern, black frock.
She stood slightly apart from the others, and when, during the
orchestra's lead-in to "String of Pearls," Towny Lee shot out
one of his long oarsman's arms, adroitly snaring Emma by the
wrist, she pulled away—trying to pull him where *she* wanted
him to go—but he wouldn't follow.

9. Mansfields, Black and Blue

The orchestra was going strong when the party was asked
to leave Myopia. Boy-Boy Blackwell and Billy Sheets had streaked
through the clubhouse, bare-assed but for cummerbund and
Converse high-tops. Everyone piled into cars and steered through
the fog. The Mansfields' house, wreathed in milky halos, riggish
with the smell of pot, filled up with boys like an outbound
ship.

On the upstairs landing, above the front hall, Mrs. Mansfield and Aunt Nutkin leaned over the railing to hand out
hellos. Innumerable black cats and raffish young men prowled
the hallway below. Throaty Mrs. Mansfield, smiling at every-

one as if she and her sister had just put in to these misty shores on the Cunard Line, called down: "Gosh! Look at you, deary! Gosh!"

"Oh, hullo!" stage-whispered the sleek, black-sheathed Nutkin, her bare freckled shoulders camouflaged with powder, her thick Irish calves and feet disguised by black sheer stockings and peau de soie pumps. "What a nice surprise to see you!" she called out randomly in her deep, mannish voice.

Every few minutes the sisters would turn away from the rail, comparing notes and gossiping, the seaside sister systematically gathering the tattle of the town from the city sister. Giggling—often cackling like hags—they passed back and forth a single filterless cigarette. Yet except for their jewelry, visible to the front door, the chin-wagging Shanahan sisters seemed to have come from different climates, worlds apart: Mrs. Mansfield's oval face glowed with health, while her older sister, square of jaw, broad of brow, looked not just older, but drier, and coarse, rouged like an aging queen.

I had never been introduced to Berry and Emma's fashionable, moneyed aunt, though often enough I'd heard about the chain of husbands ("Five so far," as Emma put it), each one richer than the last, with a Kentucky horse-breeder nosing out a Manhattan brewery heir, and a Texas oil billionaire squelching the Marquis of Mowbray. From Berry I had learned about the sensational divorces and unprecedented alimony payments, the mysterious sudden deaths and secret out-of-court settlements. From Hattie I had absorbed endless palaver about the Cecil Beaton portraits and the wild, widowed life Aunt Nutkin had lived during the sixties, jetting between Beekman Place and Palm Beach, Cheyne Walk and Cap d'Antibes. Yet, to me, the single most impressive fact about the Mansfields' glamorous aunt was that her hair remained unwashed—literally, not one shampooing—after nine Novembers.

Fresh arrivals jammed the front hall, and Emma, directing traffic, caught me admiring her aunt and immediately towed me up the front stairs to meet the Marchioness of Mowbray in person. I had never met a titled woman or a dirty-haired lady in my life.

Emma drew me alongside the rail. Lady Mowbray's back was turned. The infamous unwashed hair lay atop the widow's large head, piled, pinned, and coiled into thick, lifeless plaits of gray, with here and there a streak of yellow—an old, pale yellow, somehow promiscuous, like the yellow of stale, sour linen.

In the next instant, there was a rustling of silk, a puff of night-blooming jasmine, and all at once I was face to face with a sort of dragon lady, from whose flaring nostrils spewed twin plumes of gray-white smoke. As Emma murmured introductions, I found myself holding a dry, crooked, fingers-only handclasp and searching a wide, desiccated face for its center. But there was no center, only glittery, greenish eyes and patches of parched, powdered skin surrounding a gigantic, waxy mouth which had formed an impossibly huge O.

"Sam was one of Miss Little's first boys," Emma was telling her aunt.

"O?" said Lady Mowbray, taking me in with her smoke-cured vowel. She could see that I was impressed by her, and with her shrewd, roving eye she gave me a big, round once-over: "Oooo," she rumbled, "you must be *some man.*"

"He was the cutest one," Berry put in, appearing suddenly from the rear hall. Without breaking stride, she asked, "Has anyone seen Hattie?"

"What's happened?" said Mrs. Mansfield.

"Oh, nothing." Berry shrugged sarcastically. "No one can find her, she freaked out at Myopia, told Towny Lee he was the Devil, and started screaming about the Virgin Birth and the

245

love of God and the corruption of the flesh. I lost one of my pearl earrings, and Boy-Boy Blackwell is an asshole and thinks he can have sex with Pine Manor girls because I won't lose my virginity with him. Other than that, everything's fine—what are you guys doing?"

"Where's your father?" Mrs. Mansfield quickly asked Emma.

"How should I know?" said Emma.

"Dad's out of it, somewhere," Berry reported airily.

"I thought Berry was finished with Boy-Boy Blackwell," said Aunt Nutkin.

"As if," said Emma, flashing me a wry look.

"Well, then I guess Little Miss Merrythought knows where her Billy-Boy has gone," said Berry to her sister.

"Pine Manor," Emma returned in perfect martyrdom.

"Pine Mattress," corrected Berry.

"Oh, let's pick out a *practice* beau for Berry!" Nutkin suddenly proposed in a smoothing-over tone. "We'll have such *fun*. Oh, let's!" she urged gamely, her restless, crimson tongue darting forward to wet her lips.

Berry and Emma and their mother and I looked down on the shuffling, shaggy, tuxedoed figures in the front hall.

"Oh, can't we?" begged Nutkin. "*Can't we?* But let's! —You and I," she decided, hooking a quail-boned arm through mine. "We're such great friends! And you're so clever. Now you pick first—"

I was lost, bloated with flattery, a junior snob out of his league.

"Go on—pick." She sunk her claws into my wrist. "He's only for practice," she reminded, gaily. "I like that one, don't you?"

Held by Nutkin's raptorial grasp, I pretended not to notice the vein of rubies pulsing at her wrists and throat; the chartreuse-green emeralds budding on her fingers; the cold onyx and platinum snaking into her bosom. I couldn't help wondering what would happen when Berry got her hands on jewels like those.

"Don't *you*?" The marchioness was rattling her spangled wrist at Billy Kirby and his curly Caledonian hair, and I found my head nodding in absurd agreement.

"Ho-hum," commented Mrs. Mansfield.

"He's an *adorable* creature!" protested Nutkin.

"Mum doesn't like Billy Kirby," Emma narrated. "Mum likes Boy-Boy Blackwell, right Mum?"

"*Dreamy*," said Mrs. Mansfield, showing us her weird, distant smile.

"Sorry about that, Mum," said Berry, one field-hockey captain to another.

"Who *is* that man?" rumbled Nutkin. "He's got such marvelous hindquarters—oh, I'd try *him*, if I were Berry. That one: *there*!"

Amazingly enough, the marchioness pointed her bejeweled finger at my brother.

"Very attractive," Mrs. Mansfield agreed.

"Taken," said Berry, winking at me pointlessly.

"Yah," said Emma, "what do we think?" And we all watched Murray slow-dancing with Annie Johnston while Jimmy Cliff, singing "The Harder They Come," carried the other dancers to heights of terpsichorean frenzy.

"He's marvelous," confirmed Nutkin. "But she—she's a *cauchemar, un vrai cauchemar*."

A pause followed: My turn, I thought.

The instant I'd opened my spellbound lips, I knew right away that any remark I made would die on my tongue. It was too late to turn back: "They look like they're in heat," I observed disloyally, and no one, least of all my mother, whose voice now occupied my ringing, hollow-chambered skull ("*Oh,*

Sam! Really!"), thought me amusing, attractive, or, far less, fun.

"How about that one?" pursued Berry, making a game of picking more or less at random from the hallway pack. "I could like that one."

"The weakling?" asked Nutkin, her malediction so melodious it was indistinguishable from praise. "Or the one with the long, funny neck?"

"She meant the short, nubbly one going into the TV room: Skiddy Hornblower," said Emma.

"No—do the one with the long, funny neck," urged Berry.

"Poopsy Winslow?" asked Emma.

"He's no fun," her aunt agreed. "Too *sérieux*. You'd just break his heart."

"How do you know?" I suddenly heard myself blurt.

"One *knows*, my dear, one simply knows." And that shut me back up, mute as a nutcracker.

"How about Danny Armbrister?" volunteered Emma.

"That dark one? Handsome—but he's a highwayman. Thinks the world owes him something."

"Well, yah," Emma affirmed judiciously: "He's been going around all night, sleazily getting people's phone numbers, trying to get money out of them for some film project in Sweden."

"You see?" said Nutkin, raking my wrist, triumphant.

Emma next offered up Brad Wentworth. But no one seemed to know what to make of white-blond Wenty Bird, who was sitting at the piano bench, dandling Lili Hooper on his knee, as together they noodled the keyboard, sarcastically breaking into "Chopsticks."

"He's a rather dull night at home, what?" Nutkin said finally.

"But he's really funny," objected Berry.

"And a comfortable old shoe is nice now and then," Mrs. Mansfield countered.

"Small beer," Nutkin insisted.

"He's just a nice guy," said Emma.

"Maybe nice to have around the house, and comfortable, and fun—but after the first two years, that kind won't take you very far," decreed Nutkin, tacking on with an afterlaugh: "And they certainly won't go along if *you* do!"

This seemed the merriest thing under the sun, and we all laughed, pleased to know so much about our friends.

"Well, *anyway*," sang Mrs. Mansfield, concluding on a rising note, "Towny Lee is the one for Berry." She then extended the maternal arm to include Emma in the older sister's future happiness, but Emma carefully eluded her mother's embrace.

Emma stepped sideways, wobbling a little. Gripping the rail, she stood soundless as a silent-movie heroine for whom a stricken face and stock title cards—*Wedding Bells . . . My Towny Lee . . . Help! Help!*—must tell the tale.

"Charming boy," said Nutkin, dismissing Towny Lee with a wave. "A mama's boy like that—with those pink cheeks? Berry would crack him open like a lobster."

Berry, I suddenly noticed, was smiling—her mother's weird, unnatural, eldritch smile—and it spooked me to see her smiling that way.

"I think not," said Mrs. Mansfield.

"Yah," chimed Berry, "I think not." But she had already reached up and let down her hair.

10. Boyfriend and Girlfriend

The graveyard, webbed with mist, was dark and full of sounds. Through the trees, Emma and I eavesdropped on the party. Driveway conversations came within our hearing. A sports car had just gunned up the Mansfields' rear drive; several bodies had tumbled out and were now wrestling around, on, in, and over, Mansfield shrubbery:

". . . Pine Mattress?"

"Are you guys talking Mattress?"

"We're talking Mattress. This party sucks."

". . . Where the fuck are we?"

"I'm *outta* here!"

". . . History."

Doors slammed. Tires squealed. A car tore away, leaving a rubbery smell in the air.

Shoulder to shoulder, with Emma clinging to me as if I were the Faithful Friend of her silent dramas, we located the stone wall, and lay down, shoulders to the stone. We leaned against each other, almost impersonally at first, then with mounting coziness. I had never felt so confident with Emma.

"Do you think Billy's coming back tonight?" I asked.

"He'll be back," she said, and sighed. "We'll go on. We've got problems. But Bill loves me and he's got a good heart."

"Billy Sheets?"

"More than anyone else," said Emma, and she turned to face me, brushing at my hair in her tidy way. Against the haloed lights of the house, I could see the outline of her high forehead, knotting and unknotting. "Every boy I ever liked fell for my sister; Bill never did. Every boy—one look at Berry, and that was it; Bill never did. *You* did, hon'."

I had a feeling she was getting to that, and I was grateful she delivered the blow quickly and cleanly.

After a moment, I said: "I guess I was never sure whether you liked me."

"Of course you were, deary. I had a crush on you."

"Well, I had a crush on you."

"Then along came a spider," said Emma.

I could see with pinpoint clarity my old dream of marrying Emma Mansfield under the boughs of the Great Elm, and it still seemed so familiar, so real, I said: "Don't you think we ought to be together *someday*?"

"As boyfriend and girlfriend?—You'd be miserable with me, hon'. You'd hate me."

"I would not. We could live together. We could live on the beach."

"The beach? What beach?"

"I don't care. Any beach in Massachusetts is fine with me. Take your pick."

"*Massachusetts?*" (As if I'd chosen some especially bland sort of cheese.)

"Yeah, why not?"

"Massachusetts!" she exclaimed with her most melodious, tinkling Mansfield laugh.

"What's wrong with Massachusetts?"

"And what—?" flashed Emma, quick and defiant: "Get married? Have kids? Get fat on Dunkin Donuts? Drive the Datsun to the station to pick up some dumb guy who comes home wrecked every night?—Massachusetts!"

I asked her what she had against kids.

"Hon', I've spent my whole life in a house packed with kids. Why would I want *kids*? Why would I want one single diaper anywhere in my life?"

"But you'll get married—won't you?"

"I won't marry," she said curtly.

"You won't? Sure you will."

"No," vowed Emma, "I won't."

We were still cuddled unnecessarily close together, with Emma's cheek on my shoulder, and her sweet, tobacco-tangy breath and gingery party perfume mingling in the heat of her body. It surprised me when she nuzzled in further, breathing warm and hard, touching her nose to my throat, and said: "Anyway, I don't think we should do this."

"Do what?"

"Jeopardize our friendship."

"Why not?"

"Because," she said ominously, and lifted her head to listen, as if something she dreaded had just come up out of the burying ground, unmarked and faceless, to take our blood. Then she lowered her head, resumed position at my throat, and with new authority said: "Sex is a tricky thing."

Just the sound of it stirred me. Quickly I said, "Well, I think we'd be great together."

"Wreck us," predicted Emma.

"It wouldn't wreck us; it would save us."

"I wouldn't want it to wreck our friendship," Emma insisted, and to emphasize the point, she encircled my neck with her arms and held on tightly, as though I were the mast of a sinking ship. "I love you too much," she said.

Gladdened, full of courage, I lowered my head into kissing range. Emma drew back, but only by a few inches. Our noses were almost touching. A faint gleam of distant party light appeared on Emma's large front teeth.

My throat thrumming with fluids, I leaned in and kissed her. It was a short kiss, and strangely dry, but we lingered up close, noses touching, trying to see into each other's night-hooded eyes.

"It's impossible, deary," Emma said in her cheerless diaper-changing voice. "I'm just too fond of you. I love you too much." She reached up to my jaw, as though to feed me my worm pills. I shook the knuckly fingers away.

We sat up. Emma sighed, full of the old misery.

"Oh, hon'," she said. "I don't know."

11. Green Monsters

Fog rolled in off the water—cold, wet, smelling of caves. The party continued. People paired off on porches. People passed out on porches. People who had taken too many drugs were packed off to upstairs porches and calmed down with Tab and backrubs. Limbo Ames had not made it past the kitchen porch. He had baked and eaten so many hash brownies he could hardly speak, and for the past ten minutes the tall young man had been lying flat on his back, motionless, trying to tell Emma and Mrs. Mansfield what had happened to Hattie.

In a kind of dumb show, interpreted by the Mansfield women, it now emerged that:

"Hattie was '. . . in the Wupper's . . . Jeep,' " echoed Mrs. Mansfield, reading Limbo Ames's lips.

". . . 'Acting weird,' " took up Emma.

"And you stopped," continued Mrs. Mansfield.

". . . To pick up 'a case of Haffenreffer,' " Emma brought out. "Yah, yah, O.K.: 'green monsters.' "

"What are 'green monsters'?" asked Mrs. Mansfield, laughing delightedly.

"They lost her at a packie," Lindy Mansfield announced, winging out the kitchen door, eyes flashing, raven-black hair flying. Loud, tactless, and gorgeous, with a cigarette the constant accessory to her long-sleeved Pucci dress, the third Mansfield sister folded her arms and narrowed her eyes at the flattened form of Limbo Ames. "I can't believe," she said to her classmate, "that you lost Hattie Bancroft at a packie."

". . . 'On Route One,' " Emma calmly continued to interpret, "you 'stopped at a packie . . . on Route One—' "

"So *which* packie, honey?" Lindy howled, taking Limbo Ames by the shoulders and shaking him. "There're packies all over Route One!"

"It's O.K., hon'," Emma told Limbo Ames, babying him, urging him on with finger-squeezes. "You'll remember."

The supine young man struggled to remember, and everyone bent an ear to listen, and from among the inchoate sounds, Lindy plucked the polysyllable "Saugus."

"Saugus?" said Mrs. Mansfield. "What happened in Saugus?"

"He means the packie on the Saugus-Malden line," explained Emma: "Kappy's."

"Then why didn't the jerk just go back to Kappy's and get her?" Lindy demanded.

Alas, Limbo Ames could not clarify, and neither Emma nor Mrs. Mansfield could decode, why "the Wupper" and his charioteers had not driven back to Kappy's to find Hattie. Limbo Ames suddenly raised himself up to the porch railing, where he opened his mouth, leaned out, and booted (as Lindy put it) into the Mansfield shrubs.

"Good boy," said Lindy, exiting to the kitchen as quickly as she had entered, though not before telling everyone how grateful her father ought to be, now that she was finally bringing home boys who knew to boot in the shrubs and not in the house.

Mrs. Mansfield, overseeing the booting, gave Limbo Ames an encouraging rub on the back.

"It's the fog," Emma told her mother. "Always makes them crazy."

No matter what happened that night, there lingered the circuitous sense of incompletion. I was never where I should have been, always where I didn't want to be. Over and over, as I patrolled the Mansfields' gigantic, belittling house, I was gripped by the fear that I had somehow failed: mixed everything up, left everything undone. I clung to the insane hope that in some room, somehow, I would find Berry, and she would remagnetize me with one stroke of her lodestone. But of course I couldn't find her and of course she was everywhere, in every room.

For a while, I narrowed down my quest: I searched for cigarettes and for my brother, who, I'd heard, had been helping Mr. Mansfield fix a spectacularly clogged toilet. I looked into something like half a dozen bathrooms and still I couldn't find my brother. There was not a fresh cigarette anywhere in that house—even the menthols had been smoked—and I was more or less on the verge of sobbing when I shambled onto the main veranda.

A salty breath of air stirred the enormous, lacquered-antler chandelier which hung, swinging and creaking, from the fluted wooden ceiling. Tonight, each antler point held a short slim taper, and the candles—twenty-one in all—were lighted and shimmering, casting their flickery bands of yellow light across the house's fog-moistened skin.

Poised beneath this luminous extravaganza, Aunt Nutkin was attempting, flat-footedly, to blow out the lowest of the overhead flames. When I stepped out onto the veranda, she had just begun to make short, frustrated little jumps into the air.

"Oh, it's you," she said, her overlarge heard flung back, her lumpy hair in collapse. "What a nice surprise."

She extended her hand, and I took it, all very bright and easy, as though we'd just been picked as partners at mixed doubles. And then we stood there like the winning team, smiling our winning smiles, lifting up our flame-filled eyes to the great rack of antlers.

"I could find a stepladder—" I began.

"Oh, but no!" she cried. "No *fun!* You must leap—to *leap!*" And now my teammate stepped back, making enough room for a grand jeté. She waved me on with her glittering hand.

I stood where I was, lead-footed as a toy soldier.

"I thought you were a tall, clever boy," she teased, adding with a charming toss of her head: "Though not as tall as your dad, mmh?"

"Oh," I said, unguarded, surprised, flushing with pleasure. "Do you know Dad?"

My father lived in Washington; he wasn't exactly a social butterfly, but it seemed possible . . .

"Of course I do," she replied, and a feeling of elation swept over me. She cleared her throat and gave his name like a schoolgirl, frisking with pride over her—over *our*—easy familiarity with the subject: "Laddie Simonds: of the Marblehead Simondses. Laddie *Fahnestock* Simonds."

I think I had known all along that the Mansfields' worldly aunt had not the least idea who I was—in a social, or even a motor-vehicles-registry sort of way. Yet at the same time I had held out, half hoping that I would somehow turn out to be more than I was, and half knowing that it didn't matter.

Burning a little, I said, "Well—actually—it's *Simon:* one *s*—no *d,* and no 'Fahnestock,' I'm afraid."

"Oh," she replied. She gave me an odd, a curiously grumpy, look.

Then I blurted the rest—my name, my father's name, his land of birth—and the candles overhead seemed for a second to burn brighter; but it was only a snort of warm party air, escaping that scaly, shingled house, ruffling the flames.

"O," she repeated, steeping me in her characteristic vowel. But it was shortened now, and tepid, and with a decided narrowing of her basilisk eyes, Lady Mowbray removed herself from me and started down the veranda.

"Why not see what you can do," she suggested, "with Pa's crazy candles. I'm off—to breakfast—good night!"

It was as if we had never spoken at all. The Mansfields' titled aunt wheeled and gave me her back. Then she glided off, and as she went, she reached up to poke into the loosening mass of unwashed hair. Completely without warning, she unpinned herself.

I stood transfixed as the greasy gray coils slithered down her bare shoulders. Matted and gluey, the many-headed ends reluctantly wriggled free of each other, slinking and slithering across her hunched, vulturine shoulders and down the middle of her freckly back. The more the hair wriggled free, the more I shrank from the smell of it: a sharp, high odor, like burlap and jute.

Half turning, I sidled down the slippery porch, hurrying as fast as I could from the guttering candles and the buttery light and the slithering hair and the deep coaxing mouth. From my end of the veranda, I leapt into a hedge, and when I glanced back, Nutkin, at the far end, had paused, bowing her heavy head. In a gesture so private I could think only of women in boudoirs and changing rooms with brassieres and bathing caps, she gave a little shake and a hop, and the gruesome hair spread out into two great big glossy wings.

I shot across the grass, dropped out of sight at the lawn's lip, and plunged down into the steep, wooded declivity, slaloming through the tree trunks and the fog to a shelf of rock way down beside the water. The sea foamed and crashed, sending up ghostly plumes, soaking my thin black party shoes. The spray felt wonderful.

Bedeviled by sexy, seaweedy vapors, I made bold, daring leaps from one shadowy, humpbacked boulder to another, howling a little whenever I felt like it. The rocks were glazed with fog and spray, slick as blubber, and I slipped, of course, which was the point of the whole exercise; I careened into a dark recess between two craggy rocks and clocked myself good and hard on the head. And though I was being pretty thorough about self-pity that night, the Boy Scout in me managed to keep his head, staying clear of the rushing slides of water, checking for fractures, being prepared.

When I got back up to the house, I felt woozy and lay facedown on the lawn. The grass was soaked with dew. I ran my hands through it and wiped the jeweled moisture onto my face. I felt much better about everything when I saw some blood on my fingers and tasted it on my lips and fingered a warm, spongy wound on my forehead. Enormously pleased, I was about to get up, but someone had come over, and when I twisted around, I found myself looking up into the friendly, attentive, bespectacled face of Mr. Mansfield.

He had strolled over in an old blue work shirt, khakis, and boat shoes. He looked astonishingly neat and spruce, considering the hour, and from over the top of his rounded shoulders peered the wide-awake eyes of a small girl—Amy—who was being piggybacked across the lawn to spend the rest of that loud night at the Blanchards. Actually, I should say the wide-awake eye of a small girl, for the youngest Mansfield was wearing, for show, some Victorian grandmother's black eye-patch.

"Everything all right?" said Mr. Mansfield, his manner pleasant and formal, almost grave.

"Yes, sir, fine," I answered automatically.

"Nasty cut you've got there."

"I think it's O.K., really."

Mr. Mansfield bent over for a closer look. "Scratched yourself up on the rocks?"

"Yes, sir."

"Nearly high tide, I imagine."

"It was pretty high."

"Let's have a look," he said.

"What—? Oh, it's really no problem," I insisted.

"Nonsense," said Mr. Mansfield, and knelt down with Amy still on his back.

The former All-American unbuttoned his cuffs and turned back his sleeves. He took my head in his cool hands and peered at my forehead, squinting a little. "I don't see any swelling," he reported in his forthright baritone. He spread his fingertips along the crown of my skull and, one at a time, gingerly pressed against the skin, saying, "Fine. Fine. Fine. . . ."

During the examination, Amy pulled the black patch away from her eye, flipping it up onto her forehead, the better not to miss any of the action. Unabashed (or perhaps just unimpressed by the sight of one more flattened fellow on the premises), Amy stared, and I thought I glimpsed Emma in the large, thoughtful, gray-green eyes; and Mrs. Mansfield in the rosy, oval face; and Berry in the little, upturned nose and saucy big lips; and all of them together in the miniature air of indifference that overspread the little girl's features after a minute or so had passed and I still hadn't turned into a prince.

"Haven't done yourself any serious harm," Mr. Mansfield

diagnosed cheerfully, pressing against my froggy forehead a soft rumpled handkerchief that had about it the warmth of his pocket. The smells of bay rum and shoe polish and pipe smoke prickled my nostrils.

"Just the same," he added, "let's get you up to the house and have that cut properly dressed. I think we can find you some cotton swabs and witch hazel—and a brandy, how's that?"

Strange to say, I felt like weeping. I felt saved—saved from Emma and Berry and Aunt Nutkin and Hattie and Mrs. Mansfield—saved from everything I had feared I would become since the first day I had set foot in the green, girls-only world of Louisa Little's school. The mellow, masculine aroma in Mr. Mansfield's pocket handkerchief, like some long-forgotten transaction of love, seemed to grant permission to be myself, and to bawl, and I let loose.

I sobbed, mostly to myself, but I guess I must have made some noise because Mr. Mansfield kept patting me on the shoulder and saying, "It's fine, boy, it's fine," and of course the more awkward his touch, the harder I wept.

In a minute, I quieted, and Mr. Mansfield shook a smile out of his tight jaw. "Suppose we make that a double brandy?" he said.

We walked gently across the lawn, Amy casting solemn sideways glances at me, her father tilting back his head to look for stars.

"We'd see Saturn tonight," he said, "but for the fog."

12. Esposito's Day

Brandied, bandaged, blanketed, I slept for a while in a porch chaise. When I awoke, parched, the whistle of a Boston & Maine locomotive wailed along the tracks out behind the graveyard. Gradually, I became aware of the middle of the night—the rubbery, waterproof feeling of the skin, the increasing pointlessness of everything, the continuous reproach of half-memorized phrases: *Faith, hope, charity; these three. But the greatest of these is . . . Fourscore and seven years ago . . . But the greatest of these is . . .*

From the radio of an idling car, which was waiting for stragglers, I caught snatches of some WRKO hit, then couldn't get the cyclical chorus out of my throbbing skull: *"Na-na-na-na! Na-na-na-na! Hey, hey, hey! Good-bye! Na-na-na-na . . ."*

The party persisted on upstairs porches far into Sunday morning. For a long time, a far-off bell buoy clanged its ceaseless, solemn toll. Then, without anyone's noticing, it stopped. The night air freshened. A cool breeze sliced in from the north and the fog dispersed, leaving behind one of those dark, resinous, North Shore skies, so black that every face approaching a window caught lamplight and popped like a flashbulb.

From my chaise, I could hear waves slamming the Mansfields' weather-worn coast. Then, behind me, farther up the porch, I heard Berry's voice, riddling someone: "Are you telling me you're not telling me because you don't want to tell me if you're not telling me?"

261

I craned around and sighted up the balustrade and saw Berry's face, blazing, bright as a monument. She had put on an old sweater, one of her famous soft ones—the crimson turtle-neck—but she wasn't wearing a bra, and she looked loose and jiggly, and it gave me a tingle, I'm sorry to say, to see her like that, in that sweater again.

"Just *tell* me," she urged someone who was lying on a cot.

"How many times do I have to tell you?" came the lazy, croaky-voiced reply.

"A hundred times a day, every day."

"Come back here first."

"Solly, Cholly."

I couldn't see who "Cholly" was, but when at last he told Berry the words she wanted to hear, she sashayed over to the cot and straddled his hips. With a brisk retucking of his blanket under her chin, she sat down as if to a lobster dinner.

"Butts," she ordered, enjoying herself.

A crooked cigarette was dug out of a crumpled pack, handed over to Berry. A match flared.

She puffed. The broken butt caught, sputtered. She seized the boy's match-holding hand, drawing it closer. Now she puffed fiercely, her cheeks dimpling. The coal glowed, Berry exhaled.

She smiled. "I quit yesterday," she told the boy.

"Uh-huh," said the boy.

"I did," she insisted, "I only smoke for fun."

She watched the first long plume of blue smoke uncoil from the tip of her bent cigarette.

"I know what you're thinking," she told him.

"I'm sure you do," said the boy.

They both giggled. He reached for her, she drew back. Grabbing hold of her wrist, the boy gave a solid yank, and Berry pitched forward into the cot.

They giggled again. "You're naughty," she said, sitting up.

She continued to smoke. When she finished the butt, she stood and went to the balustrade, sat and swung her legs out, dangling them over the shrubs.

"Come here," the boy complained, and waited. "Come back here."

"I'm back," she whispered into the faintly turning gray light. "I'm back."

A little later, I went to get something to drink. I found my brother in the kitchen, sitting on the floor—absorbed, pale, rabbit-eyed.

His shoulders were rolled forward and his hands, oily and sure-fingered, were busy with what looked like a dinosaur bone from a tar pit. Beside him on the linoleum, and all around the kitchen, covering every square inch of floor and countertop, lay dozens of dewy groceries and the five-hundred-and-one oily parts of the Mansfields' industrial refrigerator innards. It looked as if, vertebra by vertebra, my brother was readying some paleontologist's crowning achievement for reconstruction. The humid air around the defrosting, dismantled hulk augured a touch of July, swampy and sweet.

Murray glanced up when I came in. "Hey, Pieman," he murmured, and without another word, calmly went back to work, as if it were the most normal thing in the world for him to be sitting on the Mansfields' kitchen floor in the dead of night, with their refrigerator arrayed around him.

"Where's Annie?"

Murray didn't answer.

"Are you going to bed?" I whispered.

"I'm trying to figure out how to put this thing back together."

I tiptoed over to the kitchen sink, which was still in its proper place. The tap water ran clear and cold. I filled a dirty glass, then lifted the water to my lips and drank. It was delicious, and I drank thirstily, and all at once, to my core, I felt overwhelmed with gratitude that my brother was my brother. *Who were these people anyway*—these smashing sisters and witches and wuppers and dragon ladies? Here was my brother, my resourceful, handsome brother, who could plant a tree, fix a tire, love a girl. Here he was, right in the middle of the Mansfields' kitchen in the dead of night—rebuilding a refrigerator from scratch.

I put down the water glass and hurried out through the back door, my cheeks crawling with tears. I shambled around the side of the house toward the lawn. A cedary scent, from some replacement shingles, wafted off the kitchen porch, and I smelled some fresh, faraway time when the house, then a sporty summer place, had been new and unrotted and fair.

"Why?" I called out, with blurry eyes turned toward Mansfield heavens.

"Na-na-na-na!—Na-na-na-na!—Hey, hey, hey!—Goodbye!" came the answer from some Wupper or Dipper or greatgrandson of Scupper, still howling on an upstairs porch.

"Why?" I mumbled to myself, sitting down on the steps to the main veranda.

"Why *what*, Pieman?"

Murray had come out on the porch, wiping his hands.

"Why do the girls I love let only men who don't love them, love them?"

"Try that again?" said Murray.

"Why don't they let *me* love them?"

"Maybe you don't love them," said Murray.

"What?"

"They're your friends, Pieman—what do you expect?"

"But I love them!"

"It's not love," said Murray. "It's just worship."

Overhead, one of the candles in the old sportsman's chandelier was still guttering along, casting faint yellow rays into the tired blue shadows. Murray sprang up, loose and easy, snapping out the flames with his fingers.

"Come on, Pieman," he said, walking out into the blue dew and the dawn. "Time for a dip."

13. Chapter Thirteen

Underclassmen, though welcome, were not expected to attend Commencement. It was a blindingly bright morning, fresh and cool. A string quartet, stationed under some dogwood trees, played a lively prelude. The river breeze brought forth the smell of trodden grass, commingled with the happy murmur of parents and teachers.

I loitered near the back of Senior Garden. Over my shoulder the chapel loomed, chalky and grand as the White Cliffs of Dover. Ahead, beyond the jam-packed rows of folding chairs, beyond the lectern and the cherry-armed captain's chairs, and the wide, granite Little Steps—out beneath the Great Elm—the graduating seniors had assembled for "Annual Ring," the traditional farewell: Every commencement morning, for one last time as a class, Miss Little's girls joined hands, forming a new ring around the bole of the ancient tree.

Singing their processional, the sweet-voiced Class of 1972 emerged from under the rich green shade, striding two by two into the vibrant light. Berry appeared near the middle of the double column. Crowned with flowers after all, she was smiling radiantly, and as Berry and her class glided out of the lush

June foliage, all but floating toward us, the sunlight burst briefly on each pair of white-frocked shoulders, feathering outward to the span of angels' wings.

Breezy Fred Harr sprang to the lectern. With laudable restraint, the headmaster told only two topical jokes as he welcomed everyone to the graduation exercises for the last girls-only class in the school's history. And bouncy the tone remained, right through the keynote address, during which the governor of Massachusetts, playing the role of Paris, handed out "Golden Apple" prizes, naming Berry Mansfield our school beauty—the "Venus" of our local heavens.

During the awarding of the diplomas, I put our local goddess of love under surveillance, but could detect no emotional change greater than a slight misting of her clear blue eyes when she dispensed secret farewell winks and waves to her friends and relations, as well as to the Wigglesworths, and perhaps half a dozen others, including Boy-Boy Blackwell and Billy Sheets, who came in with wet hair and untucked shirts during the school hymn.

I had an unobstructed view, midway down the center aisle, of the Mansfield parents and their glamorous, many-headed, lion-haired pride. From her seat on the aisle, Mrs. Mansfield covered much territory, restlessly popping in and out to record the scene on a Super-8 movie camera. Seated, seersuckered, and bow-tied, Mr. Mansfield beamed uninterruptedly at everyone and everything, and occasionally, as though to vary the rhythm, covered his beaming, ruddy face with a clean white handkerchief. Aunt Nutkin sat straight-backed beside her brother-in-law, all gussied up in a pillbox hat with fingertip veil, yellowing gloves with ivory buttons, hip-clinging suit with nipped-in waist. The gruesome unwashed hair had been bagged and snooded and tucked tidily behind the pillbox.

After the hymn, everyone sat down and the whole garden

quieted. The headmaster fidgeted at the lectern, strangely speech-less. Behind him, scattered among the Class of '72, whispers could be heard, excited and uncertain. The program indicated only that the reading from First Corinthians would come next, concluding the exercises.

A small, white-haired woman had risen from the audience—from the far end of the first row—and whispers swept the garden like gusts of wind. People sat on the edge of their folding seats, craning their necks, trying to see who, or what, everyone was making such a fuss about. You would have thought the Archbishop of Canterbury himself was coming, crook in hand, to read us Paul's first letter to the Corinthians.

Wentworth and Winslow, a few rows ahead, peered around, and I caught their puzzled eyes, and we all shrugged. To us, the old white-haired woman was a stranger.

She was so short I could hardly see her from the back. Then she stepped forward, front and center, turning her wrinkly, weather-burned face to the school, and when the school jumped instantly to its feet, I knew who it was. Louisa Little, headmis-tress from 1939 to 1971, had come out of retirement to read Chapter Thirteen.

The place went nuts. Seniors screeched and embraced. Old girls swooned, new girls showered Miss Little with daisies. Flowers piled up around the headmistress's Pappagallos. It was one of those unforeseen attacks of crowd ecstasy, so abrupt, so heart-stopping, you wonder if by chance anyone arranged for an ambulance to stand by.

Hysteria had seized the Little School. The garden trembled with applause for a full minute. The treetops roiled and spar-kled like schools of fish, now silver, now blue, now green, as though the spring run of shad and herring had eluded the Indian fishweirs and come to spawn here.

The small, stooped figure at the front returned a steady,

267

answering smile. Her dark eyes were deep in crow's feet, her cheeks as smooth and strong as darning eggs. She wore at her throat and ears a parure of pearls, and her full head of ivory-white hair ruffled in the brackish breeze. Over her shoulders hung a knitted cardigan, the sleeves of which cradled her back like guiding green arms. She held the cracked edges of a calf-bound Bible in long, bony hands speckled with sherry-colored spots.

Her head bobbed as she looked out over the faces in the garden, back along the flowerbeds and the tall privet borders, all the way back to the chapel and up to the tip of its slim white spire. Patches of the audience were still standing and clapping, and the headmistress smiled them back into their seats.

"Governor Sargeant . . ." she began. Birds chittered. Programs rustled. ". . . Mr. Chairman, Mr. Harr, ladies and gentlemen of the faculty and staff of the Little School, graduates of the Class of 1972 and their parents, alumnae, students, distinguished guests, family and friends—

"Many of you know I love surprises and hate to read prayers!"

Appreciative laughter, stopping just short of applause, greeted the crackling Yankee voice. Faces beamed, eyes glistened; the school hung on the headmistress's every word.

"I thank you," she continued, "for the honor of being asked to read the school prayer. And I thank God for the privilege to accept. But in my opinion, the person who stands up at Commencement with a prayerbook and *reads* his First Corinthians is not only cheating, but chicken!

"Of course we're all frightened we haven't got it by heart. I've had a hunch all weekend," said Miss Little, "and in my *craw* I've felt that when the time came for Chapter Thirteen, I was going to chicken out. Now that I see your faces—and so many new ones, golly!—I know I am. So please allow me to go right ahead and find my place and cheat like mad!"

The school roared its approval. With her long, angler's fingers, the headmistress plucked at a place-ribbon in her Bible, smoothed out the pages, and began to read: "Though I speak with the tongues of men and of angels, and have not love, I am as sounding brass or a tinkling cymbal. . . ."

Without warning, and perhaps without quite knowing why, everyone was suddenly blinking back tears. Most of the graduating class dissolved at once. Berry, I noticed, began to well up during the middle verses: the ones about love being patient and kind and never selfish or boastful or conceited or rude. Down front, Fred Harr sat glassy-eyed between the board chairman and the governor (both digging around in trouser pockets for handkerchiefs), and by the time Louisa Little had gotten to "beareth all things, believeth all things, hopeth all things, endureth all things . . . ," you could hear snuffling in every row, soft and steady, like the wind in the leaves.

The sun beat down. The day had turned sultry. In my overtired eyes, the light was suddenly too strong, the sky too bright, the white dresses too luminous. Strange yellow flashes rimmed my vision. Everything was happening too quickly; the earth itself seemed to be spinning faster through the clear blue empyrean. There was too much talk of the future; everyone was about to move, commence, leave. The immemorial smell of grass perfumed the air. Everything seemed to be ending.

The sound of the headmistress's voice, catarrhal and a little melancholy, put a lump in my throat. I had persisted long in my foolishness. Looking around at the school and the river and the chapel and the fields, I could see all that I had done and all that I had left undone. And as I listened to this small, sunburned woman who spoke of love in a kind, forgiving voice, I wondered if I would ever learn. I could not picture this place without Berry—easier to imagine the loss of the Great Elm, vestigial virgin, ringed wonder, blighted survivor of the first men and all who came after.

When the string quartet broke into the recessional, I skirted around the privet border and hurried to find her. The graduates and their families and teachers convened under the Great Elm's branches and bare poles, and I felt a flood of relief when Emma and Gussie and Hattie and Lili spotted me hanging orphanlike around the outskirts. They beckoned me over to celebrate *our* new solidarity: Underclassmen, we would all be coming back next year.

I started toward my friends, outwardly nonchalant, inwardly ecstatic: I still belonged to them! My heart muscles had begun their usual Mansfield contractions, every gland, every cell in my body straining like an iron filing toward a magnet, when I glimpsed Towny Lee standing beside Berry. They were holding hands. Towny Lee, chatting with Mrs. Mansfield and Ducky Wigglesworth, had just said something that made the women laugh. Berry, who hadn't been listening, begged him to repeat it. "Come on," she coaxed, peeking out at him from under her brow. "Come *on*."

But he would tell her nothing. Towny Lee stood beside Berry Mansfield in his yellowing seersucker suit, an air of seamless self-assurance stitched into every pocket, and I let myself know—I tapped myself on the shoulder, almost as if that were me standing over there beside her—that Berry Mansfield had made other plans for the summer.

Midstride, I started to veer away. Then I heard her voice approaching—how familiar it was. How dear! I recognized especially the distracted tone when she sidled up and said: "Can you believe this thing?"

I thought she meant the diploma she was carrying, and I mumbled my congratulations, hugging her delicately, grateful for any excuse to touch her. I was surprised at the strange hardness of her body.

"No, dummy, *this* thing . . ." She drew back to show me something, and as she pulled away, I burst into tears. I don't think I have ever cried so suddenly, so stingingly, in my life. Within seconds my whole face was wet and red and hot.

Berry was tilting back her head to show me, it turned out, a pimple on her chin. "Can you believe it," she said, "—at my *graduation?*"

Red-faced and snuffling, I burst out laughing. Even at Hattie's birthday in the chapel, when we'd all shown each other our most freakish body parts, Berry had not had so much as a zit. Now she had a monster pimple, big as a raisin, categorically unpoppable, more a phenomenon of the Middle Earth world of welts, wens, and verrucas than of the ordinary white-headed topography of teenage zits.

"I guess I could say a lot of heavy things, but I can't," said Berry. "Anyway, I'm sorry about the summer. I guess I should've let you know at my party, but I couldn't—I didn't know. But this isn't the end, no good-byes, because now your town's my town and next September maybe we can start all over again . . ."

Over by the tree, Mr. Mansfield was signaling: Aunt Nutkin had a plane to catch and Mrs. Mansfield needed Berry for a family photograph.

They were all lined up under the Great Elm, the smashing, glamorous Mansfields, from little Amy at the lowest end, through the motley, mopheaded boys, up through Lindy, Emma, and their dad. Berry seized my wrist and pulled me along, thrusting me into line between herself and Emma. "He's basically our little brother!" Berry announced.

Mrs. Mansfield, one eye squinting, stood ten paces away, filming her family. We were all smiling at the camera, mugging at each other, nearly on the verge of laughter. Hattie and

Gussie and Lili had joined the end of the line. The chapel bell was clanging. The air beneath the elm was cool. The girls, seized by delight, swung their right legs forward, and suddenly, blissfully, we were dancing the Nine Step.

"But the boys don't know the steps," Mrs. Mansfield complained, frowning behind the camera.

"Sam does," said Berry.

"Yah," chimed Emma, "Sam does."

EPILOGUE

For years after we left there, all my dreams about women took place at Miss Little's School for Girls. I go back to the Little School occasionally, on one errand or another, usually alone, rarely with friends. I remember once asking Emma if she wanted a ride back to a reunion—Murray and I and Paul Winslow and Charlie Crocker were going back; Lili Hooper was meeting us on the way; Gussie would be there.

"I don't think I could," replied Emma. "I don't think I believe in elitist institutions."

So what's the matter with me? Why do my dreams keep taking place at such a small green place? Why do I keep kissing the hand-stitched cover of Berry Mansfield's friendship sampler? By my age I am supposed to have put away childish things. Men at thirty are supposed to have called it quits on the past, outgrown bad habits, moved to distant cities, chalked up to experience our unrequited loves. Technically, I don't think I'm even supposed to remember their names, let alone their birthdays and bra sizes and the way they looked and smelled and sounded on a given September school night almost two decades ago.

My calendar is so full of our notable dates that I seem to have taken over where Parson Weems left off, retailing each of our gang's earliest episodes and anniversaries in the language of cherry-tree panegyric. To this day I know by heart everyone's first telephone number. I remember with sharp, unhealable pangs our expulsion from the first zip codes: 02138. 02657. 01742. There must be something wrong with me. I can't seem to forget anything.

Sometimes at night when I lie awake, fretful, conjuring disasters, I can hear those girls telling me about it. I hear Berry reporting the news and Emma concluding, "Yah . . . yah . . ." I hear them, muted, yet never quite out of earshot, talking about what's happening to us. Some nights I can almost feel what it would have been like to sleep with them, to have married and had children—to have joined with one of them in life's larger enterprises and mysteries. Other nights I realize how little I ever really knew Berry or Emma or Hattie—how little I knew of their hearts.

Eight years ago, Hattie joined an ashram. She had been in an almost constant state of apostasy since college, always forswearing, absolutely and forever, one thing for another: Harvard for Italy, opera for ballet, singing for painting, the Catholic Church for the Art Students League, a sinful father for a holy guru. With each conversion she would ask us—her old friends—to bear witness as she proclaimed her new faith. And each time, as Hattie became more painterly than painters, more operatic than opera singers, more Catholic than nuns, we would go along in support, as if it were only natural for someone's body weight to rise and fall according to creed. By the time Hattie rejected the sisterhood of Mansfields for the brotherhood of Man, I was exhausted by her tergiversations. She works in Hollywood now and lives with her guru and his disciples. I miss her.

Emma got famous. Then she got married. Then she had kids. I see her less and less every year, mostly at occasions where more and more we look once too often over each other's shoulders. I find it increasingly difficult to comprehend Emma, to see what the world sees when it lends *Boys Are Bad, Men Are Rats, I Turn Tricks* the names art and success.

But the world itself is changed, distorted. Our parents—many of them—have died. The towering trees have fallen. The towns we grew up in are so expensive we couldn't afford to live there even if we wanted to. Everything is tarted up with corporate chrome, everyone's in therapy, and the only one of us who still smokes is Berry Mansfield. She hasn't married. She seems to be a bridesmaid at practically every wedding I attend. She works in advertising and has a big salary, a corner office, and a male secretary (who, I am convinced, must smirk when he calls to ask: "Will you hold for Berry Mansfield?"). I don't know what I expected; it seems odd to find her still in some other room, on some distant porch, quarreling with some other guy she doesn't want to marry or who doesn't want to marry her. I guess I thought she'd be happier.

There have been times when I was quite sure that I was still in love with Berry. And times when, in remission from Berry, I once more fell for Emma. And also mornings when, if I did just ten more sit-ups, then, finally, one of them would—

But now several years have passed since I last wanted those girls to love me back, and I am no longer the custodian of christening cups, no more the Keeper of the Pack. My life as a worshipper has ended.

By the time the air-cushioned, eighteen-wheel moving van rumbled onto our old street the day after last Labor Day, two truckloads of stuff had already been taken to the Goodwill. Even then, 492 numbered cartons—packed and sealed for future fights—awaited removal to a roadside storage facility in Saugus, Mass. 01906.

"At least," said Murray, "we still have a Massachusetts address."

After the protracted agony of packing, the removal of the cartons went astonishingly quickly; so quickly that the unaccustomed emptiness of the house played tricks on my eyes. I kept walking into rugless, bedless, pictureless rooms, turning corners, and hallucinating onto the ringing emptiness a mirage of everything that had always been in the room. With a fresh and interested gaze, I confronted a scorch mark at the top of the stairs, where my brother had once lobbed a cherry bomb at the retreating form of Ulysses S. Grant.

At the front door, Murray was fiddling with a fancy electronic security system installed by the new owner, Mr. Lee, a multimillionaire Korean businessman. Abruptly, Murray stopped. He did not realize that I was standing behind him in the shadows of the hall, and he bellowed—this bulky, slightly balding, friendly man who is my brother—"Come on, Pieman!"

The bare walls shook so hard with his big, gruff voice that, for a second, the house felt on the point of collapse.

Through the wide-open front door I could see down to the foot of the front path. The movers had dropped a sheet of bubble-wrap, and it flapped across the yard. Indoors, a breeze stirred in the chimneys, exhaling, once more, the cool, minty smell of the hearthstones.

"Come on," Murray revised in a lower register—what he thought was his normal voice: "Time to go, Pieman."

We stepped out onto the front porch. The clean, dry wind rustled the foliage in the yard. The sharp bite of ailanthus filled our nostrils. It was September again. Murray and I stood there, our shoulders bumping, and as natural as it would have felt to have gone back inside, to get the car keys, or the dog's leash, or Mom's purse—everything was gone. Murray pulled the door closed, and out we walked, under the tree of heaven.